SAM

A Men of Clifton Montana
Novel
Book 7

Susan Fisher-Davis

Erotic Romance

Sam Men of Clifton, Montana Book 7

Copyright © 2016 Susan Fisher-Davis

First E-book Publication: July 2016

Cover design by Amy Valentini

Back cover design courtesy of Pixabay

Edited by Romancing Editorially

All cover art copyright © 2016 by Susan Fisher-Davis

ISBN: 9781076704870

PUBLISHER: Blue Whiskey Publishing

Dedication

To the Gallatin County Sheriff's Department in MT for answering any questions I had for them.

To Ariya Xie/photographer at Xie4to-graphy for the amazing photo—you know I had to have it the minute I saw it.

To Matt Oubre for being SAM—you are absolutely perfect for him.
It took me almost two years to find the right cover for this book. Every time I thought I'd found one, I'd change my mind and now I know why. It was because I was waiting for this one.

To my editor, and friend, Amy Valentini, who if it hadn't been for her SAM would have never gotten his own story. When she edited my first book, JAKE, she told me I'd better get a woman for SAM because that man was hot. Who knew so many readers would fall in love with him?

To my betas, Toby, Kelli, Dedee, & Kelly— you four ladies are the best and I treasure your friendship, and input.

Special shout-out to these amazing authors: Tiffany J. West, Cynthia Noble, Kris Nacole, Jacqueline Anne, Rhonda Lee Carver, Kathleen Ball, Chandra Crawford, Lorraine Britt, Susan Storm, Gloria Herrmann, Holly J. Gill, Renee Vincent, Tamara Hoffa, Stacy Pritt, Sherri Good, Becky McGraw, Lynda Cox, Mary Smith, Dawn Sullivan, and D'Ann Lindun—you ladies ROCK.
I love you all and I'm proud to call you my friends.

To Malinda Diehl for going the extra mile.
To Genevieve Lowe for letting me steal your name.
To Penny Culberson--just because.
To my husband Rob for putting up with me staying in my cave all day and rarely emerging. I love you.

To all of you reading this—I've said it before and I'll say it again. I wouldn't be here without you. I love my readers and love getting feedback from you.

This story was to be the end The Men of Clifton, Montana series but I'm adding more. I've had my favorites along the way, but none

of them got to me as much as SAM did. He will always have a special place in my heart. I hope you enjoy his story as much as I enjoyed writing it. Don't worry for you'll see those Men of Clifton pop up in The Callahans and The Beckett Brothers too. Thank you all for your support.
Enjoy SAM!

Prologue

Tessa stood in the cabin at the window and stared out at the snow. Covering everything it touched, it fell in a heavy blanket over the wilderness surrounding the quaint cabin. Leaning against the sill, she sipped her coffee thinking about everything that had happened in the last six months, and that tomorrow she was starting a new job in the small town of Clifton, Montana.

It was time she returned to work. After being in Kalispell, Montana for six months doing nothing but staring out the windows, it was time for her to come out of hiding and start living again. With the help of family and a good friend who was like family, she'd found a job in Clifton at the animal hospital. Trained as a veterinarian, she needed to get back to doing what she loved and that was caring for animals. Although she specialized in equine veterinarian medicine, she took care of all animals. Dr. Will Carter had hired her on the spot and in addition, had offered her the opportunity to buy the hospital when he retired in a few more months. Something she hoped to accomplish.

Tessa worried her bottom lip as she thought about everything that she'd had to endure and change, but couldn't help worrying if she would be safe there. Was it possible she could still be found?

Shaking the thought from her head, she decided that if she hadn't been found in the six months she'd been hiding with the help of her aunt Lil, a good friend and her godmother, maybe she was finally free. If changing her name, her location, and her world meant being safe then it was all worth it. Small town life had never been her thing but she might just have to change her mind on that. As long as she was safe, she'd stay put and make a new life.

Walking to the sink, she rinsed out her cup and got ready for bed. She was going to have a long day tomorrow and was grateful Lil had allowed her to stay at her cabin, but also glad for the use of the SUV in the garage. With the snow coming down as heavily as it was, she'd need it tomorrow. Lil had done so much for her and made all the arrangements for her to start her new life in Clifton, Montana as Tessa McGuire. It was a small town and not very impressive, but the few folks she'd met already seemed to have big hearts. She only hoped she'd fit in and be safe.

Chapter One

Sheriff Sam Garrett stood in his office staring through the blinds toward the animal hospital. She was in there. He'd seen her walking up the street and then entering the hospital. She was so beautiful. Blowing out a frustrated breath, he took a seat behind his scarred oak desk. He'd been sheriff for four years now and another election was coming in November. He really hadn't decided on running again yet, although he did love the job. Muttering under his breath when he heard his dispatcher/secretary Betty Lou Harper clear her throat, Sam glanced up to see her standing in the doorway.

"What is it Betty Lou?" he grumbled. He seriously loved the woman but she could drive an insane person sane.

"Don't take that tone with me, Sam Garrett. I just wanted to know if you were going to get lunch at the diner."

Sam glanced at the clock. "I didn't realize it was that late." He stood. "Yes, I'll get something. What do you want me to bring back for you?"

"I don't want anything. You just need to eat, Sam."

"Betty Lou..." Sam growled.

"Someone needs to take care of you. You don't have a wife." Betty Lou shrugged.

"By my choice. Christ, Betty Lou, let up."

"Stop swearing, Sam."

Taking a deep breath, he ran his hand down over his face then strode around the desk and grabbed his Stetson. After slamming it on his head, he moved past Betty Lou and headed out the front door. The woman was going to drive him insane. She was worse than his own mother about him settling down with a wife. There wasn't a woman he wanted to settle down with, much less marry. Stopping in his tracks, he glanced toward the animal hospital. Well, not one who wanted to settle down with him anyway. Sam blew out a breath of frustration and walked toward the diner. Many people stopped him along the way, either to complain about something or just to say hello.

Mentally groaning, he almost crossed the street to escape when he saw Lacey Cosgrove barreling down on him with a big grin on her face.

"Hello, Sam," she said as she halted in

front of him.

Sam touched the brim of his hat. "Lacey. How are you today?"

"Wonderful. How about you, Sheriff?" Her fingers ran over his bare arm. She started walking them up his arm when he wrapped his fingers around her wrist.

"I'm on my way to lunch." He smiled in as pleasant a way as possible.

"Too bad I've already had lunch or I'd join you."

Sam didn't recall asking her to. "I'll see you later, Lacey."

"Will you, Sam?"

Damn! He could have kicked himself for not thinking she might take him literally. "Figure of speech."

"Anytime you want to see me is fine with me, Sam. Anytime."

"Have a nice day," Sam said and walked away. Lacey Cosgrove had been after him for as long as he could remember. It wasn't that she wasn't pretty, she was, but there weren't too many men in Clifton who hadn't already sampled her charms. He swore as his eyes shifted toward the hospital again.

Damn it. Why did she hate him? From the minute they'd met, she'd looked at him as if he was a bug on the bottom of her shoe and he didn't know why. He'd wanted her from the first moment he'd seen her. He'd wanted to wrap her long black hair around his hand, pull it to his face, and inhale. Tessa McGuire stood tall and had the most beautiful dark brown eyes. Her lips looked so kissable that Sam couldn't help but think about tasting them. All the time. Hell, he wanted to taste *her*. All over. Every damn inch of her soft looking skin.

Christ, now his cock was getting hard. Sam stopped and took a deep breath then exhaled. He sure as hell didn't want to walk into the diner with a hard-on. Pulling the glass door open, he heard the attached bell tinkle. He nodded to some of the patrons then took a seat on the nearest red vinyl stool at the counter. Connie, the owner, came over to him.

"Hi, Sam...what would you like?"

"Burger and fries please, Connie."

The Clifton Diner was small but had the best burgers and fries for miles around. The smell of frying onions permeated the air. Connie set a glass of ice water in front of him, making him smile. She knew it was all he drank. That or coffee, and then coffee only in the mornings. Sam spun on the stool and gazed around the room. He smiled at the people who waved at him. When he spotted Joe Baker, he tensed up. Joe Baker was a drunk who enjoyed using his wife as a punching bag but Mary never pressed charges. It wasn't long ago that Sam had had a run-in with him over his cattle being on Trick Dillon's land and Sam knew it was going to come to a head one day.

Baker weaved through the tables and stopped in front of Sam. "Garrett."

"That's Sheriff Garrett to you, Baker."

Joe Baker laughed. "You love telling me that." He stared at Sam for a few seconds. "You have a nice day...*Sheriff.*"

Sam muttered under his breath as Baker walked out the door. He spun back around on the stool then glanced toward the door when the bell above it rang again. His heart hit his stomach when Tessa entered the diner. Her eyes met his but she quickly looked away, and took a seat on a stool a good way down the counter from his. Sam didn't understand why she hated him so much.

Connie returned and set his food in front of him, the aroma making his stomach growl. He hadn't realized he was so hungry. Picking his burger up, he took a bite and almost groaned. Connie smiled at him before walking toward Tessa. Sam watched as Tessa smiled at Connie when she offered to take her order, and his heart slammed into his ribs. Would she ever smile at him like that? Mentally shaking his head, he seriously doubted it. She avoided him like the plague and it really pissed him off.

After he finished his lunch, he paid for his food and left the diner. He stood outside for a few minutes. It was a beautiful day. Late-spring was warming up the little town of Clifton and it was more than welcome after the rough winter it had just gone through. Sam lifted his gaze and looked at the blue cloudless sky, the sun sitting up there all alone warming the ground. Putting his aviator sunglasses on, he turned when the door behind him open and Tessa stepped out. She hesitated when she saw him, but then nodded her head at him.

"Doctor McGuire," Sam said as he put his fingers to his hat.

"Sheriff," she said to him and the sound of her voice shot right to his dick.

Desire made him want to hear that soft voice whispering in his ear while he buried himself deep inside her. *Son of a bitch!* His cock was growing again. After giving her a terse nod, he crossed the street to head back to his office—to hell with embarrassing himself in front of her.

* * * *

Tessa McGuire watched as the sheriff

crossed the street as if the hounds of hell were chasing him. She didn't blame him for wanting to get as far away from her as fast as possible though. She'd treated him like dirt since the first minute she saw him. Her breath had left her body when she'd turned to meet him. She'd thought him the sexiest and most gorgeous man she'd ever set eyes on. Sam Garrett had just grinned at her with perfect white teeth. Her gut had told her to turn away because she knew she could never get involved with him.

Instead of being friendly, she'd frowned at him, and in reaction to her cold greeting, he'd narrowed his eyes at her. After she spun away from him, she'd heard him huff and then leave the clinic. That had been on the day she'd moved some of her things into her new place of employment as a veterinarian.

Eighteen months ago, she'd purchased the Clifton Animal Hospital from Dr. Will Carter when he had retired. She'd been in Clifton for two years now and she'd avoided Sam Garrett as much as she could. Her attraction to him was so great that she couldn't take the chance of being around him. No matter how hot he was and how she'd love to know him better, she couldn't chance it. Getting involved with any man, especially a man like Sam was out of the question. There was something about him that made it way too easy to fall in love with him, and she couldn't allow that to happen so she stayed away from him, and let him think she hated him. If she allowed herself to get involved with him and he found out her secret, he would end up hating her.

Tessa was not having a good day. As if running into Sam at the diner wasn't bad enough, now she'd lost a mare, her first, and it was killing her. The foal survived but now he was in danger of losing his life if another mare refused to nurse him or the owner, Ryder Wolfe, didn't feed him. Tessa shook her head. Surely, Ryder would take care of it. The man loved his horses. It was just such a time consuming project. Ryder had frozen colostrum on hand so he should be able to feed the foal but time was critical, as the foal would need colostrum within the first two hours of life. After eighteen to twenty-four hours, the foal would no longer be able to absorb the antibodies through his gastrointestinal tract. With orphaned newborns, the easiest method to get them to nurse was with a bottle. Their natural instincts were to suckle, so they readily were willing to nurse from a bottle.

Tessa wiped the tears from her face as she drove back to town from Ryder's place.

What kind of veterinarian are you? You're not supposed to cry over the loss of an animal.

Her dream of being an equine vet had come true right after she graduated and a large equine hospital in Pennsylvania had hired her, and then when the opportunity for her own practice opened up, eighteen months ago, she jumped on it. At first, she wasn't thrilled with the small town of Clifton but after being here for a while now, she loved it and the people in it—well, all the people but perhaps, one.

Her hands gripped the steering wheel, her jaw clenching as she thought of *him*. The man drove her crazy and as far as she could tell, he didn't like her either.

She glanced in her rearview mirror and swore aloud when she saw blue and red lights flashing. *Speak of the devil.* Tessa pulled over, got her license, proof of insurance, and registration out, and then put her window down. Glancing in the side view mirror, she saw him get out of his big SUV patrol cruiser, put his black Stetson on, and walk up alongside her car. Tessa bit her lip to hold back a groan. She handed her information out the window before he could ask for it.

"You in a hurry today, Doctor McGuire?" Sam Garrett asked in that deep voice of his that drove her nuts, even though she didn't want it to.

Tessa refused to look up at him. Way up. The man topped six foot five, and every inch was mouth-watering. "I didn't realize I was speeding, *Sheriff.*"

"Ten miles over the posted limit," he murmured. "I'll be right back."

"Take your time," Tessa mumbled.

Her eyes went instinctively to the side view mirror and watched his retreating backside—those broad shoulders. Why was he so hot? That dark brown, almost black hair was sexy enough but those beautiful blue eyes could make any woman want to jump his bones. She watched him take his hat off before getting back in his cruiser. His hair touched the collar of his khaki shirt. That wasn't very professional, but then neither was the way his jeans hugged his butt.

She tapped her fingers on the steering wheel. What was taking so long? Knowing Sam, he was deliberately taking his time just to irritate her. He was the only person in town who called her Tessa. Everyone else called her Tess or Doc Mac. Not Sam, though. He had to be different, and too damn good-looking for her peace of mind. He was the sexiest man she'd ever laid eyes on. She gritted her teeth so hard that she was surprised they didn't shatter.

Turning around in her seat, she looked through her back window at him. What was he doing? He was looking down at something then he grabbed his hat from the dash, and opened his door. She quickly turned back to the front but the longer she sat there, the angrier she got. Throwing her door open, she stepped out, folded her arms over her chest, and leaned against her car. She saw him hesitate when he saw her outside the car. His sexy mouth twitched at the corner.

"Getting impatient, Tessa?" He tilted his head.

"What was taking so long? Believe it or not, I have patients to see."

"And I have speeders to stop."

Tessa snorted. "Must get boring for you." She put her hand out. "Can I have my license back now?"

Sam tapped it against his palm. "You have an unpaid ticket."

Tessa's mouth dropped open. "I do not!"

Sam nodded. "Yep. Seems I have to take you in."

Tessa put her hands on her hips. "You will do no such thing, Sam Garrett!"

"*Sheriff* Sam Garrett." He reached for her arm.

Tessa jerked away from him. "You are

not taking me to jail for an unpaid ticket," she shouted at him, her anger getting the best of her.

"Tessa, calm down. You didn't pay the fine and so a warrant's been issued. Just get in the cruiser and I'll take you to the station. You can pay it there." He reached for her again.

"I will not go in that cruiser. I'll follow you." She clenched her jaw in defiance.

"I can't let you do that. With a warrant, I have to take you in."

Tessa poked him in the chest with her finger. "You are not taking me anywhere," she said through gritted teeth.

"Should I add assaulting an officer to the charge?" His eyebrow rose, a sense of mocking which infuriated her even more.

"Oh, you'd love that, wouldn't you?" She poked him again.

Tessa heard him take a deep breath right before he spun her around and placed her against the car. She sputtered. "What...what do you think you're doing?"

She tried to turn around, but Sam pushed her against the car again and pulled her arms behind her. Her throat expelled an exasperated gasp when she felt the handcuffs go on her wrists.

"Sam Garrett, don't you dare," Tessa

screamed at him.

He spun her around to face him. "*Sheriff* Sam Garrett and I asked you nicely, Tessa and you wouldn't do as I asked." He leaned down to look into her eyes. "You do not touch an officer of the law." He straightened to his full height. "Am I clear?"

Tessa glared at him with narrowed eyes. "*Crystal.* You want to frisk me too?"

Sam's lips rose in a slow, sexy smile. "Do you want me to?"

Her heart skipped a couple of beats at the idea of him running his large hands down her body and it was all she could do to keep from saying *yes.*

"You touch me and I'll have your badge." Tessa scowled up at that handsome face. Although he was clean-shaven, a faint shadow accentuated his chiseled jaw. Sideburns blended into the shadow, ending right before his earlobes. His nose was straight and sat over a gorgeous set of lips, a bowed upper and full bottom lip that had her wanting to nibble on them, and then gorgeous deep dimples that showed even when he spoke. His baby blue eyes, surrounded by thick lush lashes, were striking in his tanned face. Regardless, she refused to look away from him.

He shook his head at her.

"You do realize that I have every right to frisk you? There is a bench warrant out for your arrest. That gives me the right." Sam pulled on her arm to lead her toward the cruiser. "You have the right to remain silent...please do...anything you say...God help us...can, and will be used against you in a court of law. You have the right to an attorney—"

"I don't think the handcuffs are necessary, Sheriff. I'm not going to run. I need to get my purse and keys...please."

"Fine...I'll take them off, but you are still going in. Understand?" Sam regarded her as if she was going to run as he unlocked the cuffs.

"I understand....*Sheriff*." Once her hands were free again, Tessa reached into her car to get her keys and purse. After locking it, she walked to the cruiser without looking at him, and stood by the back door.

Sam strode toward her. "You can sit up front."

When she shook her head, he sighed and opened the back door. He helped her in, his hand on the top of her head for which he apologized. "Sorry—habit." Then he closed the door.

Tessa watched as he took his Stetson off, settled into the driver's seat, and set his hat on the passenger side. His blue eyes looked into the mirror at her before he put his sunglasses on. She glanced away. He started the SUV and pulled out. Tessa watched out the window as the green fields flew by. Old wooden barns stood vacant. She rubbed her hands over her cheeks, refusing to cry. Those blue eyes saw everything and she refused to let him see her cry. She leaned her head back against the seat, closed her eyes, and listened as he called the department to notify them of the *arrest.*

* * * *

Sam shook his head, and swore under his breath. He felt like a real ass for handcuffing her and taking her in but once he ran her license and the warrant came back, he couldn't let her go. It was only a misdemeanor so all she had to do was pay the fine, and then she could leave. His eyes shifted to the mirror. Her head was back against the headrest. She was the most beautiful woman he'd ever seen. Her long, curly black hair was in its usual ponytail. He'd never seen it down. Those long curls made a man want to bury his hands in them. Her hair must be nearly down to her waist, since the ponytail hung between her shoulder blades. Her bangs were the only straight part of her hair and those eyes... Sam shifted in his seat as his groin tightened. Her dark brown, almond shaped eyes made his mouth water. Her lips were lush and full, and he wanted so much to taste them but then he scowled thinking how she hated him...for some unknown reason...rather a reason known only to her. She avoided him every chance she got and he had no idea why.

Sam drove the cruiser around to the back of the sheriff's department to avoid embarrassment for her. Of course, with Betty Lou being dispatcher, it wouldn't be long before the entire town was aware of the arrest. Sam mentally groaned as he got out and knew he'd never live this down. Opening the back door, Tessa stepped out with a huff. He inclined his head for her to walk ahead of him, and almost laughed when she scowled at him then tossed her head. That long ponytail swinging as she walked into the building. When she stopped inside the door, Sam moved around her since he knew she'd follow him as he headed for his office. He hadn't even had a chance to take his hat off yet when Betty Lou burst through the doorway.

"Are you out of your mind?" She put her hands on her ample hips and stared at Sam. He took his hat off and hung it on a hall tree beside the door. Tessa took a seat in a chair in front of his desk.

"I don't need your input, Betty Lou." Sam sat down at his desk without looking at her. Betty Lou patted Tessa on the shoulder.

"I've got your paperwork done, honey, so you can get on your way." With a glaring look at Sam, she left the office. She was his godmother but at times, she really tried his patience.

Sam grumbled and ran his hand through his hair then he shuffled through piles of papers and swore when he couldn't find what he was looking for. His office was well organized and as neat as a pin. The large windows behind his desk let the summer sun shine in through the venetian blinds. Two metal file cabinets sat against the wood paneled wall and the scuffed hardwood floors along with the old wooden desk showed years of wear. Sam pushed his chair back and stood then strode from the office.

"Betty Lou," he shouted. "I need the paperwork for Tessa to sign so she can pay her fine and leave."

Betty Lou marched toward him and shoved the papers at his chest. She narrowed her eyes at him. "Your mother's going to hear about this, Sam Garrett." She spun away and went back to her desk.

Sam rolled his eyes and muttered under

his breath as he headed back into his office. He glanced over at Tessa and knew she was trying not to laugh.

"You think something's funny, Doctor McGuire?" he said with an annoyed growl and watched as she straightened up in the chair. She still wouldn't look at him as she shook her head. He gave a curt nod and took a seat behind his desk.

"Your fine is fifty dollars," Sam told her, reading the paper in front of him.

Tessa's mouth dropped open and she jumped up out of the chair. "Are you serious? *Fifty dollars?*"

"Yes, and before you go getting all pissed off, just remember you could have paid thirty-five instead...had you not tried to skirt the fine in the first place." Tessa sat back down, reached into her purse, and withdrew her debit card. Sam shook his head. "Nope...cash only."

"How am I supposed to get cash? You have an ATM in here somewhere?"

Sam grunted. "Not likely."

"Then how do I pay you? I don't carry a lot of cash." She nibbled on her bottom lip and Sam almost groaned at the effect it had on him. "I can go over...*what?*" she asked when Sam shook his head again.

"You can't leave here until you pay the

fine."

"You're crazy, Sam Garrett," Tessa exclaimed. "I can walk right across the street to the ATM. I'll be right back. Do you seriously think I'm going to run?" She was shouting now. "I live in this town."

"You tell him, honey," Betty Lou yelled in from the other room.

"Betty Lou," Sam growled. "*Shut up!*"

Tessa dropped back down into the chair. "Sheriff, please. I swear I'll be right back."

"I'm not letting you out of my sight. It's the law. But I can go with you."

"Wonderful," Tessa mumbled as she followed him through the office, and out the front of the building. "How do I get back to my car, Sheriff?" she asked as they crossed the street.

"I'll take you," Sam told her.

"It just keeps getting better," Tessa muttered.

Sam frowned. "I could have Betty Lou take you but I think I'm the lesser of two evils." He halted and looked at Tessa. "She'll talk your ear off, unlike me."

"I know that's right. You barely speak to me at all."

"I think you have that backwards."

"Whatever. Excuse me so I can get my money." She moved around him and stepped up to the ATM. Sam folded his arms across his chest, leaned against the building and hooked his boot heel against the brick. He put his fingers to his hat when Lacey strolled past him. She always seemed to be around when he was.

"Hello, Sheriff." Lacey winked at him as she spoke.

Sam smiled until he met Tessa's gaze. "What?"

Tessa shook her head. "Seriously? Lacey Cosgrove?"

"Jealous?" Sam grinned.

Tessa snorted. "Please."

Sam leaned down, close to her ear. "Oh, I could please you, angel. I can promise you that."

"You think so, Sheriff? Maybe I should make you prove it," she said before spinning around to march back across the street while Sam stood there and watched her as she did. He couldn't keep his eyes off her ass in those tight jeans. The woman was built like a brick shit house. *Christ.* His dick wanted to salute.

He jogged to catch up to her. She opened the door and went inside right before he got to her. Sam took a few deep breaths before he opened the door and entered the building. Tessa slapped her money down on the counter for Betty Lou and waited for a receipt.

"Do you want me to drive you back to your car, Tess?" Betty Lou asked, sending a scowl at Sam. He ran his hand down his face. This was getting ridiculous.

"I'll take her back. How about you do your job and that means no gossiping while I'm gone," Sam told her.

Betty Lou huffed and gave Tessa her receipt. "I'll make sure it's out of the system."

"Thank you, Betty Lou." Tessa headed for the back door to where his cruiser was. She pushed the door open and went outside. Sam blew out a breath.

"Sam—" Betty Lou started.

"Not one word, Betty Lou. Not. One. Word." He turned away from her and followed Tessa out the back door.

* * * *

Tessa made a quick call to her hospital to let them know she would be in soon then sat silently in the front seat of the cruiser as Sam drove her back to her car. When he pulled up behind her car, she hopped out without saying anything to him. She was surprised when he climbed out and called her name. Stopping beside her car, she turned around to face him as he closed the distance.

"Tessa...I'm sorry I had to take you in."

"You were doing your job. Just like I have to do mine and now you've made me late."

"*I* made you late? You're the one who was speeding and had an unpaid ticket."

Tessa glared at him. She was five foot eight in her bare feet but Sam towered over her, and she hated it. She stared up at him. "You could have let it slide just this once...*Sheriff.* I was late. I had just come from Ryder's place and his mare died while giving birth, but then I would have told you this if you'd have given me a damned chance. But no...you had to go all Robocop on me, and cuff me." Her voice rose as she spoke and she hated that he was the reason.

Sam's jaw clenched and his eyes narrowed. "I don't care if you're the damn Queen of England. If you have a warrant out on you, your ass goes in."

"Do you ever let go or are you always so...so damned *professional?*"

"You think I'm professional?" He stepped even closer to her. "I'll show you professional." Suddenly, he trapped her between his arms with her back against her car and leaned into her. When he lowered his head, she knew he was going to kiss her and knew she wanted it but then he shifted, lowered his lips to her neck, and nibbled.

Tessa bit her lip to hold back the moan threatening to escape her as his lips moved up her neck to her ear. When he took the lobe between his teeth and tugged on it, she couldn't stop the shiver that rushed through her. After releasing it, his lips moved over her cheek and his mouth hovered above her lips, with his eyes locked on hers.

"How professional was that, Tessa?" he murmured as his lips tickled against hers.

Tessa's eyes fluttered closed then flew open as he pulled away from her. She blinked her eyes as she looked at him. He grinned and touched his fingers to the brim of his hat. "You have a nice day, ma'am."

Not believing he'd left her just hanging, she watched him walk away and get into his cruiser before driving off.

Tessa watched him disappear from sight down the road. She unlocked her car and got inside. Her fingers touched her lips. He hadn't even kissed her but her lips tingled. Thinking about how close he'd been to kissing her, she swore and hit the steering wheel with her fist. How dare he? She had *not* wanted him to kiss her, or so she told herself, the self who was moaning because...she had wanted him to kiss her. Why not? The man was sex on two legs—two very *long* legs. Damn.

Chapter Two

Tessa sat in her office in the Clifton Animal Hospital. This was the part of her job she hated, the paperwork. Sighing, she stretched her arms above her head and yawned. It was late, almost midnight, and she hated being here but she had to finish up. Taking off her glasses, she tossed them onto the desk and rubbed her eyes. One of her assistants, nineteen-year-old Jodi Pearce had left hours ago and since she had fed the two horses boarded there, along with the cats and dogs in residence for care, she'd told Jodi to leave early to start her weekend.

Tessa exhaled. *It's a Friday night and here I sit. What an exciting life you lead, Doctor McGuire.*

She looked around her office and pride lifted her spirits. This place was hers. Her credentials and posters of different horse breeds hung on the walls. Tessa smiled thinking how right after she'd taken over, the first thing she did was paint the ugly green walls to blue. Noticing for the first time how much the blue of the walls matched Sam

Garrett's eyes, she dropped her head into her hands.

It had been two weeks since he arrested her, and yet it was impossible to get him out of her head. She'd seen him cruising past her building but hadn't come face to face with him since, which was fine with her. The less she saw of him, the better.

Her large mahogany desk had brochures and folders laying all over it so she made an attempt to make some semblance of order. It was late and she'd already done enough. If need be, she could catch up over the weekend. She didn't like taking her work home with her but the good thing was her apartment was just above the hospital's offices.

Tessa stood and moved to the row of mahogany filing cabinets where she opened a drawer. After stowing away the file, she pushed the drawer closed with her hip and then clumsily proceeded to drop the next file onto the gleaming hardwood floor. Groaning, she dropped to her knees to pick up the mess. It was then she heard a noise making her freeze in place.

"Hello?" she called out.

Her skin turned clammy and her breathing became harsh. There was no answer. Tessa stood and placed the file on the desk and peered around her open door. The hallway was dark, the only light coming from her desk lamp. Just when she decided she was hearing things, she heard it again.

Reaching over, she pushed her office door closed and locked it. After turning out the lamp, Tessa leaned against the wall and slid down until her butt hit the floor. She was terrified. Her gaze landed on her purse sitting on one of the leather wingback chairs that sat facing her desk. Crawling to it, she reached for it and took her cell phone out. With shaking hands, she managed to dial the sheriff's office.

"This is Tessa McGuire. I think there's an intruder in my building. Please send someone." The dispatcher on the other end assured her someone would be right there and to stay on the line. Tessa's breathing became so erratic that the operator asked if she needed an ambulance. Tessa almost laughed then tried to calm herself because she knew hysteria was setting in.

It seemed like hours but in all likelihood, only several minutes had passed when she heard someone calling her name, and then realized it was Sam. Opening her door, she ran to the entrance doors. When she unlocked them, Sam came striding in.

"Are you all right?" he asked her as he

shined the beam of his flashlight around.

Tessa rubbed her arms and nodded. "Yes, I-I thought I heard something."

Sam glanced at her. "Stay here. I'll look around."

Tessa put her hand on his arm. "Sam..." He turned back toward her and looked at her hand, making her remove it. "Be careful."

He raised an eyebrow at her then turned to walk through the hallway toward her office. A few minutes later, Sam re-emerged from the hallway. "Where did the noise come from?"

"I'm...I'm not sure. I just heard a noise." She felt ridiculous as Sam nodded.

"Could it have been one of the horses or other animals?"

"I don't think so." Tessa clenched her fists. She wanted to scream at him, it hadn't been the horses or other animals.

"Maybe you should check on all of them while I'm here," he suggested with a nod.

Tessa nodded, feeling somewhat foolish, especially if it turned out one of the horses kicked over a pail or something. After checking on the cats and dogs inside, she led the way out the back door to the four stalls housed in the back. There was nothing amiss with the horses or any of the animals. She glanced at Sam, and shrugged.

"I'm sorry I ran you over here for no reason."

Sam shrugged. "It's my job, Tessa."

Tessa had no idea what to say because she felt like a complete fool. However, she was sure she'd heard something. Sam followed her back into the building.

"Why are you on nightshift?"

"Mark and Paul are both sick. I'm working twelve-hour shifts until they get back. Why are you here so late?" Sam asked as he followed her to her office.

Tessa sighed. "I had some paperwork to do. I always put it off and I should know better."

Sam chuckled and Tessa thought it was the sexiest thing she'd ever heard. She picked up her purse, turned to leave, and ran smack into him. His hands automatically went to her waist. Her hands went to his chest.

"I'm sorry. I didn't know you were so...close." Tessa gazed up into those gorgeous eyes.

She watched as Sam's gaze traveled over her face and landed on her lips. Tessa licked her bottom lip. Sam groaned and started to lower his head. She stepped away from him.

"I want to go to bed..." Her face flamed when Sam's eyebrows rose. "Sleep. I want to sleep." She stepped around him and heard him sigh.

"I'll walk you around to your apartment." Sam's tone of voice booked no argument.

Tessa led the way out through the entrance doors and locked them once she and Sam were outside. They walked around to the side of the building and stopped at the bottom of the stairs leading up to her apartment. Tessa turned to Sam to tell him she was fine but he raised his hand.

"I'm walking you up, Tessa," Sam told her and she knew better than to argue.

Sighing, she walked up ahead of him and swore she could feel his eyes drilling into the back of her. She picked up her pace, hurried up the stairs, and stopped at her door. Sam stopped beside her.

"Do you want me to check it out?"

Tessa hadn't thought of that. "I...yes...please." She blushed when she remembered the last time she'd said that word to him.

Sam nodded for her to unlock the door. Tessa did and waited while Sam moved into the apartment, turning on lights as he walked around. A few minutes later, he came back out.

"It's all clear."

"Thank you." Tessa moved inside the door and turned to look at him. "I'm really sorry for running you over here for nothing."

"Tessa, stop...really it's fine." Then he turned to go. "Don't hesitate to call anytime you need me."

Tessa thought she saw a smile lift his lips but she couldn't see well enough in the dark. She entered her apartment, shut her door, and locked it. Her gaze swept over her living room. Everything looked the same as it had that morning when she left for work. The row of windows along one wall had hanging plant baskets instead of curtains. She liked the morning sun streaming in, lighting up her apartment. Her large red cloth sofa sat centered in the room on an Oriental rug, facing a flat screen TV. Two matching chairs sat catty-corner on each side of the sofa. She walked into her kitchen to get some water. The stainless steel appliances gleamed, as did the cherry laminate floor. The apartment wasn't large, but it was hers. It consisted of the living room, kitchen, one bath, and a large bedroom.

Tessa walked through the living room and down a small hallway to her bedroom. She groaned when she entered her bedroom and saw several pairs of her panties lying on her bed. She'd forgotten she'd left them out after dumping her laundry there. Sam had been in here. Groaning again, she scooped them up and stuffed them in her dresser drawer. She entered the bathroom and undressed, then after taking a quick shower, she climbed into bed. Before she fell asleep, she saw beautiful blue eyes surrounded by thick lush lashes that should be illegal on any man.

* * * *

Sam yawned as he drove through town, his eyes scanning the empty streets. It was a quiet night in his sleepy little town. He maneuvered down side streets, slowly checking the buildings but his thoughts continued to wander back to Tessa. What had Tessa so jumpy? He never would have thought someone like her would let a noise scare her. She just seemed tougher than that or so he thought.

He swore aloud when he suddenly thought about trying to teach her a lesson about him being professional because it had backfired on him—big time. His cock had been so hard when he walked away from her that he was surprised he was able to sit down in the SUV. *Idiot!*

Sam pulled up behind the station, parked the vehicle, and then entered the building. It was close to two in the morning, and he was dead tired. This wasn't his usual shift. Being the sheriff, he worked days only but with both of his nightshift deputies out sick, Sam had to take that shift too. He usually worked seven in the morning to three in the afternoon so the additional nightshifts were kicking his butt. His daytime deputy, Rick Stark was coming in at three so that Sam could go home and get some much-needed rest. Deputy Brody Morgan was working nightshift also until the other nighttime deputies, Mark Shaw and Paul Dixson returned. With Clifton being a town of only fifteen hundred, the five men were all it needed, usually. That is until someone fell sick or went on vacation.

Sam sat at his desk with his booted feet propped up on it and his hands clasped across his flat stomach. He had his head back and his eyes closed, but he jerked when someone cleared his throat. Opening his eyes, he saw Rick standing in the doorway, grinning.

"Hey, boss. Tough night?"

Sam grinned. "This nightshift is for the birds," he said through a hard yawn. "I forgot how much I hated it."

Rick laughed. "Yeah, I hate it too. Mark and Paul love it though. I'm sure Brody will be happy to get back to day shift too." Rick shook his head in what had to be wonderment. "I know Mark and Paul like checking out the Town Hall dances and Dewey's bar so they can see all the pretty girls."

"I wouldn't put it past them." Sam stood and walked past Rick, slapping him on the back. "Tell Teresa I'm sorry to get you out of her bed so early. I'll see you later."

Ten minutes later, Sam pulled up to the one story rancher his parents had left him when they'd moved to San Diego five years ago. He missed them but he knew it was best for them. The cold weather in northern Montana was hell on arthritis and his dad suffered from it in his hands. Sam loved the thousand acres surrounding the home. There were four horses in the barn, and one day, he hoped to get more. He smiled as he heard Bo, his Rottweiler, barking from inside the house. Sam had stopped by earlier in his shift to let the dog out for a while since it was a twelve-hour shift and no matter how well Bo was house trained, Sam seriously didn't think he'd make it that long.

Unlocking the door and expecting an excited dog, he pushed it open only to have a large black blur run past him. Bo hesitated for a second when he saw his master but he needed to find a tree so his bladder took precedent. Sam entered the kitchen and removed his gun from his utility belt, placing it on the counter, then removed the belt and hung it in the mudroom. Pulling out a chair from the table, he practically collapsed onto it. After removing his boots and socks, he stood then stripped out of his jeans, shirt, and boxer briefs and dropped them in the hamper. The dark blue marble floor in the kitchen felt cool on his bare feet. Light oak cabinets lined the wall, surrounding a window sitting above the sink. The appliances were a matching white. He let Bo back in, picked up his gun, then padded naked through the dining room, living room heading for his bedroom with the panting dog at his heels. In the bedroom, the king size bed beckoned to him. He barely had the energy to get between the sheets. After placing his Glock G17 on the nightstand, Sam fell face first into the pillow and was asleep in seconds.

* * * *

The ringing in her head wouldn't stop so half-awake, she reached out slapping at the alarm clock, but it continued to ring. Tessa sat up, rubbed the sleep from her eyes, and realized it was her cell phone. Reaching for it, she picked it up from the nightstand and answered.

"Doctor McGuire."

Turning on the light beside the bed, she sat up, and pushed her hair off her face while she listened to the caller. "I thought Beauty wasn't due yet, Gabe."

Gabe Stone lived on a large ranch outside the town limits. His wife's horse was pregnant but not due for a couple more weeks by Tessa's calculations. It was mid-June and Beauty was due mid-July. "I'm on my way, Gabe. Tell Emma to calm down."

Tessa hung up and dressed quickly. Grabbing her phone, keys, and medical bag, she ran through her apartment and out the door. After locking it, she ran down the steps to her car. It was three in the morning and the town was eerily quiet, making her shiver as she opened her car door, although it was over eighty degrees.

Tessa drove quickly out to Gabe and Emma's ranch. When she pulled up to the side of the porch, she saw Gabe standing in the doorway of the barn. Grabbing her medical bag, she headed toward him. "Is she still in labor?"

Gabe ran his hand through his thick black hair. "Yes. It's been almost thirty minutes. Follow me."

Tessa followed Gabe down the row of horse stalls to where Beauty was laying on the straw. Emma was on her knees beside her and looked up at Tessa with tears in her eyes.

"Please help her, Tess," Emma pleaded,

rubbing the horse's nose. "I can't lose her."

"I'll do what I can, Emma. Hold her head so I can check her," Tessa told her as she walked to the back of the horse. Pulling on a long sleeved plastic glove, she covered it with Vaseline, and then slowly inserted her hand into the birth canal.

"You're doing fine, Beauty. Just let me check your baby." After checking the foal, Tessa sat back on her heels and smiled. "This little one is coming tonight, or I should say this morning."

"I'll help you, Tess. Emma, go inside and take a nap. I'll come and get you when the foal is born and cleaned up," Gabe told his wife. Emma stood and after one longing look at her horse, she kissed her husband and left the barn.

"Did you make her leave for a reason?" Tessa asked him.

Gabe shook his head. "No. I just know how she is. She'd stay here as long as it takes and be dead on her feet the rest of the day. She has enough trouble running after Sophie and Joshua on her best days."

Tessa nodded and pushed down her own longing for such a problem. Sophie was Emma and Gabe's two-year-old daughter and Joshua, their son, was a year old. Tessa cleared her throat and went to work making sure this new baby had a good day too.

An hour later, Tessa stood beside Gabe and Emma watching the new filly getting nourishment from her mama. Gabe had his arms wrapped around his wife's waist from behind, his chin resting on her head. Emma looked over to Tessa.

"Thanks so much, Tess. Sorry it's so late." Emma smiled at her. Tessa smiled back.

"It's my pleasure, Emma. It's the busy season. I get calls at all hours."

Tessa picked up her medical bag and left them alone in the barn. She imagined the good feeling she had delivering a foal was much like that of an obstetrician delivering a baby. The thought of a baby gave Tessa that familiar ache in her heart wondering if she'd ever have a child of her own. Shaking her head, she walked to her car, settled in, and drove away. On the way back to her apartment, she pulled into the twenty-four hour convenience store to pick up some milk. As she stood at the counter, she saw a cruiser pull up out front. Her stomach was full of butterflies as she watched the door open but her breath whooshed out in disappointment when she saw Deputy Brody Morgan enter and smile at her.

"Late night, Doc?"

"Or early morning, Deputy."

Brody chuckled. "I suppose so."

Tessa was tempted to ask about Sam but held back. She sure didn't want it getting back to Sam that she was asking about him. Taking in the sight of his deputy wasn't hard on the eyes though. Brody was a gorgeous man at six-foot four, with black hair and brown eyes. He wore glasses, which didn't seem to detract from his overall good looks and all the women in town thought they were sexy as hell. But no matter how hot he was, he did nothing for her, unlike Sam who made her weak in the knees. Of course, Brody was head over heels in love with his wife, Madilyn and their two-year-old son. After paying for her purchase, she walked to her car and unlocked it, but as she was about to get in the hair on the back of her neck stood up. She quickly glanced around, but it was too dark to see anything. An uneasy feeling settled over her so Tessa got into her car, closed the door, and locked it immediately. Pulling out of the parking lot, she headed home, checking her rear view mirror more than a few times even though she was certain she was imagining things.

* * * *

Sam sat at his desk working on a report when he looked up to discover Betty Lou standing in the doorway. He ignored her and tried not to smile when he heard her huff. Glancing up, he raised an eyebrow at her.

"I'm taking tomorrow off." Betty Lou stared at him with her hands on her hips.

"I don't believe you have any vacation days left." Sam sat back in his chair and tossed his pen onto the desk.

Betty Lou snorted. "Maybe not, but I'm taking one. I have to help Bobbie Jo make cookies for the festival."

Sam glanced over to the calendar. The Fourth of July was in two days. *Shit!* That meant another long shift coming. He had to work the day with Rick and Brody and into the early evening with Mark and Paul. Sam exhaled. *This job is going to kill me.*

"Just what am I supposed to do if an emergency comes in?"

"What you always do. Most of the town calls you on your cell phone anyway and if it's a real bad emergency, they dial 9-1-1." She sniffed. "I know you only hired me 'cause I'm friends with your mama."

Sam smiled and rocked back in his chair. That was exactly why he'd hired her but he kept her on because she was actually very good at her job. She may be close to seventy but she was irreplaceable to him.

"I keep you because I can't see you

staying at home, sitting on your ass crocheting doilies, and when you weren't, I'd have to be chasing you and your sister, Bobbie Jo all over town."

Betty Lou cackled. "I ain't ever crocheted in my life." She turned to leave the office then turned back. "I love you, Sam Garrett." Then she disappeared back to her desk.

Sam shook his head in wonder and grinned as he remembered how he'd argued with his mother about hiring Betty Lou, but his mother had been right. Betty Lou may be a gossip and a busybody but Sam loved her and as long as he was sheriff, she'd have a job. Even if she didn't do much more than answer the phone, and call him on the radio occasionally. Picking up his pen, he returned to his report. When his cell phone rang, he picked it up.

"Sheriff Garrett."

"Sam? It's Trick. I'm at Baker's ranch because his damn cows are on my property again and he won't move them."

"I'm on my way, Trick." Sam pushed back his chair, stood, grabbed his hat, and headed for the back door then called out. "I'm headed to Baker's ranch, Betty Lou."

"You be careful, Sam. That man is a few bricks short of a load."

"I know that's right," Sam muttered.

Climbing into his patrol cruiser, he started it up, put it in gear, and pulled away from the station. As he drove out to Baker's ranch, he wondered how drunk the man would be this time. Joe Baker was a menace to society, and Sam knew things with him would come to a head one day.

Pulling into the driveway, he saw Trick leaning against the front of his truck staring at Joe Baker. Sam parked, grabbed his hat, putting it on as he climbed out of his vehicle then walked toward Trick.

"What's going on?" Sam asked.

"His cows were on my property again and he threatened to shoot me," Trick told Sam, his attitude animated and his hands waving around as he told his side.

"I just have my gun out in case he gets a little rowdy with me. Ain't that right, Mary?"

"Yes, Joe."

Trick snorted and looked to Sam. "She's so damn terrified of him, she won't go against him," he mumbled.

"I know. I've been dealing with him since I became sheriff. I know how he treats her," Sam said then looked at Baker. "Last time I'm telling you to keep your cows on your property. The next time, I'll come out here with a trailer and load them up. You understand me, Joe?"

"Yeah, yeah, I get it...now both of ya...get off my property."

Sam walked toward Baker stopping close enough that he made the man take a step back. "I'm not kidding about this. If I hear from Trick one more time that your cows are on his property, I will bring a trailer out and take them from you."

"I said I get it." Baker looked at Trick and then back to Sam. "You two have to come together every time?"

"I'm the sheriff and you're letting your cattle trespass. Trick's land is posted." Sam folded his arms across his chest and glared down at Baker. He meant to intimidate the man and he could tell the way the man shuffled his feet, it was working.

"I ain't afraid of you, Garrett," Baker said with false bravado, hiking his oversized jeans up at the waist over his belly.

"That's Sheriff Garrett, and you damn well should be," Sam told him. He looked at Trick. "You good for now?"

"Yes." Trick walked to his truck and climbed in, Sam followed behind and stopped alongside the window Trick opened. "I think he's cutting my fence...but I can't prove it."

"It wouldn't surprise me in the least. He's a shady character and I hate any man who beats on a woman," Sam muttered.

"I might have one of my men hide out to watch the fence. Funny thing is...it's always in the same area. Right where his cows are on the hill."

"I'm not lying about the trailer. You call me one more time about them being on your property and I'll load them up."

"I don't doubt that a bit, Sam." Trick smiled at him.

Sam chuckled. "I think I'd enjoy it. I'll talk to you later. Tell Kaylee I said hi, and hug that beautiful daughter of yours for me."

Trick gave him a salute and backed out of the driveway. Sam turned to Baker.

"Last warning on the cows, Baker. Do. Not. Push me." Sam walked to his vehicle and climbed in. After glaring at Baker one more time, he backed out keeping the untrustworthy man in his sights then once clear, drove back to town.

* * * *

The Fourth of July was a hot and humid day and Sam could feel the white T-shirt he wore under his khaki shirt sticking to his back as he worked the crowd. Several people stopped him to talk, and he didn't mind. It was one of the perks of the job. Wyatt and Olivia Stone stepped in front of him and he grinned. Olivia was very pregnant and Sam knew she was due anytime.

"I heard you arrested Doc Mac last month." Wyatt grinned at him with a mischievous gleam in his eye.

"You know what I'd say to you, Stone, if you didn't have your wife with you," Sam said, glaring at him.

"Shame on you, Sam," Olivia scolded him, the first finger of one hand pointing at him while the other hand rested on her swollen tummy.

Sam winked at Olivia. "I'd arrest you too, Liv, if you had a warrant out on you." He laughed when she gasped.

"Don't worry, sweetheart. I'd bail you out." Wyatt burst out laughing when Olivia glared at him.

"I think we need to stop, Wyatt. She looks pissed." Sam laughed. "Must be the hormones."

Olivia opened her mouth and then snapped it shut. "I hate you both," she muttered before she moved through the crowd, leaving the men chuckling.

Sam laughed as Wyatt ran after Olivia, but then he spotted Tessa and headed toward her. He knew the minute she saw him because she turned and headed in the opposite direction. Sam tried to get through the crowd but it was impossible. When the mayor stepped in front of him, he got the feeling that everyone wanted to chastise him for arresting the veterinarian.

"How could you?" Mayor Dexter Powers asked folding his arms across his barrel chest.

"I was doing what you pay me to do, Dex. Was I supposed to let her drive away? Maybe I should just do that for every person who has a warrant out for his or her arrest. Then you and I will be out of jobs." Sam narrowed his eyes at the man.

"Well, I...I can see your point, Sam. But it was Doc Mac, for God's sake."

"He's right, Dex. Sam was just doing his job," Tessa said from behind the mayor.

Sam raised his eyebrows. "I don't need you to defend me, Doc."

"I wasn't defending you, Sheriff...just stating a fact." She nodded at the mayor and disappeared through the crowd.

Sam wanted to kick himself. Why hadn't he just kept his mouth shut? He excused himself and headed after her. He caught up with her by Betty Lou and Bobbie Jo's booth.

"I'll take two macadamia nut cookies, please," Sam heard her tell Betty Lou.

Sam stepped up beside her without looking at Tessa. "Same for me, Betty Lou...please."

Betty Lou handed Tessa her two cookies

and her change. Tessa turned to go, and he met her eyes then he glared at Betty Lou.

"Today, Betty Lou?" Sam growled making the older woman chuckle.

"What's your hurry, Sam?"

"Forget it," he grumbled and ran after Tessa who had walked away. When he found her, she was sitting on a blanket under a large oak tree. She didn't even look up at him when he approached.

Blowing out a frustrated breath, Sam squatted down. "Tessa..."

"What?" She still wouldn't look at him.

Sam swallowed hard. "I didn't mean to jump down your throat. It's just that almost every person in this town has stopped me to chew me a new one about taking you in."

"I know. They've been stopping me to tell me you were wrong to do that," she said chuckling, and trying to hide her smile.

Sam groaned. "I was a prick that day—"

"Yes. You were," Tessa interjected, looking at him with a tilt of her head. "You could have just let me follow you, Sam. Not handcuff me."

"You're right. I'm sorry. How many times do I have to say it?"

"That was enough. I believe you." She smiled at him and his heart fluttered in his chest. "Would you like a cookie, since I see you didn't get yours?"

Sam shook his head and huffed. "Betty Lou can be a royal pain in the ass. She deliberately stalled so you could get away."

Tessa tilted her head. "I wasn't trying to get away..."

Sam grinned. "Liar." He laughed when he saw a blush move into her cheeks but then all of a sudden, her face went pale. "Tessa? What's wrong?"

Standing quickly, he glanced around but didn't see anything amiss. When he looked back at her again, she was taking deep breaths. He crouched down beside her again. "Tessa...what's wrong?"

Tessa shook her head. "I thought I..." She raised faraway eyes at him. "I thought...I was going to be sick."

Sam knew she was lying but he didn't call her on it. What had she seen? He was about to sit down beside her when a call came over his two-way radio. It was Rick with trouble at the kissing booth. Sam touched her hand and she lifted moist eyes to look at him.

"I'll see you later. Have a good time." Then Sam saw her glance around and her hand trembled beneath his. "Tessa." She looked up at him again. "If you need me, call me on my cell phone...okay?"

He handed her a card with his number

on it. She nodded her head as she took the card, but still seemed miles away.

Chapter Three

Tessa left the festival right after the fireworks were over even though she didn't enjoy them because she had the uncanny feeling of someone watching her. As she walked to her apartment, she constantly glanced over her shoulder wishing she'd asked Sam to walk her home. Hearing footsteps sound in the darkness behind her, she came to a halt, her heart pounding in her ears. Turning around, she let out a sigh of relief when she saw two teenagers walking up behind her. They said hello and moved past her. Tessa jogged the rest of the way to her apartment and up the metal stairs, the sound of her shoes clanging on each riser. After opening the door, she hurried inside and locked it behind her.

Stepping to the window, she looked down on the street. The festival lights blazed nearby but she hadn't felt safe there. Her gaze ran over the crowd but it was impossible to see if Sam was still there. Since it was way after nine, he might have gone home after his shift ended.

A sudden knock on her door startled her and she stood rooted to the floor, staring at the door. Another knock and then she heard Sam's voice. "Tessa? Are you in there?"

There was a pause and silence then she heard him start down the stairs. Knowing it was a bad idea she ran to the door and opened it. She looked down at him as he descended the stairs.

"Sam..."

Turning, he tilted his head back and gazed up at her from under the brim of his hat. "I just wanted to see if you were feeling all right," he said.

"I...yes, I am." They stared at each other for what seemed like the longest moment in history, and then Sam nodded.

"Good. I'll, uh...see you." He turned away from her to start down the stairs again.

"Would you like some coffee?" Tessa asked then mentally kicked herself. *What are you thinking?*

Looking back to her, she saw him grin. "If you're sure you don't mind."

Tessa wasn't sure of anything other than not wanting to be alone right now. She nodded and stepped back while he trotted up the stairs. When he walked past her and entered the apartment, she closed her eyes as she took in his scent, a wonderful mixture of man and aftershave.

"Please have a seat, Sam. Do you take cream or sugar?"

"I'll stand, thank you, and black is fine."

Tessa fixed him a cup from her K-cup coffee maker then handed him the cup when it was ready, and watched as he took a sip. Her gaze fixated on his mouth, watching his sexy lips caress the lip of the cup, and then she raised her eyes to look into his. Watching as he set the cup down, her pulse sped up when he stepped toward her. His hand wrapped around the nape of her neck then he leaned toward her and she knew she should stop him but couldn't move or speak. His lips hovered above hers, his warm breath barely touching hers when she pulled back slightly. She felt him grin against her lips then he closed the distance and softly pressed his lips to hers. She sighed against his mouth. He tasted of coffee and sexy man.

Their breaths mingled when he raised his head but then he lowered his head again, and gently pressed his lips to hers. This time Tessa opened to him. With a masculine groan, his arms wrapped around her, pulling her tightly against him, and he kissed her as if he was dying of thirst and she was a cold drink of water. Hesitantly, Tessa allowed her arms to snake up and around his neck. *God!*

The man could kiss. She moaned into his mouth and then he slowly broke the kiss, and lifted his lips from hers.

"Do you have any idea how long I've wanted to kiss you?" he asked in a whisper as he leaned his forehead against hers.

She smiled at the question. "How long?"

"Since the day I first set eyes on you."

"Really? I had the impression you didn't like me."

Sam grinned. "I liked you too much but after the look you gave me, I thought it best to walk away."

Tessa leaned back and ran her hand down his chest to his badge. "I knew you were trouble, Sam Garrett."

"That's *Sheriff* Sam Garrett."

Tessa laughed. "Anything you say, Sheriff."

Sam's eyebrows shot up. "Anything?"

He started to lower his head but the radio on his shoulder decided to choose that particular moment to emit a loud squawk. "Damn it."

Sam pressed the button and Tessa listened as a voice came across telling him there was trouble at the kissing booth again. He gave a sigh of obvious regret and she saw it in his eyes when he looked at her. "I'm sorry. I have to go. Every year I try to talk them out of having that damn booth."

"Duty calls, huh?" She laughed even though somewhat relieved that he was leaving.

"Yes, and its times like these, I really wish I wasn't the sheriff." He ran his hand over her hair, and she caught herself leaning into the caress. "Goodnight, Tessa. Sleep well."

When he turned and started toward the door, she heard him mumble. "I know I won't."

Without looking back, Sam opened it then closed it behind him. She heard his footsteps on the metal steps as he hurried down them. Frowning, she locked the door and thinking that what just happened had not been a good idea. Letting Sam kiss her was just asking for trouble.

Tessa was living a lie already, now she had lied to him about what had happened at the festival when she'd told him she was feeling sick. She just prayed he never found out why.

* * * *

Tessa jerked awake, her face wet from tears. She sat up and quickly glanced around her dark bedroom, wrapping her arms around her to stop her shaking. She hadn't had that dream in years. *Why now?*

Shivering, she got out of the bed and glanced at the clock—one in the morning. Sighing, Tessa put her robe on and headed for the kitchen to warm up some milk. For two years, she'd kept her secret from everyone in town, and now she prayed no one ever found out, especially Sam. Her life before coming to Clifton was the main reason she couldn't get involved with him or anyone for that matter. She'd thought him attractive from the first moment, but she'd given him a look of dislike that first day because it was the best way to keep him at a distance. She hadn't lied when she told him she knew he was trouble. Sam Garrett was trouble absolutely, trouble to her heart. The way her heart had hit her stomach the first time she saw him was proof that he'd be far too easy to fall in love with so she kept him away.

So why are you flirting with him? Would it be so bad to flirt with him? Maybe go out with him?

Tessa shook her head. She knew it couldn't go anywhere, but then again why not enjoy being with the man? A shiver raced over her as she remembered his kisses. Oh yes, Sam Garrett was definitely trouble to her heart.

The microwave rang signally her milk was ready. She took it out and carried the mug back to her bedroom. The past few days had been quiet in the hospital. Most horses didn't have problems giving birth. Since Doc Carter retired, her business had doubled and since deciding to close on the weekends, Tessa got a chance to relax occasionally unless she had an emergency.

Moving to stand by the window, Tessa sighed as she sipped the milk and looked out to the street below. A sheriff's cruiser drove by slowly, but she knew it wasn't Sam. He always drove the SUV cruiser. She couldn't get his kiss out of her head. The man knew how to kiss, there was no doubt there, but he scared her. He was so inquisitive, silently questioning, and she wondered how she could keep her secret from him and not have him hate her if he found it out. Lying by omission was still lying.

Shaking her head of the wishes filling it, Tessa felt her eyelids getting heavy. After setting the mug down on the nightstand, she crawled back into bed leaving the bedside light on. After pulling the quilt up to her chin, she fell asleep.

* * * *

Betty Lou held her hand over her nose and scowled. "You stink, Sam Garrett."

Sam narrowed his eyes and blew out a breath. He and Brody had spent the last two hours trying to round up twelve pigs that had gotten out of the fenced in area on Barton's farm.

"If you were rolling around with pigs you wouldn't smell like a bed of roses either. As soon as Brody gets back from cleaning up, I'm going home to shower."

"Whew. Please do." Betty Lou waved her hand at him and backed out of his office.

Sam chuckled then sat down at the desk and filled out a report sheet for escaping pigs. He was just finishing when Betty Lou hollered at him from the front.

"I'm heading out for lunch."

"Why can't she just use the damn intercom?" Sam grumbled.

"Because I don't like it, and stop swearing," she shouted back, making him chuckle.

The woman could hear a pin drop a mile away but at times, she had selective hearing when he asked questions she didn't want to answer. Sam glanced up when Brody walked in, his hair still damp from his shower.

"Damn, Sam. You stink." Brody grinned at him.

Glaring at his deputy, Sam walked past him and headed for the door. When he reached the door, he looked back over his shoulder. "Just for that smartass remark, I'm done for the day."

Laughing when he heard Brody swear, Sam went out the back door of the station, got into his cruiser, and had to put the window down because of the smell filling the interior. Who knew pigs could smell so bad?

Sam chuckled as he thought of him and Brody running around trying to catch the pigs. Sam had burst out laughing when Brody fell in the mud, but when Sam caught a pig that had apparently rolled in manure, Brody took out his revenge by laughing at him. Jim Barton, the owner, stood next to his truck watching them, telling them he was too old to be running around trying to catch pigs and Sam wondered if it was just an excuse to get them to do the dirty work.

Sam drove down the street then took the road to head home, smiling when he happened to see Tessa's SUV ahead of him. He hadn't talked to her since the kiss they'd shared after the Fourth of July Festival. The kiss that he'd wanted to continue had he not been called back to take care of drunks at the kissing booth. That had been a week ago now, and he'd wanted to talk to her but he wasn't sure what kind of reaction he'd get.

Mentally shrugging, he knew there was only one sure way to find out, so he flipped the lights on to pull her over and grinned as he imagined her reaction as she steered her car over to the side of the road. Pulling up behind her, he shoved the gear into Park, grabbed his hat, stepped out, and set his Stetson on his head before sauntering toward her vehicle. Sam stopped beside the window. She already had it down and threw him a quick gaze up at him before turning forward again.

"I wasn't speeding....*Sheriff*," Tessa said staring straight ahead.

Sam laid his arm on the roof of her car and leaned down to look in at her. "I know. I just wanted to see how you were. I haven't seen you since the night of the festival."

"I'm fine, Sam." He loved hearing her say his name. "You, however, need a shower...phew!" Tessa placed her hand over her nose.

Sam chuckled. "Sorry. Jim Barton's pigs got out. Brody and I had to round them up. I'm on my way home now to get cleaned up."

When she gazed up at him, their eyes met and held. He watched as a slow smile lifted her lips. Sam groaned and tapped the top of her car. "I'll let you go, Tessa. Have a good day."

With a grin, he walked back to his vehicle without another word.

* * * *

Tessa watched Sam in her side view mirror as he sauntered back to his SUV cruiser, not taking her eyes off his tight butt and the way his jeans hugged it. She saw him take his hat off, toss it into the passenger seat then run his fingers through his thick hair, before getting into the vehicle. The man was far too sexy with those blue eyes that could make any woman's panties melt and those lips...she moaned thinking of his delicious mouth and hard body that made her want to climb it like a tree and kiss everything on the way up. The thought of doing just that thrilled her. Sam Garrett was the most eligible bachelor in Clifton and surrounding towns. Would it kill her to have some fun with the man? Keep it casual.

When Sam's cruiser drove by, she wanted to follow him home and climb into the shower with him. Tessa put her fingers to her lips remembering his kiss, and wished he hadn't had to leave that night but she knew it had been for the best since just the thought of his sexy mouth against hers made her shiver with desire.

After checking for traffic, she pulled her SUV out onto the hot blacktop and drove to Ryder's ranch. She needed to check on the foal he'd been taking care of and to give the foal the inoculations he required. Sam's vehicle had long since disappeared from view. She smiled when she thought about him chasing pigs and rounding them up. Tessa laughed aloud at telling him that he needed a shower, but then the laughter died when she thought about him being naked in that shower. Imagining him standing there as the water glided over that tall, hard body, and she imagined every bit of it was hard.

Tessa had seen him shirtless last year when he was at Wyatt's ranch, helping stack hay. She had gone there to check on a pregnant mare and Sam had been in the barn, tossing hay bales as if they weighed next to nothing when Tessa knew they could weigh close to eighty pounds. His hard chest had gleamed with sweat, the light smattering of hair that traveled down his stomach and disappeared into his jeans, glistened, and fascinated her. She was sure her mouth had dropped open and in embarrassment, she had quickly scurried into the other barn but she hadn't been able to get the image out of her mind. His jeans had hung low on his lean hips and remembering how he looked, Tessa groaned as she pictured that sexy V that seemed to capture her full attention. She didn't know what was below those lean hips but if the sight were even half as sexy as the top half, she'd never survive the view or be able to keep resisting him. There wasn't an ounce of fat on him. Sam was all muscle.

Her hand slapped the steering wheel. Now *she* needed a shower—a cold one.

Later that night, Tessa was sleeping soundly when her cell phone woke her. Groggy and silently cursing the person on the other end, she reached for the phone.

"Doctor McGuire," she answered her voice hoarse with sleep.

"Tessa? It's Sam. Look, I'm sorry to call at this time of night but one of my horses has a bad cut on his leg, and I can't get him to calm down enough to check it."

Tessa sat up, now fully awake, and pushing her unruly hair from her face. "No problem, Sam. You need to calm him down though. Call Wyatt or Ryder. I know Trick's out of town but Wyatt or Ryder can help you. They're almost as good as Trick when it comes to talking a horse into anything."

"I'll call one of them... Shit. It's three in the morning."

"Sam. Please, call one of them. They'll understand. I'm on my way." Tessa hung up and dressed quickly. Grabbing her keys and medical bag, she ran down the steps to her SUV. She was sure she'd left tire marks on the road as she tore out of the parking spot.

Tessa hoped Sam had called Wyatt or Ryder.

Not long after, she pulled into Sam's driveway and drove up to park near the barn. After shutting down the engine, she stepped out of her vehicle, bag in hand, and ran to the barn. When she reached it, Olivia Stone, Wyatt's wife was standing by the door.

"Liv?"

Olivia turned and nodded toward the back doors of the barn. "They're both in the stall. I just wanted to come outside for a breather. The heat in there is stifling."

"I'm sorry Sam had to wake you and Wyatt up at this time of the morning." Tessa smiled noting how Olivia wore her long hair in a messy top knot and fluffy slippers on her feet.

Olivia grinned at her. "We weren't sleeping. I heard sex will induce labor."

Tessa laughed. "I should have known you'd tell me something I really didn't need to hear, Liv."

Olivia snorted. "I know you probably don't want to hear this either, but you seriously need to jump Sam's bones," she said following with a loud sigh. "I know I've said it before but that man is so hot and if I wasn't in love with Wyatt, I'd go after the sexy sheriff myself." Olivia grinned at her. "He has a great ass too, you can't tell me you haven't noticed the way he fills out those jeans. Talk about ten pounds of sugar in a five-pound sack. *Whew.*"

Tessa burst out laughing and shook her head. Thankfully, the men came out from the stall just then. She snickered when she heard Olivia sigh.

"Have you ever seen two sexier men in your life? Let's see, all we need to add is Jake, Gabe, Ryder, Brody, Riley, and Trick." Olivia giggled as she ticked off the names on her fingers.

Tessa saw Wyatt raise an eyebrow at Olivia then he grinned and winked at his wife.

Sam glanced at Tessa with worry furrowing his handsome brow. "His leg is still bleeding but Wyatt calmed him down."

"I'll check him," Tessa said and then looked at Wyatt. "Thanks for helping Sam out."

"No problem. I've been there." Wyatt said with a grin and a nod.

Tessa entered the stall and slowly walked toward the horse. She rubbed her hand over the horse's neck, talking to him softly to keep him calm. Sam came to stand beside her.

"So how long has the leg been bleeding, Sam?" Tessa asked.

"I'm not sure. Bo was acting crazy, so I

got up and when I let him out, he ran to the barn. I followed him."

"Bo?" Tessa raised an eyebrow.

"Bo is my dog."

"Well, I think Bo must have heard the horse making a fuss," Tessa told him as she gave the horse an antibiotic shot.

Sam exhaled in relief when she wiped the blood away from the cut. "Thank God," he said, shaking his head. "I'm glad it's just a small cut. I thought it was bigger since it was bleeding so badly."

"It looks like he was kicking the rails for some reason. A snake may have been close or a mouse could've scared him."

Just then, Wyatt and Olivia popped their heads in to bid them goodnight. Tessa watched them stroll down the barn toward the doors, their arms around each other. She shook her head, snickered, but then sobered when she saw Sam looking at her.

"What's so funny?" he asked her.

"I seriously doubt those two will go home and sleep. Liv mentioned that you didn't wake them up when you called."

Sam chuckled. "Yeah, she informed me of that too, when I apologized to her. Apparently, she thinks sex will induce labor." He rubbed his hand around the back of his neck. "I'm sorry, Tessa."

"For what? To use your words...it's my job." She smiled. The smile left her face when her eyes met his. Olivia was right. The man was hot. She almost groaned and knew she shouldn't be standing so close to him. Crouching down, she picked up her medical bag and almost lost her balance. Thankfully, Sam caught her and pulled her up.

"Are you all right?"

Tessa nodded. "Fine. Thank you."

"So polite," Sam muttered.

Tessa glared up at him. "What's that supposed to mean, Sheriff?"

Sam shook his head and glanced away. "Nothing, Doc." His gaze shifted back to her. "Come on, I'll walk you to your car."

Tessa spun on her heel. "Don't bother."

She marched down the aisle of the barn and came to a complete stop when she saw the huge Rottweiler standing in the doorway. She knew not to move especially since he was the biggest Rottweiler she'd ever seen and he was growling. The fur on the back of his neck stood up as he snarled at her.

"It's okay, Bo," Sam said from behind her and immediately, the dog sat down and quieted.

"Hi, Bo." Tessa put her hand out and the dog gave her his paw making her smile.

"He's a big teddy bear," Sam said.

"He's the biggest Rottie I've ever seen. Why haven't I seen Bo before this?"

"I take him to the vet in Hartland and before you say anything about why I called you tonight, that vet doesn't make house calls and doesn't specialize in equine."

Tessa squatted down in front of the dog and he panted at her. "You're a sweetheart, aren't you?" She laughed when Bo suddenly licked her face. It felt as if her entire face was wet from one swipe. Tessa stood, and looked everywhere but at Sam. "I still don't understand."

"I didn't think you'd want my business, Tessa. I thought you hated me."

"No, it's not like that. If only..."

"What does that mean?" Sam stepped closer to her.

"It means that you are trouble with a capital T, Sam Garrett but if you ever need me to see Bo—"

Sam grinned. "I'm trouble?"

Tessa laughed. "To me you are. There's not a single woman in town who doesn't want you. Probably some married ones too."

Sam cupped her face in his hands. "I'm only interested in one woman wanting me and that's you, Tessa." He leaned down and pressed his lips to hers causing her to moan and wrap her arms around his neck. As his tongue entered her mouth, he pulled her against him so that she could feel his hard shaft behind the fly of his jeans. She pressed her hips against him making him groan into her mouth then he slowly lifted his lips from hers. "You'd better go."

"Yeah, I should. I'll go so you can get back to bed."

Shit! Why did the mention of a bed around Sam make her cheeks flame hot?

Grabbing her bag, she moved past Sam and headed toward her car.

"I'll stay up now. I have to start my shift in two hours anyway." He was directly behind her following her out of the barn. Tessa knew she had to get out of here before she did something stupid. Something like what Olivia said and jump the sexy sheriff's bones.

"Tessa."

She turned back to face him. "Yes?"

"Have dinner with me."

"I'm not sure that's a good idea, Sam."

"I do," he said then exhaled as he stepped closer. "All right...think about it and let me know." He leaned down and kissed her quickly. "Goodnight, angel."

Tessa watched him as he strode away with Bo following him.

Chapter Four

Mid July let everyone know what hell was like. It was unbearably hot. Heat waves rose from the street in the middle of the day and little bubbles popped up in the blacktop. The little town of Clifton looked deserted since people were staying indoors to escape the heat.

Sam stood from his chair in his office to check the air conditioning for what felt like, the hundredth time. The thermostat showed seventy-two but it felt like one hundred and seventy-two. *Christ! It was hot.* He hadn't been outside since he arrived this morning and he had no desire to go out again yet his T-shirt was sticking to him. Walking out to the front office, he saw Betty Lou sitting in her chair fanning herself looking as uncomfortable as he was.

"Are you all right, Betty Lou?" Sam asked her concerned that the heat might be having a harsh effect on his old friend.

"I just can't seem to get cooled down, Sam."

"Do you want me to take you home?"

Betty Lou glared up at him. "Did I say I wanted to go home, Sam Garrett?"

Sam ran his hand over his mouth. "No, ma'am."

Betty Lou grumbled. "If I want to go home, I can drive myself. I just said I was having trouble cooling down." She narrowed her eyes at him. "Just go back to your office."

Sam hid a grin as he turned then headed back to his office and was about to sit down when a call came in. When he heard the Bakers were at it again, he groaned and swore as he slammed his hat on his head then headed out the back door.

"You be careful out there, Sam. That Joe Baker is crazy," Betty Lou yelled as the door shut behind him.

Shaking his head, Sam knew she was right. Joe Baker liked using his wife as a punching bag but no matter how many times they tried, Mary never pressed charges. She'd just have him hauled in to spend the night in jail and the next day, she'd bail him out. As Sam stepped out the back door, the heat slammed into him making sweat trickle down between his shoulder blades before he even climbed into the cruiser. He called Brody on the two-way radio to let him know where he was heading.

"Sam, I should tell you that Doc Mac is

out there too. She had a call about one of the horses. Jodi mentioned it when I was talking to her about Madilyn's cat."

Son of a bitch! Sam cursed Joe Baker. "Get out there, Brody. I'm on my way. Run the lights and siren."

Brody acknowledged he was close, and was on his way. Sam tore out of the parking lot with his lights and siren going, all the while hating the idea of Tessa being out there if Joe Baker was on a tear. Going around a turn so fast, he swore he was driving on two wheels but he had to get there for Tessa.

* * * *

Standing with her hands on her hips, Tessa glared at Joe Baker. "Leave her alone, Joe."

Baker swung around and pointed his finger at her. "You just do what you're here to do and leave us alone," he said in a snarling tone then turned back to his wife. "You get in the house, Mary. This ain't over between us yet."

"Mary, you stay out here if you want," Tessa told her. She hated seeing a woman pushed around. Tessa glared at Joe.

Joe let go of his wife's arm and marched toward Tessa but she stood her ground. No man was going to make her back down. As long as he didn't touch her, she was fine.

Most bullies were cowards and sure enough, he stopped within two feet of her.

"You ain't got no business running your mouth, Doc Mac. This is between me and my wife." His eyes narrowed as he looked at her.

"No way. I'm not going to stand here and watch you browbeat Mary," Tessa said between clenched teeth.

Joe jerked back. "Brow...what?"

"Browbeat." Tessa stared at him with narrowed eyes. "You're a bully, Joe Baker. Why don't you pick on someone your own size?" She watched him as he eyed her up and down.

"You look about my size."

Actually, she was taller than he was but if he touched her, she knew she'd lose it. Her bravado was all for show and she hoped he wouldn't call her bluff. In the distance, she heard sirens. Thank God, her call had gotten through. When she'd placed the call, she had to talk fast before Joe caught her.

At the sound of sirens, Baker spun around and glared at Mary. "You called the cops?" he accused her, his voice filled with anger.

"No...Joe. I-I was here the whole time," Mary stammered stepping back with her hands up in front of her.

Joe glanced back to Tessa. "You?"

Tessa straightened up to her full height. "Yes, I called. I'm not going to stand by and watch you hurt Mary."

Mary Baker was a tiny woman, thin, and not quite five-foot-tall, where Joe was almost five eight and in comparison, towered over her. Tessa could see Mary was frightened of her husband, because any time he spoke to her she obeyed him. Tessa had seen her flinch whenever Joe got near her or yelled at her. She hated coming to the ranch but Mary had called about her horse not eating, and Tessa couldn't ignore a sick animal.

Now Tessa sighed with relief when she saw two vehicles with flashing lights pull into the driveway—one was Sam's patrol cruiser. Her heart fluttered when he stepped from the vehicle and strode toward her with his aviator glasses hiding those beautiful eyes.

"What's going on?" He looked to Joe and then to Tessa as Brody joined them.

"I'll tell ya what's goin' on. Mary and me was talking and Doc Mac stuck her nose in where it don't belong."

Sam removed his shades putting them in his shirt pocket, glanced at Tessa, and raised an eyebrow. "Tessa? What's going on?"

"I told ya—" Joe shut up when Sam turned his attention to the man.

"Mary called me out here to check on her horse. We were in the barn talking and he..." Tessa pointed to Joe. "Started yelling at her and told her to get into the house."

"Have you been drinking again, Joe?" Sam asked him.

"He drinks every day—" Mary started to say until Joe suddenly backhanded her.

Sam grabbed Baker and slung him to the ground only Joe swung a fist connecting with Sam's jaw and knocking him back. Brody ran over but before he could grab Joe, the man reached to pull a gun out from the back of his pants.

"Gun," Brody hollered pulling his weapon from his holster. Sam was even faster.

"You draw that weapon and your ass will be in jail for quite a long time, Baker," Sam said as he stood over him pointing his weapon at the man. Now Brody also had his weapon pointed at the man lying on the ground.

Tessa was terrified as she put her arm around Mary. "Tell Joe not to draw his gun."

Mary shook her head. "He won't listen to me, especially when he's drunk.

Tessa shook her. "Try."

Mary cleared her throat. "Joe, please don't pull your gun. You're gonna get hurt."

Joe laughed. "I don't think so. I ain't goin' to jail."

"You pull that weapon, Joe and you're either going to jail or to the morgue," Sam said in a low tone of voice telling the man he meant business.

Joe pointed at Tessa. "It's her fault. She should've minded her own business."

"You're wrong, Joe. She was just protecting Mary from you. You want to hit someone, I'm right here." Sam spread his arms wide.

Tessa's breath left her body. "Sam...please don't, he's dangerous."

Sam smiled and holstered his weapon. "We have a history, don't we, Joe? How many times have I dragged your ass to jail for hitting Mary or drunk driving? Hell, I've put you in jail so many times it's almost like a second home."

Joe laughed. "You're sweatin', Sheriff. You scared of me?"

"It's hot as hell today. My sweating has nothing to do with you, Joe. I'm not afraid of a man who beats women. Try beating on a man, let's see how you do."

"I'd love to but I know the minute I hit you, your deputy will shoot me."

Sam glanced at Brody. "Let him go, Brody, back down." He nodded when Brody complied. "Okay, Joe. Come on. Deputy Morgan won't do a thing to you. In fact, if you kick my ass, we'll both leave without arresting you."

Tessa could see Joe's bravado seeping out of him. She hated men like him. They were typical bullies who only felt big when they beat on a woman. They backed down from confrontation with a man, especially a real man like Sam, a man who was big and strong. She saw Sam narrow his eyes at Joe.

"But it will give me great pleasure to kick your ass and drag you to jail. So come on, Joe. It's too fucking hot to piss around." Sunlight flashed off his badge.

Joe stared at him with anger in his eyes. Tessa was so afraid for Sam, not that she thought Joe could beat Sam but because the bastard still had his gun within reach. She could feel Mary shaking.

"Mary, you have to press charges against Joe. It's the only way you're going to stop him from hurting you," Tessa whispered to her.

Mary shook her head. "He'll kill me."

"He won't get the chance. Press charges, Mary and you'll never go through this again. He could spend a year in jail, and you could start a new life." Tessa looked into her eyes. "Do it."

Mary's eyes filled with tears. "I can't."

Tessa sighed. "You'll feel better about yourself."

Mary didn't say anything. Tessa watched Sam staring Joe down. Joe had a nasty grin on his face. Sam didn't move as he kept his eyes on Joe.

"I'd love to kick your ass, Sheriff but I don't trust your deputy," Joe told him climbing to his feet and holding his hands out to his sides. Brody moved forward and grabbed Joe's gun from the back of his pants. Joe growled at the deputy.

Sam walked forward and stopped within a foot of Joe. "Try it," he said in a deadly voice.

Joe looked away for a moment then swung his fist but before it could connect, Sam punched him and knocked him out cold.

"Joe," Mary screamed, and broke loose of Tessa running to where her husband lay on the ground. Tessa had tried to stop her but Mary was unbelievably strong.

"Son of a bitch," Sam growled as he stared at Joe. "Let's get him inside, Brody."

Tessa watched as Sam and Brody carried Joe into the house with Mary following them. Once they were out of sight, she dropped to the ground. Tears streamed down her face as she wrapped her arms around her waist and rocked back and forth. Joe could have shot Sam.

* * * *

"Damn it, it's too bad you had to hit him. I'd rather have seen his ass in jail than in his house, lying on the couch," Brody said from beside him.

Sam blew out a breath. "I know but I didn't have a choice. I'll charge him with assaulting an officer. He *was* thinking about shooting us, after all."

"He was thinking about shooting *you*, you mean," Brody reminded him. "He doesn't care for you at all. You've run him in so many times."

Sam nodded as he watched Mary hover over Joe. Unable to understand the woman's loyalty to a man who beats her, he walked outside and it was then he saw Tessa on the ground, on her knees, rocking back and forth. After what she'd experienced, it was possible that shock was setting in. Taking a deep breath, he strode toward her.

"Tessa," he said softly. She didn't acknowledge him as he squatted down in front of her. "Tessa?" Sam gently touched her shoulder but she jerked away and looked up at him, her face was ghostly white and her eyes wide in her face.

"I'm okay," Tessa whispered as she

glanced away from him.

"I don't think so." Sam frowned.

"I...he's a bully." She gazed up at him. "He was going to shoot you, Sam."

"I wasn't going to let that happen. I knew I could hit him before he realized what was happening." Sam tilted his head. "Are you all right?"

Tessa nodded her head and glanced around. "I...uh, I feel sick." She tried to stand and Sam helped her but then Tessa ran to a row of bushes and threw up. Sam was beside her.

"It's hard seeing something like this go down," Sam whispered as he held her ponytail back. Her hair was as soft as silk in his hands.

Tessa gazed at him wiping her mouth. "He deserved it but I don't think Mary will press charges." She shuddered. "That's the course of domestic violence. It's so dangerous. I..."

Sam frowned. "What?" He helped her stand.

Tessa shook her head, and gazed up at him. "Nothing," she said suddenly looking away. "I need to leave, Sam."

She started to move away from him but he kept a hold on her arm.

"Tessa, I'll need you to come in and file

a report," Sam said as they walked toward her car. She nodded, told him she would then got into her SUV, and drove off without looking at him.

* * * *

It had been a long day—damn Joe Baker. Sam finally had a chance to head home. Joe Baker was a loose cannon and Sam hated how he treated Mary. The woman was terrified of him. Just as Sam had thought so many times before, it would all come to a head one day. Right now, he just wanted to get home and relax.

Just as he headed out home, a call came over the radio about a woman in labor who wasn't going to make it to the hospital. So much for heading home, the location of the emergency was in the direction Sam was heading, so he called in that he was close but told the dispatcher to send the ambulance.

As he came around a curve in the road, he saw a pick-up truck alongside the road. Slowing down, he thought it looked like Wyatt's truck. Pulling in behind it, he opened the door, stepped from the cruiser, and walked toward the truck. When he heard a woman scream, he quickly pulled his weapon. Sam had to make sure this was the woman in labor and not something else— something far more dangerous.

Slowly walking to the back of the truck, he stopped and called out, announcing himself.

"Hello? Sheriff's department."

Wyatt Stone came around from the side toward the back of the truck looking disheveled. Sam had never seen him like this but lowered his weapon.

"Sam. Thank God, help me," Wyatt said as he took his hat off, raked his fingers through his hair, and resettled his hat.

Sam holstered his weapon and stepped forward. "Wyatt? What the hell is going on?"

"Olivia. She's in labor."

Sam blew out a laugh. "Oh, is that all? I thought you were in trouble."

Wyatt narrowed his eyes at him. "Is that all? I am in trouble. Her water broke and she says the baby's coming."

Sam tried his best not to grin. "Calm down. I'll help. If her water broke, she most likely won't make it to the hospital."

"If you two could quit chit chatting and get your asses up here to help me, I'd appreciate it," Olivia called out then let loose a scream that sent a shiver down Sam's spine.

Sam pursed his lips. "Coming, Liv. Wyatt, keep her calm. I need to get some things from my patrol cruiser." Walking back to his vehicle, he opened the rear hatch, and pulled out blankets and towels then returned to Wyatt's truck. He peered in at Liv with a grin.

"Hey, Liv. How are you doing?"

"I'm having a baby in a pick-up truck on the side of the road, how do you think I'm doing, *Sheriff*?"

Sam dipped his head down then turned to Wyatt. "Was it you who called 9-1-1 about her being in labor?" At Wyatt's nod, he went on. "Go around to the other side to help her sit up if she needs to push." He watched Wyatt run around the passenger side of the truck. "I'm glad you were able to get in the backseat. More room." Sam glanced at Liv to see her glaring at him. He winked. "We need to get your pants off, Liv."

Olivia stared at him then burst out laughing. "Sam Garrett, of all the times I might have fantasized of hearing you say that, this was not the way I thought it would go."

"Excuse me?" Wyatt growled from behind her.

"Oh, please. You know I love you, cowboy, but you also know I've always had a crush on Sam."

Sam shrugged when Wyatt glared at him. "I could leave..."

"Not a fucking chance, Garrett. Right now, I don't care if she professes her undying love for you as long as you help with this baby."

Sam chuckled. "Sure. Maybe you should come around here and take her slacks off?"

"Yeah, okay." Wyatt moved back around to where Sam stood and told Olivia to lift her hips. He tugged them down and off, then tossed them onto the floor. Olivia started laughing. "What the hell is so funny?"

"You taking my pants off *is* what got me into this predicament in the first place." She laughed but then her guffaw ended in a gasp. "Shit. Cramp." She groaned loud and grabbed at her belly.

"Let's get this towel under you, Liv. Wyatt, go back around to help her sit up. The ambulance should be here soon." Sam sure hoped so anyway.

"Have you done this before, Sam?" Liv asked him looking a little worried.

"Yes, ma'am. You'll be my third."

"Damn, I was hoping to be your first," she said then giggled and winked at him.

"Jesus, Olivia. I'm right here," Wyatt said.

"I love you, Wyatt, and you know it...but I'm a hopeless flirt." She shrugged.

Sam grinned. No truer words were spoken. Olivia Stone loved her husband and no one doubted that but she was, indeed, a flirt.

"I hear the ambulance," Sam said, never more glad to hear that sound as now.

"Thank God," Wyatt muttered.

"You don't have faith in me?" Sam asked with a scowl.

"Sure I do, but my wife seems to enjoy being around you without her pants on far too much," Wyatt said with a frown then chuckled when Olivia burst out laughing. Her laughter died fast though when she inhaled with a hiss.

"I need to push," she said between clenched teeth.

"Sit her up. Push when you're ready, Liv," Sam told her as he glanced out the back window to see the ambulance flying down the road toward them. He looked back to Liv to see the head crowning. "Ambulance is here, but so is this baby."

Olivia grasped the back of the front seat with one hand and Wyatt's hand with the other as she pushed. All Sam really had to do was take the baby once it arrived. The ambulance pulled to a stop beside the pick-up truck. As the paramedics ran toward them from the vehicle, Sam laid the baby on the towel between Liv's legs and grinned at Wyatt.

"It's a boy! Congratulations, you two."

He looked at Liv and Wyatt to see them both with tears on their cheeks.

"His name is going to be Caleb Samuel. For you, Sam," Liv told him with a happy smile.

Sam grinned. "That's nice but my name isn't Samuel. It's Jonathan Sam."

"No shit?" Liv asked with raised eyebrows.

"No shit," Sam said laughing.

"Okay. Then Sam will be his middle name. Thank you so much, Sam."

"You're welcome, Liv. Wyatt? You all right?"

"Yeah, Sam. I'm great." Wyatt grinned at him with the usual pride of a new father.

Sam slapped him on the back and once he made sure the paramedics were taking care of mother and baby, he cleaned up then climbed into his SUV and finally, drove home.

* * * *

Tessa sat in her office, staring at the wall while tapping her pen on the desktop, and knowing she needed to go to the sheriff's department to fill out a report on what she'd witnessed at the Baker ranch. Why couldn't Sam just take a statement over the phone? Why did she have to go there? It was getting harder and harder for her to be close to him.

He made her feel things she couldn't afford to feel.

Tessa put her hands over her face and groaned. The man was too...*male.* A sudden knock sounded on her office door startling Tessa. She looked up to see Jodi stick her head in and smile at her.

"I'm leaving, Doc Mac. I'll see you Monday."

Tessa nodded and glanced at the clock. It was ten after six. "I didn't realize it was so late."

After shutting down her computer, she grabbed her purse. "I have to go over to the sheriff's office to make a statement about Joe Baker," Tessa said with a grimace.

"It's too bad you had to go through that but any excuse to see Sheriff Garrett would almost be worth it." Jodi giggled. "I mean, I know he's older, but he's so hot."

Tessa burst out laughing. "I believe he's only thirty-four, Jodi."

Jodi frowned at her. "Yeah, I know. He's an older man." She looked at Tessa as if she'd grown a third eye.

Tessa shook her head, smiling. "I won't tell him you said that."

Jodi laughed. "Please don't. All the girls my age have a huge crush on him. See ya." She gave a wave and walked out the door.

Tessa's mouth twisted. It wasn't just girls Jodi's age with a crush on the sexy sheriff. She was twenty-nine and she had one hell of a crush on the man. Sighing, she pulled out her keys. She might as well go and get it over with since Sam was expecting her. Tessa locked up the hospital and headed up the street. The hairs on the back of her neck stood up making her stop and glance around, but she didn't see anything or anyone out of the ordinary. Shrugging, she crossed the street and entered the sheriff's department.

Betty Lou glanced up when Tessa walked in. She was wearing a frown on her face but it quickly turned into a smile when she saw Tessa.

"Hi, Tess. How ya doin', hon?"

Tessa smiled. "I'm good, Betty Lou. Is Sa—uh, Sheriff Garrett in?"

"Nope. He's out patrolling. He's working late today." Betty Lou shook her head.

Tessa tried to stem the disappointment. "I'm supposed to fill out a statement about Joe Baker."

"I can get it for you." Betty Lou stood up and motioned for Tessa to follow her to Sam's office. She walked to the file cabinet, pulled out a form, and handed Tessa a pen. "Just sit here at Sam's desk, fill it out, and leave it there, that way he'll see it when he comes back." Betty Lou left her alone in Sam's office.

Gazing around the room, she inhaled deeply. It smelled like Sam's aftershave. She lowered herself into the chair and began filling out the paper. When she heard the door at the back of the station open and close, she hoped it was Sam. When he came to stand in the doorway, she knew he was there before she even looked up. Her pulse went into overdrive. He cleared his throat and Tessa lifted her eyes to look at him.

"Hello, Tessa." His voice ran over her like warm honey.

"Hi, Sam. I'll be done in just a minute."

Sam nodded. "That's fine. I need to see Betty Lou a minute anyway, so take your time."

Tessa silently chastised herself for acting all loopy over Sam and for sighing with disappointment when he stepped away from the doorway. Why did he have this effect on her? The last thing she needed or wanted was to get involved with him, but it would be so easy to do. He was interested, that she was sure of, which made Tessa shiver remembering the times he'd kissed her. No man had ever kissed her the way he had. She sighed again, finished the report, and stood just as Sam entered the room and smiled at her.

"All done?"

Tessa nodded. "How is Joe by the way?"

Sam frowned. "He has a black eye and is threatening to sue, which is nothing new when it comes to him." He strode around his desk and stood in front of her.

Tessa looked up at him and allowed her gaze to travel over his face. The crow's feet that fanned out from the corners of those blue eyes were even sexy. The stubble on his lower face, neck, and strong jaw was growing thicker as the day progressed, which made her want to trail her fingertips along it. She'd seen him clean-shaven, and with stubble, and there was no way she could choose which was sexier if her life depended on it.

Tessa squeezed between him and the desk then headed for the office door but stopped when his deep voice grabbed her attention.

"Have you decided about having dinner with me, Tessa?" he asked her, making her breath catch in her throat. She'd forgotten all about his asking and as much as she wished she could...

Tessa shook her head and turned toward him. "I don't think that's a good idea, Sam."

Sam tilted his head as he gazed at her.

"Why not?"

Tessa dropped her gaze to the top of his desk where his hat rested. "Because...I'm not looking for any type of relationship."

Sam sat down in his chair, leaned back, and clasped his hands across his stomach. "It's only dinner but you can't deny the attraction between us, Tessa."

Tessa clenched her teeth. "You have no idea what you're talking about, Sheriff Garrett."

Sam sat forward and leaned his arms on the desk. "Yes, I do. If you say you don't feel it, then you're lying to yourself and me."

Tessa refused to address his allegation because he was right and she didn't know what to do about it. She gave a huff and marched from the room. Betty Lou glanced up as she passed her desk but Tessa didn't address her, she was too flustered. Sam had no idea what he was talking about but he did, which made her moan as she pushed through the doors.

Tessa knew he was right. There was a deep attraction between them and as much as she'd love to go for it with him, she knew she couldn't. She didn't have the right to get involved with anyone, even just for fun. Stepping outside of the department, she took a deep breath as the heat of the evening hit her. It was almost six-thirty at night and still unbearably hot. She jogged across the street, heading for her apartment to spend yet another weekend alone.

Chapter Five

Sam sat back, rubbed his eyes then swiveled his chair around, and pulled up the blinds. It was early August and still hot but in another month, the cooler weather would be moving down from the Glaciers. Being in northern Montana the cold weather moved in early. Sam gazed at the mountain range and knew they would be snowcapped in another month. Standing, he stretched his muscles. The day had been a long one so far with nothing much happening around town.

He wondered about Tessa, though. She still hadn't let him know about the dinner date he'd requested, and it had been over two weeks since he'd asked her. Should he ask her again? *And get shot down.* No man liked that and he'd wanted her for so long. Those few kisses they'd shared only enhanced his need for her.

Sam gazed over toward the animal hospital. It looked quiet. He reached for the phone, dialed the number for the animal hospital, and waited. He had to ask her out again, he just had to try or claim defeat.

"Clifton Animal Hospital, how may I help you?" a feminine voice answered.

"Is Tessa around? This is Sheriff Garrett."

"Oh hi Sheriff." A giggle came across the line. "Doc Mac had a call out at Jim Barton's."

"How long has she been gone?" Sam wanted to know with the hope that he might know if she was going to return soon.

"She just left about ten minutes ago. Do you want to leave a message for her?"

"No. Thanks." Sam hung up, grabbed his hat, and headed for the back door. "Betty Lou, I'll be back in a little while."

"Are you going for lunch?" Betty Lou hollered from her desk.

Sam halted and exhaled. "I wasn't, but do you want me to bring you something?"

"Not if it's a problem, Sam Garrett."

Sam muttered under his breath as he headed toward the front office and folded his arms atop the counter. "Do you want me to bring you something or not?" he asked again.

"Why are you in such a snit?" Betty Lou glared up at him.

"I'm sorry. I just need to go out for a minute." He gave her one of his most charming smiles, but it didn't work on her.

"I'll get my own lunch, thank you very much." She turned her back to him and continued working on a crossword puzzle.

"Damn it, Betty Lou. I can bring you something back if you want me to." Sam was trying very hard, desperately even, to hold on to his temper and sanity.

Betty Lou slowly rose from her chair. "Don't you dare swear at me, Sam Garrett—I know your mama, remember?"

"How the hell can I forget when you remind me every damn day?" Sam glared at her, spun on his boot heel, and headed out the back. "You go right ahead and get your own lunch. I'm sure whatever I'd bring back wouldn't suit you anyway." Sam heard her gasp as he slammed the door behind him. Rolling his eyes to heaven as he headed for his vehicle, he knew he'd pay for that later.

Sam climbed into his SUV and began the drive to Barton's ranch. Although Tessa's specialty was equine, she was still a veterinarian to all animals. Sam didn't think Jim Barton had anything other than pigs on his ranch but he knew since Doc Carter retired, everyone now turned to Tessa for their animals' welfare. Well, except him, and she already knew why. Now, if Tessa needed time off, Doc Carter stepped in. Sam was tempted to run the lights but he knew he couldn't do that. If he showed up with his lights on just to ask her out, she'd think he was crazy for sure. However, he flew down the road, well over the posted speed limit not wanting to risk missing her. When he reached the entrance to Barton's farm, Sam slowed down and pulled into the driveway but stopped his vehicle there. *What the hell am I doing?*

Spotting Tessa's SUV parked up by the barn, Sam shifted into Park, watched, and waited. He took his sunglasses off and tossed them on the dash, rubbed his eyes then pinched the bridge of his nose. Pressing the button for the window, he lowered it, and shut the truck engine off. The August air smelled of cut hay, and pigs. Sam shook his head, turned the key, and put the window back up. He laughed softly. How did old man Barton stand it? The man was probably used to the reeking aroma after a lifetime of smelling it. Although, Sam didn't think it was possible for anyone to get used to that stink.

He sat up when he saw Tessa walking from the barn with Barton following her. She stood by her SUV caught up in conversation with Barton. They were both smiling. Sam sighed. Did he really want her to see him sitting here like some kind of stalker? Reaching for his sunglasses, he put them on, and started up the engine. Sam swore. *You really have it bad, buddy.*

He'd wanted Tessa since the first time he saw her, and the experience was like a sucker punch. Sam shook his head as he remembered her looking at him like she hated him on sight, and now he knew why. She thought he was trouble. Of course, his response hadn't been any better since he'd frowned at her, and there had begun their relationship. It wasn't until recently that he'd gotten close to her. Sam wanted to be closer— so much closer. He wanted to bury himself deep inside her. *Christ!*

His cock twitched and he knew then he needed to get the hell out of here. Swearing, he backed the vehicle up onto the road and sped off, slamming his palm against the steering wheel. It hurt, but he did it repeatedly.

* * * *

Tessa pulled out of Barton's driveway and headed back to town. With all scheduled surgeries done for the day, Tessa had taken the call to check out one of Barton's pigs that had cut its snout on the barbwire fence. Having never worked on a pig's snout before, she still couldn't help but laugh remembering how bad Sam had smelled the day he had to round up the pigs. Now she knew why. Those little buggers really stunk. They rolled in mud along with anything else that was in the filth. She'd rather not think about what else might be in it.

Now as she drove down Main Street, she decided to stop in at the diner and grab a turkey club sandwich to take back to the office. She picked up her cell phone, called Jodi to see if she and the techs wanted anything and of course, they did. After parking in front of the diner, Tessa stepped out into the heat. She hurried into the diner and when she entered, everyone waved or called out to her. Tessa glanced around and smiled at everyone as she took a seat on one of the red vinyl stools at the counter.

Glancing over her shoulder when the bell above the door announced another customer, she had to stop herself from throwing her arms around Sam as he sauntered in. He grinned at people who stopped him to talk while Tessa kept her eyes on him. Sam glanced at her and her heart hit her stomach when those blue eyes clashed with hers. He nodded at her, and then took a seat on the stool next to hers.

"How are you?" he asked her leaning in close.

"I'm fine. What about you?" Tessa toyed with the metal napkin holder on the counter.

"I've been thinking about you," he said as he leaned in even closer to her.

Her eyes closed of their own volition when the scent of his aftershave and natural aroma filled the air around her. "Have you?"

Sam chuckled. "Always, sweetheart."

Tessa's heart slammed against her ribs at the endearment. Hearing it shouldn't make her heart speed up, but it did so she smiled and glanced at him. "Really?"

Sam groaned. "You're killing me, darlin'."

Tessa laughed and looked away. "I don't want to do that."

"Hey, Sam...what can I get you?" Connie asked him looking from him to Tessa and back again.

Sam looked to Connie. "A burger and a water, please Connie." He smiled at her, and then his gaze shifted back to Tessa meeting her eyes again.

Connie set Tessa's orders on the counter in front of her, drawing her attention so she handed Connie some money, waved away the change, and stood.

Tessa leaned down alongside Sam. "I'm still thinking about that dinner, Sheriff." With a sly grin, she headed out the door knowing Sam was watching her go.

* * * *

Tessa sat at her desk, taking deep breaths trying to calm her still racing heartbeat. She couldn't stop thinking of Sam and his eagerness to have dinner with her. She really shouldn't go out with him but she wanted to, she wanted to get to know him better—she simply wanted him. If his kisses turned her on, she had to wonder what it would be like to go to bed with him. She wasn't a virgin by any means, but there was something so heart stopping about him that he scared her. He was too much man for her, far more than she'd ever experienced before.

"Are you all right, Tess?" Kaylee Dillon asked from the doorway.

Tessa looked up at Kaylee and nodded.

"Yeah, just a rough day," she answered with a smile. "I'll be fine. What are you doing here?"

"I know we haven't known each other long but I know when you're lying, Tess." Kaylee folded her arms across her chest. "You can tell me anything, you know. It would go no further than this room."

"I know that, Kaylee. It's nothing really...just something I'm trying to talk myself out of." Tessa tried to smile.

Kaylee sighed. "All right but if you want to talk... I just brought the dog in for his shot and wanted to say hi. I'm on my way out of here. Patrick will be happy I'm home early from the hospital, for once."

Tessa smiled. "I'm sure he will be."

Kaylee laughed. "He'd better be." She sobered. "Seriously, Tess, if you need to talk, I'm here for you."

"Thanks Kaylee. I may take you up on that. How's that beautiful daughter of yours?"

Kaylee beamed with maternal pride. "Great, and absolutely spoiled rotten by her daddy."

"I'm sure. Trick was so excited when she was born. She is beautiful but that's no surprise, look at her parents." Tessa grinned.

"She looks like her daddy with that black hair and those black eyes. She's going to be a heartbreaker when she grows up."

Tessa laughed. "No doubt about that. I'd love to come out to see her again."

"Tess, you are welcome anytime. The only problem you'll have is if you want to hold her...getting Patrick to let go of her. Harlee has her daddy wrapped around her little finger."

"Daddy's should spoil their daughters. I'll try to stop by next week."

Kaylee smiled at her, waved farewell, and left. Tessa could hear Kaylee and Jodi talking as they walked out together. Jodi yelled out goodbye and Tessa walked to the waiting area to lock the door behind them. She leaned back against the doors soaking in the sudden quiet of the reception area, but then let out a small scream when someone suddenly tapped on the glass behind her. Tessa spun around and sighed with relief and a bit of annoyance when she saw Sam standing there. She unlocked the door, let him in, and turned away from him, not able to meet his eyes.

"Tessa?"

"Sam, what are you doing here?" She moved away from him, wishing he hadn't come by.

"I can't seem to stay away. I wanted to see you."

"Sam..."

"Tessa, what is it going to hurt to go out to dinner?"

She gave a sarcastic laugh. "What's it going to hurt? I told you, I'm not looking to get involved with anyone, especially a man like you—"

"A man like me? What the hell does that mean?"

"I don't need the complication, and you'd be far too easy to fall for, Sam."

He strode toward her and stopped in front of her. "Is that so?"

Suddenly, Sam moved his hand around to capture the nape of her neck, and then pulled her toward him as he lowered his head taking her lips with his in a deep kiss. Tessa moaned as she wrapped her arms around his neck. His tongue moved into her mouth and when she sucked on it, he growled low in his throat.

"Sam," she said as she pulled her lips from his.

"You keep saying that. I want to hear you say it when I have you in my bed."

Pulling back, she gazed up at him. He stared down into her eyes and Tessa watched as his gaze roamed over her face. His dark lashes hid those beautiful eyes as they settled their attention on her lips.

"I want you, Tessa," he whispered, the words sending a thrill through her she couldn't deny was pure desire.

"I want you too," she whispered back, only realizing after she breathed the words how dangerous they were but she couldn't hold them back.

When his lips touched hers, they were gentle at first then she sighed against his lips, and his hungry mouth moved over hers. A deep, masculine groan tore from his chest as he took possession of her mouth. Sam cupped her face in his hands and tilted her head, deepening the kiss. Tessa had never felt anything like it. She tossed his Stetson to the floor and ran her fingers through his thick dark hair.

Sam pulled back from her. "Christ, I want you more than I've ever wanted any other woman." He pressed his lips to hers again.

Tessa couldn't stop the groan that tore from her as Sam's hands ran down her ribcage to her waist, around to her butt and pulled her tightly against him. His hard shaft pressed against her stomach and she moved against him, and then smiled when a gruff moan tore from him.

"You're enjoying yourself, aren't you?" he whispered against her lips.

Tessa laughed softly. "I am." She put her hand on his cheek reveling in the feel of its masculine texture.

Sam's eyebrows shot up. "I never realized you were so wicked, Tessa McGuire."

She stepped back from him, thinking she should stop this now but feeling just as wicked as he accused her. "Oh, Sheriff, you have no idea."

"I think I do." He tugged on her ponytail. "Do you ever wear this down?"

"When I go to bed," Tessa said then blushed at what that implied.

"Is that when I'll see it down? When I have you in my bed?"

Tessa stared up at him. "Is that what you're trying to do? Get me into your bed, Sheriff?"

Sam grinned. "Yes, didn't I just say that?"

Tessa burst out laughing. "At least you're honest."

He ran the pad of his thumb over her bottom lip. "Do you know how long I've wanted this?"

She frowned. "Wanted what?"

"This smile," Sam said shaking his head. "I saw you at Dewey's Bar one night and you were with Mitt Ashby. I had to watch you slow dancing with him. You were smiling at him. I wanted you to smile at me like that. I wanted you smiling for me."

"You were with Riley that night and had a blonde sitting beside you." Tessa frowned remembering how the girl kept running her fingers and hands over his chest, back, and leg. She hadn't liked it at all.

"I didn't want to be with her. I wanted to be with you."

Tessa blinked back tears. "Oh, Sam...I'm so sorry." She should be sorry for not stopping this now, but she wanted to be with him. She needed to feel alive again and he was man enough to give her that, but at what cost?

"It's all right."

"I never hated you." She placed her palm against his cheek again.

"I've wanted you since the first day I saw you, Tessa." Sam's voice was husky sounding and sexy.

Tessa put her hands on his chest. "I wanted you too, but didn't want to get involved—can't get involved. It's too complicated."

"So...dinner? Dinner's not complicated, is it?"

Tessa blew out a breath. It was only dinner. "All right. When?"

"Saturday night? I'll pick you up at six."

"That's fine. Now, I'm going to my apartment and take a hot bath. It's been a long day."

"Too bad I can't join you. I know...I know," he said with a groan when she raised an eyebrow at him. "I have to head home and do some work around the ranch."

Tessa blushed thinking how sinfully delightful it would be for him to join her in a bath, but she still needed to keep her distance. "Right. Let me lock up."

"I'll walk with you, Tessa." Sam waited while she locked the front doors then followed her down the hallway, and out the back door. He stood waiting beside her while she locked them then they climbed the stairs to her apartment. After she entered her apartment and closed the door, he remained standing on the stoop for a moment longer but then she heard him leaving, his heavy footfalls on the metal stairs. It took every ounce of her willpower not to call him back.

* * * *

The next day, Tessa was sitting at her desk when Jodi told her she had a call. Thanking her, she picked up the phone.

"Doctor McGuire," she answered with a smile.

"Hey, Tess...it's Olivia Stone. We have a sick mare."

"Is she standing, Liv?"

"Yes. Wyatt and Gabe are both out there with her, but she's listless."

"It's not a pregnant mare, I take it?" Tessa asked as she picked up her medical bag while getting ready to head toward the door.

"No, she's not pregnant. Wyatt thinks she got into some wet hay that wasn't meant for consumption," Olivia explained. Tessa knew this could be serious and needed to get there fast.

"I'm on my way. I know Wyatt and Gabe know to keep her up but please make sure they do." Tessa hung up, called to Jodi telling her where she was going, and headed out the back door. As she approached her car, she saw Sam's SUV driving down the street, coming toward her. It didn't surprise her at all when he pulled into the parking lot, stopped alongside her SUV but she hadn't really time for his flirtations. He put the passenger side window down and smiled at her. She leaned down to look at him.

"Hey Sam, don't have time to chat, I have to get to Wyatt's—a sick horse."

"Do you want me to go with you? I'm heading in for a late shift tonight."

Tessa hesitated, but she had to admit that she'd feel better with him going with her since another pair of hands couldn't hurt. "Yes. They could use help keeping her up," she explained very quickly that Gabe was helping, but Olivia had said the horse was listless.

Tessa climbed into her vehicle and waited for Sam to climb into the passenger seat beside her then sped out of the parking lot before Sam even had time to buckle his seat belt. She pulled hers over her shoulder and buckled it as she drove.

"You do know you should have that on *before* you take off like a bat out of hell?" Sam scowled as he struggled to get buckled up in the passenger seat.

Tessa laughed. "Yes, *Sheriff*." She

chuckled when she heard him muttering under his breath. "Did you say something, Sam?"

"I said you are a smartass."

Tessa burst out laughing and drove to Wyatt's taking curves in the road so fast she had Sam hanging on for dear life.

"*Christ!* I need to give you a damn ticket," Sam shouted as he grabbed the suicide handle above the door.

Tessa glanced at him. "I have an emergency, Sam."

"All right. I'll give you that one." Sam reached out to brace himself against the dash while hanging tighter to the handle above the door making Tessa laugh harder. She sped down the road, pulling onto Wyatt's ranch when she reached it, and coming to a stop by the barn. Sam and Tessa both jumped out and ran inside to see Olivia waving at them from the back of the barn. They both hurried toward her.

"Did they keep her up?" Tessa asked.

Olivia shook her head. "They tried but she went down." She had tears in her eyes.

Sam moved past the women and entered the stall, with Tessa and Olivia following. The women each grabbed a section of the strap wrapped around the mare's stomach and pulled alongside the men. All of them did their best to get the horse to stand—little by little, the mare tried to get her legs under her. It was literally a life or death situation.

"How long has she been down?" Tessa asked feeling sweat drip down her back as she pulled with all her strength.

"A few minutes." Wyatt grunted as he pulled on the strap.

Tessa nodded her head. The horse still wasn't on her feet but at least she wasn't on her side anymore. The position would have to do for an examination. She slowly let go and reached for her medical bag. "Hopefully, not long enough to hurt her. Keep her still while I examine her."

Moving to stand at the back of the horse, she put on long latex gloves and examined the horse for impaction, a main cause of colic. "Olivia, could you please remove the food and water."

Olivia did as she was asked and then went back to grab onto the strap.

"I'm going to give her an antispasmodic injection. It will help with the cramping. Poor thing is impacted too, so I'll give her something for it but we have to get her up before she starts rolling."

All of them tugged on the straps and finally, they managed to get the mare to her feet but she continued to nip at her stomach.

Tessa rubbed the mare's belly hoping to ease the beast's discomfort.

"The shot should be helping soon. Wyatt, do you think you could walk her a little?" Tessa smiled when he nodded then gently led the mare from the stall. She glanced at Sam to see him staring at her. Their gazes met and held.

Out of the corner of her eye, she saw Olivia and Gabe leave the stall. Tessa felt her cheeks growing warm. She bent down, picked up her medical bag, and then felt Sam beside her. Tessa gazed up at him.

"You love what you do...don't you, Tessa?"

"Any vet would do the same," she whispered, trying to resist his presence because being so close to him had her hormones raging.

Sam shook his head. "You really care about the horses. It's not just a job to you. You love it." He tugged on her ponytail. "I saw it in your eyes, the fear of possibly losing the horse and the determination not to. It was amazing to watch."

"You've seen me do it before, Sam. I helped your horse," Tessa reminded him.

"My horse wasn't nearly as bad as this mare. Mine just had a small cut on his leg. This horse was down less than a few minutes and she could've died."

"All horses are different. Some take longer before they go down and some don't go down at all." Tessa shrugged. "Any good owner knows to get the horse up before it starts rolling, twisting the intestines, and harming its internal organs."

"See? You love it."

Tessa smiled. "I do. I've always loved horses."

"And yet, you don't have one of your own. Why is that?"

"In case you've forgotten, I live in an apartment. I can't keep a horse there."

"You could keep one at my place. I have plenty of room."

Tessa widened her eyes. She had thought of boarding a horse, but hadn't looked into it yet. Now Sam was offering her a place to keep one. Tessa was about to tell him she'd think about it when Wyatt led the horse back toward her.

"She seems better already, Doc," Wyatt said smiling at her. Olivia and Gabe stood beside him, nodding. Olivia held a baby monitor in her hand.

"I'm glad. Just keep the food and water away from her, and I'll be out tomorrow to check on her." Tessa rubbed the mare's nose. "You be a good girl, Coco. I'll see you tomorrow." Turning back to face them, she smiled at Olivia. "I wish Caleb was awake so I could see him."

"Next time," Olivia told her before giving her a hug.

After saying good-bye, Tessa and Sam headed for her vehicle. Tessa stopped before she got in and glanced over her shoulder to see Sam talking with Wyatt. They shook hands and Sam strolled toward the passenger side. Tessa almost groaned watching him move. He was so sexy. The tight jeans cupping his sex left little to the imagination along with his khaki shirt fitting tight across his chest and the short sleeves wrapped tight around his biceps. Dear God, the man had a body. The black Stetson sat low on his forehead and his sunglasses hid those incredible eyes. Stubble covered the lower half of his jaw making her lick her lips and her fingertips tingle at the thought of caressing his cheek.

Tessa climbed into the SUV and took a deep breath in an attempt to calm her racing heart. She wanted him. She wanted him so much so, that she wiggled in her seat. Her wanting him, desiring him was wrong—so very wrong. Her life was far too complicated and living a lie was something that if he found out about, he'd hate her and that scared her to her very core. Tessa glanced over when he climbed into the seat beside her. Sam looked over and smiled at her. When she didn't smile back, a frown marred his forehead.

"Are you all right?"

Tessa nodded and started the vehicle then pulled out of the Stone's ranch without saying another word. After a silent ride back to town, she parked by the back door of the hospital. Staring straight ahead, she wrapped her fingers tighter around the steering wheel. She knew Sam was looking at her and he was probably wondering what in the hell was wrong with her. Taking a deep breath, she glanced over to him.

"Thanks for going with me, Sam," she said in a low voice not too much louder than a whisper.

"It was no problem, Tessa," he said in a low tone of voice and not making a move to exit the vehicle.

Tessa cleared her throat. It was now or never. It was only dinner. "Would you...would you like to come for dinner tonight, instead of going out tomorrow night," she said then added quickly, "as a way to thank you."

"No. But I will come to dinner...for dinner," Sam told her.

Tessa looked over to him and smiled.

"All right. After your shift?"

Sam nodded. "As long as nothing major happens, my shift should end around seven tonight. Mark's on vacation. Is that too late?"

Tessa wanted to tell him she didn't care if he showed up at midnight. "That's fine. The hospital closes at six."

Then she saw Sam shake his head. "You know what? It might be better if you come to dinner at my place. How's that? I'll have to go home and shower after my shift anyway." He grinned. "Who knows? I may have to round up more pigs before the day is over."

Tessa laughed and nodded. "All right then. What time should I be there?"

"Seven thirty? I'll call you if something comes up." Sam smiled at her and climbed out of the vehicle.

Tessa watched him stride over to his cruiser with her eyes instinctively going to his butt. She bit her lip to stop the groan bubbling up in her throat, and then climbed out and stood alongside her SUV. She watched him drive away then entered her hospital, all the while thinking about meeting him tonight and hoping to have the courage to come clean about who she was, and her life before Clifton, Montana.

Chapter Six

Tessa pulled onto Sam's road and drove up to his house. She thought she'd be more nervous than she was but she was just happy to be seeing him again. After parking, she sat there for a few minutes. *What are you doing? This is so wrong. Someone is going to get hurt.*

Probably both of them because she was so close to falling for the man but if he fell for her, and learned the truth...she shook her head. It was best she just not get involved with him then there was no reason for her to tell him the truth at all. It was only dinner, two friends, or rather two people becoming friends, and she could handle that—she hoped. She stepped out, carrying a bottle of wine and walked up to the house. When she knocked on the door, she smiled at hearing Bo barking.

The door opened and when she saw Sam, she nearly forgot to breathe. His hair was still damp from his shower, his feet were bare, and he didn't have a shirt on. He smiled at her as he opened the door wider.

"I'm running a little late, Tessa. Come on in."

Tessa smiled and strode past him. The aroma from the pan simmering on the stove was mouthwatering. At least she thought it was until she turned to tell Sam she'd brought wine, and he was right behind her. His scent, clean, masculine, and sexy surrounded her and her hand instinctively went to his chest, and they both froze. Tessa slowly raised her eyes to his and watched as Sam slowly lowered his head. She knew it was to give her time to move away if she wanted and even as her internal voice screamed at her to move, she couldn't.

When she didn't, he pressed his lips to hers and Tessa's head tilted back as he deepened the kiss. His tongue entered her mouth slowly touching hers. Tessa moaned and ran her hand up his chest around his nape and into his damp hair. Sam's hands moved to her hips and pulled her against him and she could feel his erection pressing against her belly. They jumped apart when Bo nudged between them. Sam lifted his head slowly and those sexy lips lifted into a smile. Tessa grinned and then glanced down at Bo.

"We're not going to be friends if you keep doing things like that," she scolded even as she was glad the dog had interrupted the embrace.

Sam chuckled. "I second that, Bo."

The dog sat down and gazed up at both of them with adoration in his eyes since he was now getting their attention. Tessa cleared her throat.

"I brought wine. I wasn't sure what you were fixing, so I just picked up a nice Chardonnay."

"That's fine. I made spaghetti."

"One of my favorite foods," Tessa said with a grin.

Sam stepped back from her and pulled his T-shirt on over his head. "I'll be right back. I need to put my boots on."

"Or I could take my shoes off," Tessa suggested.

Sam halted in mid-stride and turned to face her. "Sure, if you want."

"Why not? We'll be more comfortable." Tessa pulled a chair out from the table and took a seat, then toed off her sneakers and tugged her socks off, wiggling her toes as she smiled up at Sam.

"Red toenails, huh?" Sam folded his arms over his chest as he gazed down at her feet. "Sexy."

"One of my many secrets," she teased then realized just how many secrets she was hiding from him and looked away.

"How many more do you have, angel?" Sam crouched down in front of her, lifted her foot, and put it in his lap then massaged it slowly. "I'd love to know all of them."

Tessa took her bottom lip between her teeth, and then crooked her finger at him as she leaned toward him. Sam moved closer.

"I like sexy bras and panties," she whispered then laughed when Sam groaned.

"I saw some of those sexy panties. How about we just skip dinner?" Sam suggested even as she felt the heat of a blush rush over her face remembering how he had seen her panties that night in her apartment.

"Oh no, Sheriff...you promised me dinner."

She almost changed her mind when Sam kissed her again while his hand wrapped around her ponytail. "I want to see this down."

"Hmm...maybe you will," she said against his mouth.

"Promise?"

She gazed into those amazing blue eyes and wished she could promise him that but she knew she couldn't.

Sam stood, his eyes not leaving hers so she dropped her gaze only to see his erection straining against the zipper of his jeans. She glanced away even when she didn't want to then lifted her gaze, and smiled up at him. He put his hand out to her and helped her stand.

"You go sit in the living room and I'll bring dinner in when it's ready. I don't need you here distracting me."

Tessa laughed softly. "All right, Sheriff. Let me know if you need help with..." She couldn't resist giving a quick glance at his fly then back to his face. "Anything."

Sam growled making her stifle a laugh. "Go."

Blushing, Tessa headed in the direction Sam pointed her and entered the living room with Bo on her heels. Taking a seat on the large sofa, she picked up the remote, turned on the television that hung above the red brick fireplace, and then glanced around the room. It was definitely a man's home. A large overstuffed brown plaid recliner faced the matching sofa. On the mantel sat photos of Sam and his sister, Kaitlyn, and Kaitlyn and her daughter, Sadie. There were also pictures of his parents, and all of them at Kaitlyn and Riley's wedding. Scattered rugs covered the cherry hardwood floors. It was a very comfortable looking home.

You shouldn't be here! I know! She tried to quiet her inner voice, and had just about convinced herself to leave when Sam carried two plates in, piled high with spaghetti. After setting them on the coffee table, he walked back to the kitchen and returned with hot garlic bread. The smell of it made Tessa's stomach growl so she decided to stay. After Sam sat down beside her, they both dug in and Tessa couldn't help but moan when the flavors hit her tongue.

"Oh Sam. This is fantastic."

"My mother thanks you. She taught me how to make it years ago. Other than steak, this is about all I cook."

"Well then you must eat a lot of spaghetti and steak," she said leaning back to stare at him. "You sure don't look like a starving man."

"Oh, I'm a starving man all right, darlin'...just not for food." He stared at her, and she knew exactly what he meant.

Tessa's eyes met his. "Sam..."

"I love the way you say my name." He leaned forward and kissed her, tasting of spice, tomatoes, and garlic...he was nearly as delicious as the food on her plate. "I want you so much Tessa," he whispered against her lips.

"It's not that I'm not interested... Sam, I just don't think it's a good idea."

"Well, I think it's a hell of an idea."

"I'm not looking for a relationship, Sam...although, you're very tempting."

Sam stared into her eyes. "Glad to hear it."

Tessa leaned away, looked back at her plate, and then continued to eat even though her appetite had abandoned her. She couldn't do this, the idea of having sex with Sam was something she just couldn't do, no matter how badly she wanted him. If she thought she could keep it simple, casual it would be one thing but there was something so special about him. One minute she had herself convinced to go for it, to tell him about her past, and then the next she was too afraid to do anything.

Taking a deep breath, she chewed her food while her inner voice pleaded with her to tell him the truth. What if she did, would he hate her. Had she waited too long now so he would think she was leading him on? Just then, she realized he was staring at her so she turned her head, and looked into his eyes stifling a groan.

"Your eyes are beautiful, Tessa. Your eyes were one of the first things I noticed about you. After that it was your beautiful face."

"Do you know what I first noticed about you?" Tessa tilted her head at him.

"I believe it was my badge."

Tessa laughed. "Okay. The second thing I noticed."

"What?"

"How gorgeous you are."

Sam snorted. "I'm just a man, Tessa."

Tessa laughed. "Ha! If you look up tall, dark, and handsome in the dictionary, I have no doubt that your picture would be there."

Sam shook his head and chuckled. "If you say so."

"I say so, and so does every other woman in town. Sam, you shave every day, don't you?"

Sam frowned at her with an expression of confusion. "Yes. Why?"

"Obviously, you have to look in the mirror." Tessa shrugged. "You have to see how good-looking you are."

"Good-looking? A minute ago, I was gorgeous," he said in a teasing tone.

Tessa narrowed her eyes at him. "You know what I mean. You *are* gorgeous, you're so tall, that dark hair, your body is perfect, you have such sexy lips, a gorgeous smile, and those blue eyes are killers."

Sam shrugged. "They're just blue, Tessa, and how are my lips sexy?" He frowned as he picked up his wine. When she didn't say anything, he glanced over to her. She stared at him and lifted an eyebrow at him. "What'd I say now?"

Tessa burst out laughing. "Oh my God, you're humble too. Christ, Sam. You're perfect."

"I am *not* perfect," Sam growled making Tessa laugh harder. He set his plate on the coffee table, stood, and strode to the fireplace.

"I'm sorry, Sam. I didn't mean to make you angry," Tessa said softly, suddenly feeling self-conscious. *Now might be a good time to leave.*

Sam huffed. "You didn't. It's fine." He turned to look at her. "But I'm far from perfect, Tessa. I'm just a man, nothing more."

Tessa shook her head and stood. "You're a *good* man, Sam. You're nice, very good-looking, and you have a great sense of humor. You're hot and your lips are beyond sexy..."

Sam strolled over to her. Stopping in front of her, he tilted his head as he gazed down at her. "How are my lips sexy?"

He had asked her that question before and now, as she stared up at him then looked at his mouth, she smiled thinking of just how perfectly sexy his lips were. Setting her plate on the coffee table alongside his, she came to her feet and stepped around it to stand in front of him.

"They're perfect," she said putting her hand over his lips when he started to say something. "You may not think *you're* perfect, but these lips are." Tessa ran her fingertip over them tracing their shape. "Perfect," she murmured. "This upper lip..." She caressed it with her fingertip. "Is bowed just right, and then this lower lip," she murmured continuing as her eyes traced along with her fingertip, "makes a woman want to nibble on it."

"Do you want to nibble on it, Tessa?" Sam whispered, making her insides flutter and flip with nervous excitement.

"Oh yes, I do, Sam." She stood on her tiptoes, took his lower lip between her teeth, tugged on it, and then nibbled.

Sam groaned and put his hands on her waist then he moved them around to her butt, and pulled her closer to him.

"And you go to the left," she said against his lips.

"What?" He pulled back from her, looked down at her, and raised his dark brows in question.

Tessa smiled up at him. "Most men lean to the right when they kiss." She shrugged. "You go to the left."

"You've kissed so many that you know

this for a fact, huh?"

"Enough."

"I'd rather not talk about how many men you've kissed. Just keep kissing this one."

"Sam..." she whispered. *Now is the time to tell him.*

"God, what you do to me when you say my name. Stay with me tonight, Tessa," Sam said as he kissed his way across her cheek and down along her neck sending delicious shivers over her skin.

No! Tell him now!

Tessa pulled back from him. "I-I can't, Sam, not until I..." She swallowed, her courage escaping her. "Please give me time to think about this."

Sam took a deep breath and blew it out. "All right, but I'm not giving up."

Tessa smiled. "I hope not. I'd better go. We both have to work tomorrow."

"I'll walk you out." He picked up the plates, and she followed him to the kitchen.

Once in the kitchen, she pulled a chair out and sat down to put her socks and shoes back on. When she stood, Sam took her hand in his, walked her out to her vehicle, and kissed her softly.

"Thank you for dinner and for helping me earlier today."

"Anytime for both. Go home before I

do whatever it takes to keep you here."

"Against my will, Sheriff?" She smiled raising her eyebrows.

"I do have handcuffs, remember?" Sam pressed a kiss to her forehead.

"I remember very well. Goodnight, Sam."

Tessa pulled away from him and climbed into her SUV. After starting it, she put it in gear, glanced out the window at him wishing things were different then silently cursed her old life and without looking at him again, drove away. On the way back home, she wondered what in the world she was doing, because getting involved with Sam was so very wrong but every moment she spent with him, she fell that much more for him.

You have to tell him!

"I will...I will," she muttered at her inner voice trying to shut it up. As she drove home, she thought about Sam, the evening, how much she'd wanted to stay with him and knew she had to find the right time, the right way to tell him because she was running on borrowed time before he somehow found out.

Chapter Seven

A week later, Tessa entered the exam room and even as she internally cringed, she smiled at Gwendolyn Barnes. The biggest gossip this side of the Mississippi. The woman simply lived for it and everyone in town knew it.

"Hello, Mrs. Barnes. How are you and Boots doing today?"

"Boots is here for his rabies shot," the older woman said in a haughty voice.

Tessa tried to smile. "Please take him out of his crate while I fill out the form for him."

When she heard the older woman clear her throat, Tessa knew the woman wanted to ask something but she kept her back to her.

"So...Doctor McGuire...you and the sheriff, huh?"

Tessa bit back a nasty retort and exhaled a relaxing breath. "Yes. Sam and I just started seeing each other." Since it was none of the woman's business, she refused to say more than she needed to.

"Did you know he dated my niece

Sandy, until you came along?" Mrs. Barnes sniffed.

Tessa spun around. "Yes, I did, but I'm sure Sam dated quite a bit before we met."

Mrs. Barnes laughed and it grated on Tessa's nerves. "Oh dearie, they more than dated. They spoke of marriage. It just broke Sandy's heart when Sam broke it off with her. She's still very much in love with him after all. He's quite a catch, you know. I may be seventy-seven years old but I know a good-looking man when I see one." She huffed. "But because of you, her dreams are now shattered."

Tessa held her temper. After all, Mrs. Barnes was a client, so she smiled at her. "I'm sure she'll be fine—"

"Of course, *you* think she'll be fine. Her family doesn't, however. Imagine talking marriage with the man you love, and then he breaks it off because of some...*veterinarian.*"

Tessa almost laughed. Mrs. Barnes made it sound as if veterinarian was another word for whore. "Obviously, Sam didn't feel the same way or another woman wouldn't have caught his eye."

"It wasn't his eye that was caught, missy. Everyone knows he spent the night at your apartment last night and you should be ashamed of yourself."

"Well, I'm not ashamed of anything, and not that it's any of your business or anyone else's in this town, but he spent the night *on my couch.* He had spent most of the night at the scene of an accident on Copper Ridge. With my apartment being closer, he went there instead of trying to drive home as tired as he was. Maybe it would be better if you started taking Boots to another vet." Tessa headed toward the door and then stopped, glancing over her shoulder. "Let Jodi know who you want his records sent to. Have a nice day, Mrs. Barnes."

Leaving the horrid woman alone in the exam room, she closed the door softly behind her and headed straight for her office. She needed some cooling down time before seeing the next patient. She wasn't sure how long she'd sat there when she heard Sam's voice.

"Rough day, Tessa?"

"Apparently, I'm the town whore."

"Excuse me?"

Tessa couldn't help it, she laughed, more out of frustration than humor. "Mrs. Barnes—"

"Stop right there. Saying that woman's name is enough. She loves to stir up trouble."

"She says everyone knows you spent the night at my apartment and because of me, you broke her niece's heart."

Groaning, Sam shook his head. "We can talk about that later. I just stopped in to tell you I'm heading home to get some more sleep. I appreciate you letting me sleep for a few hours on your couch though."

Tessa nodded. "No problem, Sam. I'll talk to you later. You do look more rested but be careful going home."

Sam grinned and her heart hit her stomach. "Worried about me, darlin'?"

"Of course."

Sam walked around the desk, took her hand, and pulled her to her feet then cupped her face in his hands and leaned down. His lips were barely touching hers when he whispered. "I'm glad to hear that." He pressed his lips to hers and kissed her quickly. "That should hold me over. I'll call you later." He kissed her again and left the room.

Tessa listened as his boot heels clack down the hallway. Did Mrs. Barnes tell her the truth? Was Sam going to marry Sandy? Tessa sat down behind her desk again and put her hands over her face. The thought of him with another woman was bad enough but to talk marriage with her was heartbreaking. She knew Sam had been with other women and it was in the past but...*marriage?* He said they'd talk about it later and she wanted to hear it but she was also afraid to know. Had he been in love with Sandy? She snorted. Of course, he had if he talked about marriage with her, but then who was she to complain about his past. So deep in thought about Sam and his past, Tessa about jumped out of her skin when Jodi spoke her name.

"What is it Jodi?"

"Are you all right? Mrs. Barnes about threw a fit in the lobby, yelling about taking her business elsewhere."

"I told her to get with you on where to send the records for Boots."

Jodi's eyebrows shot up. "For real? I'd love to have been in that exam room. I'm glad. She's a mean old bitch."

"Jodi! I've never heard you swear before." Tessa laughed.

"Just tellin' it like it is." Jodi laughed. "She said she'd call me later to tell me where to send them. I'd like to tell her where she can shove them." Jodi grinned and walked back toward reception.

Tessa chuckled. Apparently, she wasn't the only one whose skin Mrs. Barnes got under and it made her feel somewhat better. A shiver crawled over her though when she thought of Mrs. Barnes having a field day gossiping if the secret Tessa was hiding came out. Sighing, she stood and headed for the next patient, hoping the day would get better.

* * * *

Sam was walking toward his cruiser when he saw Gwendolyn Barnes bearing down on him. He mentally groaned but he forced a smile, and put his fingers to his hat when she got to him.

"Mrs. Barnes."

"Sheriff. You need to speak with your...girlfriend about her rudeness. She told me to take Boots to another vet."

"Mrs. Barnes, I have no control over something like that. It's Doctor McGuire's business who her patients are. I have no say in it."

"You're seeing her, so of course you have a say in it. The next vet is a county over. It would take me forever to get there."

"Then I suggest you apologize to her," Sam said between clenched teeth.

Mrs. Barnes gasped. "I will do no such thing. It's because of her you broke Sandy's heart."

"Look, I don't mean to offend you, but it's none of your business." He raised his hand when she started to interrupt. "I will agree it's because of Tessa I broke up with Sandy but not the way you think. I stopped seeing Sandy long before I started seeing

Tessa. Sandy and I were going nowhere and she knew it as much as I did. Now, if you'll excuse me, I'm going home to get some sleep. Tessa's *couch* is not the most comfortable place to sleep and the cots in the department are too short for me." He turned from her then turned back. "And don't think I wouldn't have slept in her bed if she'd asked me." He gave a terse nod and strode away from her, hearing her gasp her indignation.

Mentally, he shook his head. Why in the hell did he have to add that? The woman needed put in her place but he knew he just added fuel to the fire. Most people in Clifton avoided her since all she wanted to do was gossip or spread rumors. She'd let him know several times how she blamed him for breaking up with Sandy when it had been a mutual breakup. Yes, Sandy had been a little upset but she knew the relationship was stalling. Now because of the old busybody, he had to tell Tessa about it before she started thinking he was seeing her when he was also seeing Sandy.

Sam pulled his cell phone out and called her office. "Dinner tonight at my place?" he asked once Jodi transferred him.

"Sounds good. Do you want me to pick up some steaks?"

"Yes, if you don't mind. I'll see you around six-thirty, Doc." Sam hung up and headed home to his own bed.

At six-thirty that evening, he stood on the porch leaning against a post with his arms folded as he watched Tessa's SUV pull up and park. She stepped out, and after giving him a smile, she walked up the steps carrying a grocery bag. He could swear his heart stopped.

"Hello, Sheriff," she said as she stopped on the top step. "I come bearing steaks."

"Good. Hello, beautiful." He put his hand out to her and after she placed her hand in his, he pulled her toward him and lightly kissed her lips.

"Are you hungry?"

Sam allowed his gaze to travel over her length. "Starving," Sam said, and then chuckled as he watched the blush move into her cheeks.

"I meant for food."

Sam raised an eyebrow. "So did I."

When she swatted her hand at him, he laughed while leading her into the kitchen. As soon as she entered the room, Bo came running toward them.

"Sit," Sam commanded. Bo slid slightly on the floor but sat down, and stared up at Tessa.

Squatting, she rubbed his head. "Hi, big boy. How are you doing, Bo?" The big dog laid his big paw on her lap and licked her face making her laugh.

"It's a good thing you like dog kisses."

"Bo's a good kisser, aren't you, boy?"

"He is, huh?"

Tessa stood and wrapped her arms around Sam's neck. "Not as good as you though. He loses a little something in the technique."

Sam dipped his head and pressed his lips to hers and nibbled on her bottom lip then took it between his teeth making her groan. "I hope I don't lose something in the technique."

"You've got it down perfect, Sam Garrett," she whispered.

Sam grinned against her lips. "*Sheriff* Sam Garrett."

"Well, Sheriff, I love how you kiss me."

Sam cupped her face in his hands and stared into her eyes. "I could kiss you a thousand times a day for a thousand years and it still wouldn't be enough."

"Sam, you say the sexiest things," she whispered, and delighted in seeing her blush again as she reached down to pet Bo again.

"I'll say anything to get you into bed," Sam said grinning when her gaze lifted to meet his.

"Sam, I can't say I wouldn't like that and honestly, all you'd have to say is that you want me and I'd be so very tempted—"

"I do want you, Tessa, every minute of every day."

He watched her blush again, but then she suddenly held up the grocery bag. "Do you want to start the steaks or have a glass of wine?"

Sam gave her a look that told her he was disappointed and she turned away to hide her laugh, but not before he saw it. "I'll start the steaks. I'm not big on wine unless it's with spaghetti."

"I'll have a glass and watch you then."

"You do realize you can't drink and drive? I'll have to put you under house arrest if you try to leave before you've slept it off."

"I'm sure one glass of wine won't do anything more than make me relaxed and if it does more than that...well, you can put me under house arrest," she whispered against his lips.

Sam groaned. "Can't the steaks wait?"

"Nope. You get them started, and then you're going to tell me about Sandy."

Sam nodded. He figured she was going to want to know after what happened with Mrs. Barnes. "All right."

After he seasoned the steaks, he took them outside to place them on the grill, which he'd already started. Tessa followed behind him. Out of the corner of his eye, he saw her take a seat at the table and sip her wine. Turning down the heat on the grill, he moved to the table, took a seat beside her, and took a deep breath.

"I met Sandy about two and a half years ago. I was making the rounds at Dewey's and she was there with a friend of hers. She came up to me and started talking. I liked her, she seemed nice, and she is. Sandy is a great person. She gave me her number and I called her a few days later. We went out together and soon it was just us exclusively." He sighed. "I wanted to fall in love, but I didn't. She just wasn't *the one* for me."

"Her aunt said you were going to marry her."

"No. We never talked about getting married. If her aunt said that, it's either her own lie or Sandy lied to her—although I can't see Sandy doing that. I was never in love with her. Six months before I kissed you that first time on the Fourth of July, I broke it off with her. I couldn't do it anymore. I knew I was going to hurt her, but I couldn't avoid it either. I wanted you from the minute I saw you, Tessa. In all honesty, I led her on way too long as it was. I guess I wanted it to work because you seemed to hate me and I knew I'd never be with you, but it wasn't working no matter how much I wanted it to or tried to make it work. I just didn't love her and I couldn't continue on knowing that. It was the same with Lydia. I dated her before I met Sandy. It wasn't going anywhere either and I knew she was in love with me. She moved back to Louisiana right before Katie and Riley's wedding."

Tessa stood and walked to him then she sat on his lap and kissed him. "I never hated you, Sam. I know it seems like I did but I didn't want to get involved with anyone. I shouldn't..."

Wrapping his arms around her, he leaned his head on her shoulder. "I know that now, Tessa, but I didn't then. I thought for sure you'd never want me." He shrugged. "In my mind, I knew I had to find someone else but in my heart, I wanted it to be you."

Tessa pressed her lips to his and moaned when he deepened it. Slowly moving his tongue inside her mouth, he tangled it with hers. Her fingers combed through his hair. Sam growled low in his throat.

"Are you sure those steaks can't wait? I want you so much. The only thing I'm hungry for is you."

"I want you too, Sam, but—" she whispered against his lips.

"No buts...if you have something to say it had better be something like 'more Sam'," Sam growled, pushing out of his chair, lifting her into his arms while kissing away any objections.

He turned off the grill, closed the lid, and carried her to his bedroom where he laid her on the bed. He stood staring down at her. When she leaned up on her elbows and started to speak, he raised his hand and shook his head.

"You're perfect. You don't need to think about this. Just let it happen," he said before lying down beside her. He cupped her cheek in his hand and lowered his lips to hers as his hand moved under her shirt to her stomach. Tessa moaned into his mouth even as she shook her head. "You drive me crazy, Tessa."

"But Sam..." He pressed hot kisses against her neck and heard her moan. "You make me lose all coherent thought," she whispered and he hoped he'd won.

"I hope so," Sam told her as he lifted her top off over her head and stared down at her naked breasts. "No bra?"

She laughed softly. "It was hot...there's something—"

Her words stopped when his lips surrounded her nipple and suckled then licked it until it stiffened into a tight peak. "Sam..."

His name just a breath on her lips was driving him insane. Sam groaned and put his hands on her waist and pulled her closer to him.

He kissed her deeply then tugged on her ponytail gently pulling the band from her hair and running his fingers through the long silky curls. He slowly lowered her down and when he saw her hair spread over his pillow, he almost wept. For so long, he'd wanted this. It was as beautiful as he'd imagined. She rolled to her side with her back to him.

"Hold me for a little while, Sam."

"Anything you want, angel."

"Why do you call me that?" Tessa whispered.

"Because it's what you are to me," Sam whispered back.

"Oh, Sam...I'm not...you don't know me..." Her voice trailed off and he wondered why she trembled. Sometimes he wondered if something from her past made her afraid. He'd even done a search of her on Google, but found nothing. She didn't seem to have any kind of online presence, which actually was fine with him—the less people knowing his or her business, the better. It was bad enough having Gwendolyn Barnes nosing around in their lives.

They lay together for a while longer—neither speaking. Sam had his arm around her and she snuggled back against him, finally relaxing. Sam began to nuzzle her hair with his nose, inhaling the vanilla scent of it. His arm tightened around her and he pulled her closer. Her breathing began to change.

"I want you so much," he whispered alongside her ear and heard her sigh.

Tessa rolled to her back and gazed up at him. "I want you too, Sam, but there's things about me—"

Kissing her lips, he stopped her words then he whispered. "I don't need to know...yet. I don't care about your past or whether you snore...I just want to hear you scream my name."

"Really?" She smiled up at him as she swept his hair back from his forehead.

"God, yes, darlin'. Most men, real men, want to know they're pleasing their woman and how do we know if you don't tell us in some way?"

Tessa stared into his eyes. "Maybe I want to hear you scream mine."

Groaning, Sam closed his eyes. "I have a feeling you will."

"Sam—"

"I love how you say my name. It's husky and sexy as hell." His heart skipped a beat when she smiled and he buried his face in her neck. "You make my dick hard just by saying my name and that's the truth." He raised his head and gazed into her eyes. Tessa blushed and Sam chuckled. "You're the most beautiful woman I've ever seen, Tessa. You make me want to bury myself in you so deep," he whispered as his hand moved over her hair and down her neck to her breasts.

"God, you're so fucking gorgeous," he murmured as his hand went down to her flat belly to the snap of her jeans. Sam kissed her. "Touch me, Tessa. I want to feel your hands all over me."

With trembling hands, Tessa caressed his shoulders and down his biceps, then to his chest. He appreciated that she was nervous, and her touch made his skin quiver. He took her jeans off her and groaned when he saw the red panties.

"You're killing me."

Tessa laughed softly then frowned as her hands fell away but then when he pulled his T-shirt off over his head, her eyes widened and her fingers ran over his hard pecs and down his six-pack stomach. Without prodding, she kissed his nipples and ran her tongue over them then she followed the hair surrounding his belly button, until it disappeared into his jeans. She looked up at him with large eyes.

"You have a fantastic happy trail."

Sam burst out laughing then hissed in a breath when her hand went to the snap of his jeans. He was so hard she had trouble getting the zipper down. Sam sat up and pulled his boots and socks off then shucked his jeans and boxer briefs. He leaned over her, and kissed her long and deep.

"I want to be inside you." He nudged his cock against her. "I want to love you all over, Tessa."

Tessa's eyes fluttered closed and he saw her swallow then he heard her speak in a barely audible whisper. "Please, Sam."

Those two words were all the permission he needed. "I told you before I could please you and I will."

Sam rubbed his nose against her hair then moved his mouth to her neck and down to her collarbone, slowly to her breasts. When he took her nipple into his mouth, her fingers gripped his hair as he circled his tongue around the firm nub, and then pulled it into a peak rubbing his teeth against it. Not wishing to neglect the other companion nipple, his thumb rubbed over it making Tessa moan.

"It feels so good." She blew out a breath. "It's wonderful. Please don't stop."

"Anything you say, darlin'," he said as he grinned against her breast before moving to her other breast so as to give it similar treatment. The more he tugged on her nipple with his teeth, the more she moaned. At one point, she pulled his hair so hard he had to tell her to let up.

Tessa released him. "Sorry, I didn't mean to...it's just I love what you're doing to me, Sam."

Sam smiled against her stomach as he moved lower running his tongue over the butterfly tattoo on her left hipbone, which had surprised him when he first saw it. She said there were things about her that he didn't know. Well, if those things were more delights like the tattoo, he was looking forward to learning all about them. Right now, he knew if he didn't slow down he was going to explode.

Sliding her panties off, he kissed his way down her thigh to her knee then moved to the other leg, and kissed his way back up. The black curls beckoning to him from between her legs were glistening. Sam closed his eyes in desired wonder. She was wet—for him. *Shit!* He wanted more than anything at that moment to thrust into her hot, wet body but knew he couldn't—not yet.

Sam buried his nose in her curls and breathed in deeply. She hissed in a breath when his tongue touched her, making her jerk against his mouth then she bent her knees for him and moaned his name making him smile. Sam moved his tongue against her clitoris then put his mouth over her and sucked. Tessa arched against him so he moved her legs over his shoulders as he continued sucking on her. His tongue moved down her slit, to inside, then back up to her sensitive nub. Sucking it and moving his teeth against it until it threw her over the edge. Tessa fisted her hands in his hair and screamed out his name as she came.

Sam kissed his way back up her body to take her mouth in a deep kiss, her nectar lingering on his lips. Then he reached into the bedside table and withdrew a condom. After sheathing himself, he moved between her legs. Tessa was still breathing hard from her orgasm, her eyes closed, and a smile gracing her delicious lips.

"Look at me, Tessa," Sam whispered. She opened her eyes and looked into his. "You must be what sin tastes like."

Tessa moaned deep in her throat. "God

Sam, that was amazing. I had no idea—"

"We're not done yet, darlin'." Clenching his teeth, he slowly inched into her making her gasp.

"You aren't lacking anywhere, Sam Garrett."

Sam huffed out a laugh. "*Sheriff* Sam Garrett." He kissed her as he moved into her. When he was in as far as he could go, they both groaned. Sam began moving his hips. "Wrap your legs around me." He growled low in his throat when she did. "God, you feel so fucking good. I knew you would."

Tessa arched her hips and met him thrust for thrust. The moans coming from her urged him on. Sam slipped his hand under her to pull her tight against him and moved faster and harder as he did.

"You with me, Tessa?" he groaned against her neck.

"Yes. Oh yes, Sam," she moaned as her hands moved all over him.

Sam groaned and thrust harder, his muscles straining against the tension building in him. Tessa stayed with him and he could feel her inner muscles tightening around his cock right before she cried out his name again. Sam groaned out her name as he came hard then relaxed against her. It had never been like this before—not with any woman.

His elbows kept his weight off her but he kept his face buried in her neck, breathing hard. Tessa threw her arms around his neck.

"That was fantastic, Sheriff," she whispered against his ear.

"You got that right, Doc." He kissed her and rolled off, but then pulled her against him.

Tessa sighed and threw her arm across his waist. "You're a wonderful lover, Sam."

"Takes two, darlin'." He hugged her to him. "I like the butterfly." He felt her stiffen but then relax a moment later.

"I-I love butterflies." She took a deep breath and she seemed to withdraw a bit or perhaps it was his imagination.

"I like it," he repeated and then kissed the top of her head.

"No tattoos for you, Sam?"

"No. I've never wanted one." Sam shrugged. "I guess I was too busy. As soon as I graduated from high school, I went to college, and then right into the US Marshals."

Tessa sat up and frowned at him. "You were a Marshal? How long were you a Marshal?"

"Seven years." He blew out a breath, relaxing against a pillow. "Then four years ago, my parents wanted to retire to San Diego—Dad has arthritis pretty bad in his hands. They wanted me to come home and take care of the ranch." He shrugged. "I did and when it was time to elect a new sheriff here in Clifton, I ran and won."

Tessa snorted. "That's probably because all the women voted for you."

Sam chuckled. "Would you have voted for me, Tessa?"

"Yes...yes, I dare say that I would have." She laughed then and seemed to relax again.

Sam ran his finger over her tattoo. "I do like this."

"I do too. Maybe you should get one," she said teasing him and running a fingertip along his jawline.

"Well, if I decide to get one, it sure as hell won't be a butterfly—something of significance, maybe." Sam kissed her nose.

Tessa grinned and then sighed. "Okay. I'll hold you to that."

"Tessa, as long as you hold me, I'll be fine." Sam grinned mischievously as he rolled out of bed to head for the bathroom to dispose of the condom. He glanced over his shoulder at the beautiful woman lying in his bed and thanked heaven that she was there.

"How about a shower, Doc?"

Chapter Eight

A few hours later, Tessa woke up feeling a bit disoriented since she didn't recognize immediately where she was but then she smiled, and moved her lips across Sam's lightly whiskered cheek to his earlobe. She tugged on it with her teeth then moved down his neck. Nipping at his shoulder lightly with her teeth, she moved to his chest. Her hands ran down his hard pecs to his rippled stomach and his hard cock. Wrapping her hand around it, she gently squeezed. Sam fisted his hands in her hair and groaned. Tessa moved her lips down his stomach and ran her tongue along his hard length before taking him into her mouth. When Sam moaned, she glanced up to see his head back against the pillow and his eyes closed.

Feeling powerful, she wanted to please him as he'd done for her earlier. They'd taken a shower together then crawled back to bed, and promptly dozed off. She knew this would be a wonderful way to wake him. Taking him deep in her mouth, she sucked on him while stroking her hand up and down his hard length, and gently kneading his balls with her other hand. When she moaned, he shuddered. Tessa didn't stop until Sam grabbed at her shoulders.

"Tessa...please stop. You have to stop," he growled tugging at her.

Raising her head, she looked at him. "Why?"

Sam exhaled in sudden relief. "You know the answer to that."

Tessa grinned. "Yes. I do." Then put her mouth back over him causing him to tangle his fingers in her mop of hair.

Sam hissed in a breath. "Tessa, no...I'm too close."

"I want you all the way there, Sam. I want to do this for you," she said around his hard flesh.

"Tessa, I'm—" A sudden groan tore from deep in his chest as he lifted his hips and came. Tessa kept up her attention to him until he lay spent then crawled up his body, and kissed him.

"Are you all right?" She laughed softly when he groaned again.

"No. I'm dead." His eyes remained closed but a smile played on his beautiful mouth.

"You're not dead, you're talking," she whispered, smiling in triumph.

Sam opened one eye and grinned. "God, that was amazing. You didn't have to do that but I loved it. Thank you."

"You're welcome. I enjoyed doing it for you."

Sam hugged her. "Anytime you want to—" She swatted him gently making him laugh, but then he rolled her under him and the heat in his eyes made her tremble. "I think a payback's in order."

"Sam, you don't have to. I wanted to show you how much I care about you before—"

"I know, baby but now, I want to show you." Sam moved his lips to her neck but Tessa pulled his hair. "Ouch! What was that for?"

"Can't you just let me do something for you?" Tessa pushed at his shoulders until he rolled off her. She sat up and glared at him, feeling disappointed that he couldn't just accept her generous gesture.

Sam burst out laughing. "I just did." He sat up, wrapped his arms around her, and pulled her back down spooning her against his hard chest. "Let's just lay here a minute, all right? Then we'll see about payback. I always pay my debts, darlin'."

Tessa sighed and rested her cheek on his chest. "All right."

When are you going to tell him? You need to tell him before things get even more complicated. I know! I know! Her inner voice was right but she wasn't ready to let this end yet and once Sam knew the truth, she feared it would end. She knew that for sure.

"Good," Sam murmured against her hair as they both drifted off to sleep.

* * * *

The next morning, Tessa woke up with her head on Sam's shoulder. Her arm was across his waist. One of his hands held her wrist across his stomach and the other was in her hair, with his cheek lying on top of her head. They fit together perfectly was the first thought that ran through her sleepy head. She smiled then the truth of things smacked her in the face.

"About time you woke up," Sam's deep voice rumbled above her ear and she raised her head to gaze up at him. He looked so happy. Now was definitely not the time to divulge her secret.

"Good morning, Sam," Tessa whispered as she leaned forward to kiss him.

"I've been waiting for you to wake up." Sam smiled at her, and then he closed his eyes as if in discomfort.

"Why is that?" she murmured with a frown. Had she talked in her sleep?

Sam rolled to his side to face her. "I think that would be obvious." He moved her hand to his hard cock. Tessa almost laughed in relief.

"How do I know that isn't just morning wood?"

Sam laughed. "You love using euphemisms, don't you? Happy trail? Morning wood?"

"Okay, laugh then...it doesn't matter if it's morning wood or evening wood, as long as it's...wood." She wrapped her hand around him and smiled.

"Damn, Tessa." Sam groaned.

Tessa moved her hand up and down his long, hard length. "God, Sam. You really are hung well."

"You surprise me. You never came across to me as brazen." He kissed her. "Stay again tonight, Tessa."

"I'm brazen as hell but we both have to work tomorrow, Sam."

"So? We'll go to your apartment and get you some clothes for tomorrow. I want to go for a ride with you today."

Tessa hesitated for many reasons, but the thought of sleeping in her bed alone wasn't at all tempting anymore. She smiled. "Are you talking horseback riding?" She laughed when he groaned.

"Yes, I was talking horseback riding, but we can do the other too. Stay with me."

She contemplated having a long discussion with him now or enjoying the day with him. She wasn't ready to end this and if she told him what she needed to tell him, it would end.

"Okay, Sam. Let's get some breakfast and go to my apartment."

Sam grinned. "That's my girl."

Tessa blushed and watched him climb from bed, naked and glorious. She wanted to be his girl for as long as he wanted her. She sighed, knowing she was a coward. Tessa knew she was falling for him and she knew, without a doubt, she was not going to come out of this relationship with her heart intact. *Tell him! I will!*

* * * *

The day was already very hot, and the air conditioning in her vehicle took a while to cool it down. Tessa held her ponytail up and fanned her neck with her hand. As soon as it started cooling, she drove out of the yard. She'd enjoyed her time with Sam but as good as it was, she knew she had to sit down with him and tell him everything. Their growing relationship could only get better but only with the air cleared between them—or end before it got more serious.

Once on the road, she picked up speed, grinning as she wondered if Sam was trying to catch speeders this morning as he had left the house a while ago. Pressing the gas down a little more, she laughed when she saw his patrol cruiser close in behind her with the lights and siren on. After she pulled over onto the berm of the road, she put her window down glancing in the side view mirror while chewing her lower lip as she focused on his fly as he sauntered toward her.

Oh, that man is hot. Tessa glanced over her shoulder and pretended to scowl at him.

"Is there an emergency, Doctor McGuire?" Sam asked as he leaned an arm along the top of her vehicle.

"No. No emergency....*Sheriff.*" Tessa tried not to grin.

"Then what's the hurry?" His fingers thrummed on the roof.

"I didn't get any coffee this morning after I got out of bed, and I want to stop at the diner and pick some up before I get to work."

Tessa noticed Sam was smiling as he glanced away even though those damn mirrored sunglasses hid his eyes. She was really beginning to hate them. Sam slapped his hand on the roof making her jerk.

"Better get going then." He turned to go

then turned back to her. "Of course, if you'd gotten your ass out of bed earlier, you would have had coffee." Sam put his fingers to his hat. "You have a nice day...ma'am."

Tessa laughed and watched him walk back to his cruiser, admiring his butt in those close-fitting jeans. She groaned thinking how hot he really was, even if a smartass, since it was *his* fault she was so late getting out of bed. After checking for traffic, she hit the gas and pulled out, spinning tires and throwing gravel. Tessa grinned when she looked back and saw Sam throwing his hands up in the air as if to say 'what the hell'.

* * * *

Sam climbed into his vehicle and watched Tessa drive away shaking his head. She had claimed he was trouble...nope, that woman was absolute trouble with a capital T. He chuckled. She had to know he was out here and that was why she was speeding, she'd wanted him to stop her. That made Sam smile as he pulled onto the road and followed her to the diner. A cup of coffee sounded good right about now. He drove into a spot beside where she'd parked at the diner, and stepped from the vehicle. Tessa grinned as she looked at him over the hood of her SUV.

"Are you following me, Sheriff?" She

teased with an innocent expression and an adorable tilt to her head.

Sam stopped beside her and gazed down at her. "Yes."

Tessa laughed. "I don't think I've ever met a more honest man than you, Sam."

Sam chuckled and took his sunglasses off. "I don't lie." Her expression suddenly changed and all playfulness left her. "What is it?"

"Nothing. Well, if you must know, I hate it when you wear those sunglasses," she told him with a sudden smile.

"I'm not wearing them now."

Tessa looked away then back and looped her arm through his. "Let's have coffee, Sheriff then I have got to get to work."

Sam stared at her and shrugged. He wished he could understand why she sometimes seemed to lock down. Was it about him? Was he moving things too fast for her? She'd said she didn't want any involvements. Maybe he needed to slow down. "Sure."

They enjoyed their coffee together talking about events on the news channel running on the TV mounted on the back wall then Sam leaned over, and kissed her quickly before leaving the diner to head to the office.

* * * *

Tessa sighed with a grin she couldn't hold back as she watched Sam walk out of the diner then she turned back to her coffee only to find Connie smiling at her. Tessa raised an eyebrow.

"So...you and Sam, huh?" Connie inquired in a low voice.

"I-I'd like to think so, Connie," Tessa said making her friend laugh. "It's kind of complicated and I have no idea how he feels."

"Well, if he isn't interested, he's missing a good opportunity because there is a lot of sexual tension between you. *A lot.*"

Tessa smiled wishing it were that simple. "Could I have a coffee to go?"

She watched Connie pour coffee into a Styrofoam cup, put a lid on it, and hand it to her. Tessa paid her, left the diner, and climbed into her vehicle to drive the short distance to the hospital, and a long day of appointments.

Later that night, Tessa walked into her bedroom planning to go to sleep. She was tired but not sleepy. It was close to midnight and she hadn't talked to Sam since she'd seen him that morning. She moved slowly to the window and gazed down at the street. It had started raining earlier and the street had taken on an eerie look. Main Street was empty, but the streetlights glowed and reflected off the dark pavement. The rain moved through the light in a downpour.

Her breath caught when she saw a figure standing under a lamppost. The person seemed to be looking up at her window. She blinked quickly and the figure was no longer there. Was she imagining things again? A nervous shiver crawled through her so she quickly changed into her lounge pants and T-shirt then crawled between the sheets.

Her bed seemed overly large because she already missed sleeping with Sam after only two nights of being in his arms. Tessa didn't think she'd fall asleep but the stress of the day finally caught up to her, and she drifted off to sleep. When she woke up later screaming, she sat straight up quickly glancing around the room. Reaching over, she turned on the bedside lamp to see that the room was empty.

Tessa placed her hands over her face rubbing the sleep from her eyes and the fear from her pounding chest then looked at the clock—it was almost two. Her thoughts went to Sam who had to be sound asleep but she needed to hear his voice. Reaching for her cell phone, she dialed his number before she lost her nerve.

"Sheriff Garrett," he said in the way of

answering even though his voice sounded rough and sexy from sleep.

"Sam," Tessa whispered.

"Tessa, what is it?" Sam's voice sounded concerned but now wide-awake.

"I...I miss you, Sam." She choked back tears.

"I miss you too, Tessa. Why are you still up at this time of night?"

"I had a bad dream and now I'm too scared to go back to sleep. I wish you were here with me."

"I asked you to stay here...remember?" His huff came over the phone reminding her of her own decision not to stay.

"Yes. Maybe I shouldn't be so stubborn. Next time I won't be." She sighed. "Sam, do you think everyone in town thinks like Gwendolyn Barnes? I mean...you know...that I broke you and Sandy up."

"If they're all so blind as to believe that old busybody, that's their problem. You don't believe her, right?" Sam asked then paused, waiting for her answer.

Tessa took a deep breath. "Of course not but...is...well...is marriage something you see for your future?"

Sam didn't answer right away and she thought that maybe she'd said the wrong thing. Leave it to her to ruin things without trying.

"Marriage...marriage is a big step...for anyone, but I suppose someday...if the right woman came along and she wanted it too, I suppose it could be," Sam answered. "If the right woman came along...I'd want her to be mine and all mine. Does that answer your question?"

"Yeah...it does. Thanks Sam. I'm okay now. I just needed to hear your voice. Goodnight, Sam. Thanks for listening. I feel better now."

"Goodnight, baby."

She heard him yawn just before he hung up and she immediately missed him again.

Tessa smiled as she put her phone on the nightstand, turned out the light, and laid back against the pillows. Pulling the covers up to her neck, she thought about the figure on the street and Sam's words. He would want her to be his and only his. Now she didn't know what to do. Telling him the truth could end something good and the idea of that scared her. She closed her eyes trying to make sense of what to do and promptly fell back asleep.

After a night of tossing and turning, Tessa rolled out of bed at six in the morning and entered her bathroom to shower. Pulling her hair up into its usual ponytail while still damp, she dressed quickly, applied her make-up, and then ran down the stairs after locking her door. She wanted to grab some breakfast at the diner but when she reached her SUV, she stopped mid-stride. Groaning when she saw the flat tire, she pulled her cell phone from her pocket, and dialed the local garage. Thank goodness, they were open but only just. They told her someone would be there within thirty minutes, which gave her just enough time to walk over to the diner, get some coffee and a bagel or something, then meet the repair guy back here. Her first appointment might have to wait a bit but she'd let Jodi know so she could tell them.

Returning from the diner, Tessa leaned against the car and waited. Ten minutes passed when she saw a sheriff's unit coming down the street. Straightening up, she watched it pull in behind her car. Her heart began beating double time as the door opened and Sam stepped out. Tessa knew at that moment he was coming to mean a lot to her in just a short time. She grinned as she watched him fold his arms and lean against his SUV. He had those damn sunglasses on and if she ever got the chance, she was going to throw them away. Nothing should hide those beautiful eyes.

"Don't tell me you don't know how to

change a tire, Doctor McGuire." Sam tilted his head while a smirk played around his beautiful kissable lips.

Tessa shrugged. "All right, I won't tell you."

Sam shook his head and strolled toward her, stopping close to her. She tilted her head back to gaze up at him. Her eyes roamed over his gorgeous face and landed on those sexy lips and pure instinct drove her to her toes to kiss him. She felt him grin against her lips.

"Good morning, Sheriff," she murmured, feeling his hands go to her waist.

"Good morning, Doc," Sam said against her mouth. "Why are you standing out here with a flat tire?"

Tessa stepped back. "The garage is sending someone to change it. I need it fixed in case I have to take a call." She smiled. "I may live above the hospital but I still need my SUV."

Sam's eyebrows rose above his sunglasses. "You're serious? You really don't know how to change a tire?"

"Nope." Tessa tried not to smile.

Sam grinned at her. "Call them back and cancel. I'll change it."

Of course, he would change it. Men love to show a woman how macho they are.

"Thank you." While Sam went about working on changing the tire, she called the garage and canceled the repair request. When he was done, he put the flat tire in the back of her SUV and wiped his hands on a rag.

"You do realize you owe me now, right?" Sam's mouth twitched as he fought what she suspected was a smug smile of satisfaction.

Tessa gasped. "That's why you changed it for me...payback." Moving closer to him, she put her hand around the back of his neck. "Okay then...just what do I owe you...Sheriff?"

Sam glanced away and then back to her. "I'm sure I can come up with something." With a sly sexy grin, he jerked her to him and kissed her. His tongue slowly moved deep into her mouth. Tessa groaned as she ran her other hand up his chest and around his neck and plastered her body to his. They sprang apart when a car went by blowing the horn.

Tessa laughed softly, reached up, and took his sunglasses off.

"I hate when you wear these. I love seeing those baby blues," she said teasing him.

Sam's mouth flattened as he gazed back at her. "Can I have those back, please?"

Tessa shook her head, making Sam frown. "Only if you promise to take them off when you're around me...please."

Sam stared at her for a few seconds. "No problem, darlin'."

Tessa handed the glasses back to him. "I'm looking forward to paying you back for helping me...Sheriff."

Sam blew out a laugh. "Not as much as I am." He kissed her quickly. "I have to run. I'm sure Betty Lou will have the entire town out looking for me if I don't get back to the office soon. Tonight?"

Tessa stood on her toes and kissed him. "Yes."

Sam gave her a nod then put his glasses back on as well as his hat, and then climbed into his vehicle, giving her a wave as he drove off. Tessa walked around the building to go to work with a huge grin on her face.

* * * *

Entering the station by the back door, Sam walked into his office and took his hat off, hanging it on the hall tree, and strolled around his desk. As soon as he took a seat, Betty Lou filled the doorway. Sam mentally groaned as he ran his hand down his face.

"What is it, Betty Lou?" he asked looking up at her.

Betty Lou had a huge grin on her face.

"You and Tessa, huh?"

Sam was sure his mouth dropped open. "Jesus Christ, Betty Lou...I just left her."

"Don't you swear at me, Sam Garrett," Betty Lou scolded and folded her arms across her ample chest.

"How the hell...heck, did you find out?"

Betty Lou snorted. "This is Clifton, for heaven's sake. It was all over town when you kissed her at the diner yesterday then again this morning after you changed her tire."

Sam groaned. "People around here need to get a life and stay out of mine."

"Aww, Sam. Everyone thinks it's great. Tessa's a wonderful woman and you're such a good man." She laughed. "It's about time. You deserve each other."

Sam muttered and grabbed some paperwork. When she didn't leave, he glared up at her. "Was there something else, Betty Lou?"

Shaking her head, she cackled as she left his office and headed for her desk. Sam leaned back in his chair, spun it around, and gazed out the window. He looked toward the animal hospital and knew Tessa was in there. His lips rose in a grin as he remembered her kissing him first this morning.

* * * *

Later that day in her apartment, after

long hours of taking care of animals and dealing with their owners, Tessa was getting ready to take a shower when there was a knock on her door. Glancing to the door, she hesitated then walked slowly to it and peered through the peephole. Relief rushed over her and made her smile when she saw Sam standing there. Opening the door, she stared at him hiding her smile of delight.

"Hi, sweetheart," he murmured.

Tessa grinned and reached up to take his sunglasses off. "Hello, Sheriff. What can I do for you?"

Sam smirked. "You have no idea." His gaze ran over her. "Can I come in? We have a debt to discuss."

"I thought we were going to discuss it tonight?" Tessa nibbled on her bottom lip as she opened the door wider for him to step in.

Sam strode through the doorway and stood by her couch. "Come here, Tessa."

Shivering at the sound of his deep sexy tone, Tessa walked to him and stopped within inches of him then gazed up at him. "I'm here, Sheriff."

Sam gripped her hips and pulled her to him. She could feel his hard cock through his jeans. "Do you feel what you do to me?"

"Sam..." Tessa moaned leaning in.

"God, Tessa. You have me in the palm

of your hand." He lowered his head and kissed her. His tongue moved into her mouth making her groan against his caress. She threw her arms around his neck and he backed her up to the sofa. "I want you so much...so very much. Kiss me, Tessa," Sam whispered against her lips.

"You are such an amazing man," she whispered in his ear. "I was planning to take a shower. Care to join me?"

Sam groaned as if in pain. "Yes."

He picked her up and carried her to the bathroom. Sam set her on her feet and cupped her face in his hands, pressing his lips to hers as his hands moved down her shoulders to her waist and the bottom of her T-shirt. Sam pulled it off over her head and kissed her, taking her mouth roughly. Tessa's hands went to the buttons on his khaki shirt but her fingers were having trouble with them. She started to laugh, making Sam pull back from her and raise an eyebrow.

"I can't get these damn buttons undone." Tessa chuckled.

Sam laughed and pushed her hands out of the way. He reached behind him and pulled the shirt off over his head, not bothering with the buttons. Tessa then lifted his T-shirt off over his head and ran her hands over his pecs before slipping her fingers down along his rippled stomach to the snap of his jeans, reveling in the way he sucked in his breath as she did. Looking up into his eyes, she unsnapped them and lowered the zipper slowly. Sam groaned.

"You're killing me," he growled.

"I'm just unzipping your jeans, Sheriff," Tessa said innocently.

"Just unzipping my jeans—yeah, that's it." He took a deep breath. "You're touching me, Tessa, and that about kills me every time I feel your hands on me."

Tessa stood on her toes and kissed him. "You say the sexiest things, Sam."

"I'm not trying to be sexy, for God's sake, Tessa. I'm just saying what you do to me."

Tessa ran her hands around his waist. "You just have no idea how sexy you are, Sam Garrett."

"I don't know if I will ever get enough of you, Tessa. You're so beautiful."

Stepping back from him, she removed her jeans then her bra, and slowly lowered her panties and stood naked in front of him. She watched as he closed his eyes as if he couldn't take looking at her. When he opened his eyes, she gasped at the heat in them. Tessa moved to the shower and turned it on. With what she hoped was a sultry glance over her shoulder, she stepped into it. As she lathered up the soap, she watched as Sam finished undressing and she was so excited to have him, she moaned. He stepped in behind her and took the soap from her. Lathering up his hands, he slowly ran them over her back, on down to the dip above her ass. His hands ran over the cheeks of her ass and then encircled her waist. Sam dipped his hand to her mound. Tessa's head went back against his shoulder. His mouth ran along her collarbone sending shivers of pleasure over her skin.

"Sam...please," she pleaded with a long moan.

"Please, what? I told you before I could please you. I have, haven't I, Tessa?"

"Oh God yes...you have, Sam."

His breath came across her ear. "I want to please you again, Tessa."

Tessa moaned. "Yes...Sam, please..." She gasped when his hand moved between her legs and he rubbed a finger between her slit.

"God, you're so wet, Tessa."

"For you, Sam...only for you," she whispered, then groaned when he moved his hand behind her and slipped it between her legs to her very core. He inserted a finger deep inside her. Tessa bucked against him as his other hand moved over her clitoris while he moved his lips along her collarbone. She clenched her legs around his hands.

"Sam..." She placed her hands on the shower wall and leaned forward as Sam's hands worked their magic. Her orgasm hit her hard so that she groaned out his name as wave after wave of pleasure crashed over her then she cried out again as she came again. Tessa fell back against him, her hands going up into his hair.

"That was amazing." She spun around and wrapped her hand around his hard cock. Moving her hand up and down the length, she watched as Sam closed his eyes and pumped into her hand. He wrapped his hand around hers and opened his eyes.

"Tessa," he whispered her name making her shiver. She continued moving her hand up and down his hard length. Sam's hand tightened around hers guiding her and making him groan.

Watching him close his eyes in pleasure, she slowly stroked him and moved her thumb over the tip feeling a slick drop of moisture. She continued to pump her hand as she pressed her lips to his. Sam moaned into her mouth.

"You're close, Sam," she murmured against his lips.

"I want to be inside you," he groaned.

"Not this time. Let me do this for you." Tessa pressed her lips to his and kissed him with all the passion she had for this wonderful man. Her tongue entered his mouth. Sam pumped his hips against her hand as their lips clung together. As he grew harder in her hand, she kneaded his balls with her other hand until a groan tore from his throat and he turned from her coming against the shower wall. He took deep breaths then looked at her.

"Damn, you didn't have to do that."

"I wanted to. You do it for me," she said against his lips.

Sam leaned down to kiss her then yelled and jumped back. The water had gone cold. Tessa giggled. She was behind him so the cold water hit only him. Sam grabbed her and turned her around making her squeal when the icy water hit her. Sam chuckled.

"Sam Garrett, that's not funny," Tessa growled.

Sam pulled her to him. "That's *Sheriff* Sam Garrett."

Tessa laughed, pushed away from him, and stepped from the shower. "I'll get you back for that."

Sam grinned. "Looking forward to it, angel."

Chapter Nine

September had arrived, turning leaves red and gold and bringing cooler nights. Sam and Tessa had been seeing each other nearly every weekend since late July. This evening they lay in the back of his old pickup truck on a blanket, out in a pasture, staring up at the stars, and Tessa thought life couldn't get any better.

"They are so beautiful. There's so many of them," Tessa said in awe of the night sky filled with sparkling pinpoints of light.

"Thousands, maybe more. I love coming up here and just laying here looking up at them." Sam clasped his hands behind his head.

"How many women have you brought up here for star-gazing?"

"Only you. I never bring women to my home."

Tessa laid her head on his shoulder. "You brought me here."

"Yes. You aren't like the other women, Tessa. You have to know that by now."

Tessa bit her lip. *Tell him!* Her inner

voice seemed to scream at her nearly every day but dear God, she couldn't. Not yet. *When?* She wished she knew when the time was right. He was such a traditional man that it terrified her to think of his being disappointed in her. They'd been seeing each other almost two months now and all she'd managed to do was deceive him. He was going to hate her when he found out the truth about her, and he would—eventually. There was no way she could keep this a secret much longer—not from a man like Sam. They were getting too close and she was falling in love with him. She blinked her eyes quickly. It was all going to fall apart and it would be no one's fault but hers.

"Are you going to run for sheriff again?" she asked, hoping to change the subject.

"I haven't made up my mind yet. I love the job, but I'd also like to make the ranch into something again. My parents raised cattle for beef. I'm not interested in that so much but maybe instead, raise and sell horses. I need something to do when I retire someday."

Tessa let out a relieved breath that he'd gone along with her change of subject. "You need to make a decision soon, Sam. The election is November and you'll need to campaign."

"I know. I'll probably run again. I'm just thinking of what to do. Maybe something will happen and it will make my decision."

* * * *

A few days later, Sam got what he'd wished for—something that would help him make his decision about running. Sitting at his desk filling out paperwork, he glanced up and saw Rick standing in the doorway looking uneasy. Sam tossed his pen down and leaned back in his chair. When Rick still didn't say anything, Sam raised an eyebrow at him.

"Problem, Rick?" Sam frowned at the worried expression on his deputy's face.

Rick moved into the room and took a seat in the chair across from the desk. Sam began to feel uneasy, especially when Rick cleared his throat and glanced around the room then back to Sam.

"I'm going to run for sheriff," Rick announced without his gaze actually meeting Sam's eyes.

Sam was stunned. "What did you just say?" He sat forward, laid his arms on the desk, weaving his fingers together, and narrowed his eyes at Rick.

"I'm running for the office, Sam. It's something I've always wanted to do."

"I thought we were friends, Rick. Other than you being my deputy, and one of my best ones at that, I thought we were friends."

"We are, Sam. This has nothing to do with friendship. It's just something I want. I've wanted to be sheriff long before you came back. I was going to run against Jefferson but you decided to...and I knew I couldn't win against you...then."

Sam sat back, clasped his hands across his stomach, and smirked at Rick. "And you think you can now?"

Rick stood quickly. "Actually, I think I have a hell of a shot at it."

Rising slowly from his chair, Sam placed his hands on the desk leaning forward, and stared at him. "You'd better hope you win. Otherwise, you'll be out of a job." He sat back down, picked his pen up, and went back to his paperwork. "Now get to work. I'm busy." He didn't raise his eyes as Rick left the office.

Once Rick left, Sam swore softly. He couldn't believe Rick was going to run against him in November. Feeling the walls seeming to close in on him, Sam knew he had to get out of the office. He stood, then headed out the door, grabbing his hat along the way.

Betty Lou glanced up at him. "Are you going out, Sam?"

"Yes."

"Okay. I'll call you if I need you or

anyone else does," she said in a matter of fact tone.

"I'll be back in a while." He stepped outside and took a deep breath of fresh crisp fall air.

Son of a bitch! Of all the people he had to worry about running against him, Rick hadn't been one of them. Sam glanced toward the animal hospital and knew he needed to see Tessa. Crossing the street, he followed the sidewalk without looking up at anyone. When he reached the entrance, he entered the hospital, and ambled up to the counter.

"Hi, Jodi. Is Tessa busy?" He smiled at the teenager and saw a blush darken her cheeks.

"Let me check. I know she just finished a surgery." Jodi picked up the phone and called Tessa's office. After hanging up, she gazed up at Sam. "She'll be right out."

"Thank you." Sam moved away from the counter and nodded to the two women sitting together in the waiting room with their pets. He knew they were talking about him since they kept glancing at him, smiling, and whispering. Finally, Tessa came from the back and greeted him with a smile that made his heart skip a beat.

"Hi, Sam...so what are you doing over

here this time of day?" Tessa moved to stand in front of him blocking the view of the two women who already had their heads together. He appreciated the move and that she was acting very professional, but he needed the ease of being alone with her right now.

"I-I—" He stopped, glanced over her shoulder at the two women, then Jodi, and then back to Tessa. "Can we go to your office?"

Tessa raised an eyebrow. "Of course." She looked over to Jodi. "Please hold any calls for me, Jodi."

Jodi nodded at her and smiled up at Sam. "No problem, Doc Mac."

Sam looked at Jodi and smiled then followed Tessa to her office. Once inside, he wrapped his hand around her arm and turned her to face him then pulled her into his arms to hold her.

Tessa pulled back from him and gazed up at him. "What's wrong, Sam?"

Taking his hat off, he ran his fingers through his hair then resettled his hat and huffed out a frustrated breath. "Rick just told me he's going to run against me in the election."

Tessa gasped with wide eyes. "Why would he do that?"

"He said it's something he's always

wanted. I have to admit that I'm in shock. I'm sorry to bother you but I just needed to get out of there. I was standing outside when I looked down this way and knew I had to see you." He pulled her back to him and held her tight. Her arms wrapped around his waist.

"I'm sorry, Sam. I know you and Rick are friends, and this has to hurt. So...I guess this means you are definitely running again."

"Yeah, I guess I am. I hadn't realized how much I still want the job until Rick said he did. I just can't get over it. Of all the people to worry about running against me, I didn't expect him. I can't help but feel betrayed. I thought he was a friend." Sam shook his head but when he felt Tessa tense in his arms, he tried to read her expression. She gave him a quick kiss.

"You'll win, Sam. You're a great sheriff. Clifton loves you," Tessa told him with a nod and a smile.

Sam shook his head. "I hope so. You know what, I really like the job, but if I lose then I'll run the ranch instead."

"Could you go back to the Marshals?" Tessa tilted her head back to look up at him.

"Not if it means not seeing you," Sam whispered.

Tessa's eyes widened then she stood on

her toes and kissed him. "You're a wonderful man, Sam Garrett."

Sam leaned down and put his lips close to hers. "*Sheriff* Sam Garrett." He captured Tessa's laughter with his mouth. Her arms circled around his neck and he lifted his lips from hers.

"Are you going to be able to come out to the ranch after work? We can stargaze some more—or make-out." He winked at her.

She laughed. "I can't. I'll need to check on the dog I just did surgery on. I had to amputate her front leg, and she'll be in pain when she wakes from the anesthesia. She should sleep most of the night but I want to make sure everything's all right."

"I understand. I don't like it, but I understand." Sam sighed. "I need to get back to the office. I just needed to hold you for a minute."

"I got it. You needed a hug, Sam." Tessa laughed.

Sam muttered under his breath. "If you say so." He kissed her quickly and left her office.

When Sam strolled back through the doors of the sheriff's department, he felt better. Just being near Tessa did it for him every time. Anytime he was feeling bad, all he had to do was be close to her and it went away.

"Nothing happened while you were gone," Betty Lou told him glancing up at him.

Sam halted and stared at her. "I figured that out when you didn't call me."

"Don't take that attitude with me, Sam Garrett." Betty Lou huffed, and then frowned at him. "What's got your panties in a wad?"

"Did you seriously just ask me that?" Sam narrowed his eyes.

"I did." She stood. "You were fine earlier, then Rick comes out of your office like he's mad at the world and you ain't far behind him. He storms to his desk and you storm out the door."

"I did not *storm* out the door." Sam rolled his shoulders. "I went to see Tessa for a moment."

"That's nice. She obviously put you in a better mood."

"Betty Lou..." Sam started.

"Yeah, yeah, I know. I'll mind my own business. But there's a reason you went to see her in the middle of the day. None of us are blind, Sam."

"I have work to do," Sam mumbled and strode back to his office to take a seat at his desk. Once there, he leaned back and stared at the wall.

What *would* he do if he lost the election? Could he actually make the ranch profitable again? His parents had raised cattle for beef and even though the ranch wasn't quite as large as the Morgan ranch, it had done all right.

Sam shook his head. He couldn't think like that. There was no way he'd let Rick beat him in the election. He hadn't realized how much he wanted to remain sheriff until Rick told him he was running against him. Sam *was* the Sheriff of Clifton County and he intended to stay that way. He mentally groaned when he looked up to find Betty Lou standing in the doorway. Sam leaned back in his chair.

"What now?"

Betty Lou moved into the room and closed the door then she took a seat in the chair across from him. "What's wrong Sam? I've known you since you were in diapers and I know when you're mad or upset about something."

Sam ran his hand around the back of his neck because he could feel the muscles tensing up there. "I suppose you'll find out soon enough. Rick's running against me for sheriff."

Betty Lou stared at him. "Why? Why would he do that?"

Sam shrugged. "He has the right to run. I hate that we're going against each other but there will be others too."

"You'll win, Sam. There's no one who could run against you and win." Betty Lou stood. "You'll see." She opened the door and walked out.

Sam hoped she was right. This town was his home, and it was his job to protect it and the people in it. As long as he was sheriff, Clifton would be safe. He'd stake his life on it.

* * * *

Tessa hated sleeping at the hospital but she wanted to be close to her patient, a dog who had to have emergency surgery. The sofa in the back office was the only place to sleep unless she slept on the floor. Tessa sighed. The floor was not an option so the sofa it would be.

Before closing up tonight, she retrieved a blanket and pillow from her apartment and upon returning to the hospital that evening, she'd tossed them onto the sofa. Now that everyone had left, she made sure the doors were secure. Although she'd done this plenty of times, she really despised it. Even with several animals there, it was eerily quiet. She knew she could have asked one of her techs to do it, but if something went wrong Tessa needed to be here and she'd never ask anyone else to do it anyway. She enjoyed taking care of the animals but wasn't thrilled about spending the night here.

After making sure everything was secure, she headed down the hall to check on Sheena, the dog with the amputated leg. Silently, she pushed the door open to the recovery room and stepped in, then squatted down and peered into the cage. Sheena gazed up at her with sad eyes.

"Hello, pretty girl. I just want to make sure you're feeling all right," Tessa said softly as she opened the door to examine the dog. Sheena whimpered and licked her hand. "Aww, girl, I'm so sorry. I'll get you some pain meds."

Tessa retrieved the medication and administered it through the IV. As she watched, Sheena closed her eyes and slept. As Tessa quietly left the room, her cell phone vibrated in her pocket.

Oh, please no emergency calls tonight.

"Doctor McGuire," she said when the call connected.

"Hello, Doctor McGuire. Sheriff Sam Garrett here."

Tessa bit her lip to keep from laughing. "Just what can I do for you...Sheriff?" she asked in a sultry voice but ruined it by laughing when Sam groaned.

"Damn it, Tessa. Don't ask me something like that when you're there and I'm here," Sam muttered.

"When the sheriff calls, it usually means he, uh...wants something."

Sam's chuckle came over the line. "Oh, I want something all right. I want you."

Now it was Tessa's turn to groan. "Sam..."

"And that right there is what gets me," Sam whispered. "I'm going to hang up now, Tessa. I just wanted to tell you if you need me, call me." He hung up without giving her a chance to answer that she'd always need him.

You are playing with fire, Tessa. You are in so deep and he's going to hate you when he finds out that you've done nothing but lie to him. You have to tell him!

She stared at the phone. She'd fallen in love with this man and it was all built on a lie. Then again, she could only hope that if he loved her the way she did him that he would understand.

She hoped. The alternative—losing him forever—was what terrified her.

* * * *

By the end of October, Sam was so tired of campaigning, he wanted to say the hell with it all and let someone else be sheriff. It had started with three other men running against him. Now it was down to him and Rick. Sam swore, picked up his coat, and strode from his office. Betty Lou gazed up at him as he entered the lobby.

"You all right, Sam?" she asked him with a worried furrow of her brow.

"Yes. Just restless, I suppose," he told her knowing she meant well with her concern.

"You'll win, Sam."

Sam turned to look at her. "You think so?"

"Not a doubt in my mind. You made Rick look like he didn't know what he was doing at the town meeting last night."

Sam smiled thinking she was right. "It's not my fault he didn't know how to answer about how dangerous Copper Ridge is."

Betty Lou laughed. "You did, though. I'm proud of you. You'll win."

"You just want me to win so you'll have a job," he teased.

"There is that." She laughed and then sobered. "Only a few more days, Sam."

"I know. I feel confident, but you never know."

Betty Lou stood. "I know, Sam Garrett. You're going to win."

"I hope you're right, Betty Lou. I'm going to lunch. Do you want anything?"

"No, thank you. Bobbie Jo is bringing me lunch."

"All right. I'll be back in an hour. Call me if you need me."

"Sam?"

"Yeah?" He turned to look at her.

"I'm real happy about you and Tess."

"So am I, Betty Lou." He gave her a salute and walked outside.

Damn, it was cold and it seemed like summer had just been here. Had he only been seeing Tessa since July? A little over three months yet it seemed longer. As if she'd always belonged to him. The cold wind blew his coat open as he walked down the street to the diner. Entering the warm aromatic eatery, everyone called out to him. Grinning, he gave a wave and took a seat at the counter.

"Burger and fries, Sam?" Connie asked him with her usual smile.

"Please."

Setting a glass of water down in front of him, she yelled his order through the window behind the counter to the cook. Sam swiveled around and his eyes scanned the room settling on a stranger in a back booth. It was nothing new for strangers to be here in the summer months since the Clifton Bed and Breakfast had opened, but it was a little unusual to see a stranger this time of the year. Of course, the man could just be passing through. He watched him for a moment or so but the man just seemed to be enjoying his meal. A few minutes later, Sam spun back around on the stool when Connie set his meal down on the counter. He picked up the burger and bit into it. Connie stood at the counter staring at him so he winked at her, making her laugh as she walked away. She always waited to see if he liked his burger. Glancing to the door when the bell above it rang announcing a new customer, he grinned at Wyatt Stone who took the seat beside him.

"Hey, Sam. Ready for election day?"

"No. I hate the waiting."

Wyatt chuckled. "You got this, no problem. There's no way Rick's going to beat you."

"I hope to hell you're right, Wyatt." Sam raised his eyebrow. "Where's that beautiful wife of yours?"

"Why is it that's always the first thing people ask me?"

Sam chuckled. "Because we like to give you a rough time. Hell, you know Liv is only interested in you."

Wyatt grinned. "Damn straight, but she

does seem to have a crush on you. What about you? Where's that beautiful veterinarian of yours?"

Sam chuckled. "Working. I'll see her later tonight."

Wyatt glanced up at Connie. "Burger and fries for me, Connie. Olivia wants a fried chicken salad with ranch dressing."

"So Liv is meeting you here? Is she bringing Caleb?" Sam asked. He had to admit he'd like to see the little fella.

"No, Emma has Caleb. Olivia wanted to do a little shopping. She stopped in *Paige's* on the way here." He wiggled his eyebrows. *Paige's* was a lingerie shop known for its racy underwear.

Sam burst out laughing. "Why? It'll just end up on the floor."

Wyatt chuckled. "Yeah, but getting it to the floor is the fun part."

He and Wyatt were still laughing when the door opened and Olivia entered. She narrowed her eyes at them when they stopped laughing and glanced away from her.

"Why do I get the feeling I was the topic of conversation just now?" she asked taking a seat on a stool beside Wyatt.

"Probably because you were, sweetheart," Wyatt said smiling then nodded at the bag she set down at her feet. "What did you buy me?"

Sam chuckled. "He just wants to see what he'll be taking off you later."

"I believe you're right, Sam," Olivia said laughing before leaning in to give Wyatt a kiss.

Sam was about to comment further when his cell phone rang. "What's up Betty Lou?" Sam answered, listened then stood and paid Connie as he held the phone to his ear. He swore, told her he was on the way, and hung up.

"Problem, Sam?" Wyatt asked.

"That damn Joe Baker is at it again. I need to head out there. You two have a good day and an even better night." He waggled his eyebrows, grinned, put his fingers to his hat, and walked out. He jogged across the street, climbed into his patrol cruiser, and tore out of the parking lot.

When he arrived at the Baker's ranch, he drove up toward the barn. As he stepped out of his unit, he heard a gunshot, and quickly drew his weapon.

Using his shoulder mic, he called it in, "Shots fired at the Baker ranch, send backup."

As he slowly walked toward the barn, he saw Mary Baker come running out of it. Sam ran to her when she fell to the ground.

"Mary?"

Sam rolled her over and swore aloud when he saw her bloodied and swollen face. "Where is he?" he growled. Mary pointed toward the barn. "I'll be right back."

He stood and using his mic again, he called for an ambulance while he cautiously made his way through the barn with his weapon drawn and at the ready.

"Sam?" He heard Brody call for him in a low voice from outside.

"In the barn, Brody," Sam yelled back in a loud whisper. It wasn't wise to draw attention to yourself when trying to locate a dangerous man with a gun. He glanced in each stall leading with his weapon as he slowly made his way toward the back of the barn. When Brody caught up to him, he didn't turn to look at him but kept his sights trained on the spaces in front of him. "You must have been close by."

"Just down the road. It looks like he beat the shit out of her," Brody muttered from behind him.

Sam threw a quick glance over his shoulder to see Brody sweeping the closed stalls on the other side of the barn with his weapon held out in front of him.

"Yes, and I think I'll do the same to him when I find the son of a bitch. You hear me,

Baker. Come out, you bastard, and face me," Sam called out.

"Sam," Brody said to him, and when Sam glanced over, Brody jerked his chin toward an open stall. "Looks like you're not going to get the chance."

Sam frowned, strode across the barn, and looked into the stall where Brody stood already holstering his gun. Joe Baker lay in the hay with a bullet hole in his chest. Sam holstered his gun and moved to stand over him.

"I can't say he didn't deserve it." Sam took a deep breath and blew it out as he squatted down beside Joe pressing two fingers to the man's neck to check his pulse. "He's dead all right." Sam looked up at Brody. "Call the coroner. I already called for an ambulance for Mary. I'll question her at the hospital. I just hope I don't have to arrest her."

"Everyone knows how he beat her."

"I know, and I hope to hell it was self-defense." Sam stood and walked out of the barn to where Mary sat on the ground where she'd fallen. He crouched down beside her. Tears rolled down her face as she stared at the ground in front of her. "Are you all right, Mary?"

Sam gently touched her shoulder but she

flinched away from him.

"I couldn't take it any longer, Sheriff. He was going to kill me this time, I just know it."

"I believe you but once we get you to the hospital, I'll need to question you about what happened, okay?" Sam glanced up when the ambulance came tearing up the drive and came to a halt throwing dust all around.

She stared up at him. "What happened is I killed the son of a bitch. I'd just had it."

"I know but I'll need details, Mary. Let the paramedics check you out then we'll talk."

Mary nodded as tears rolled down her battered face. If the bastard weren't already dead, Sam would have killed him. He hated men who beat on women. His thoughts went to Tessa. Sam clenched his fists at the thought of anyone hurting her. He swore if he ever saw her wearing a haunted expression such as Mary always wore there was no telling what he'd do to the man who caused it. He strode back to his vehicle and took a deep breath as he watched the paramedics look Mary over. One of them walked over to him.

"She refuses to go to the hospital."

"Damn it," Sam muttered as he strode back toward her. "Mary, you have to go to the hospital. I want you checked out and photos taken. Trust me it will help your case."

She stared up at him, seeming to give some thought to what he said, and then sighed. "All right, Sheriff." She stood and then lay down on the stretcher. The paramedic rolled her to the ambulance.

"I don't think it's hit her yet what she's done or even that he won't hurt her anymore," Brody said from beside Sam.

"I know. The son of a bitch finally got what he deserved. I'll follow the ambulance. You wait for the coroner. I'll see you back at the office." Sam watched as Brody walked away then he climbed into his vehicle and drove to the hospital.

At the hospital, Sam walked behind the paramedics pushing the stretcher carrying Mary. Sam wanted to kill Joe Baker for doing this to her but she'd beaten him to it. He stood outside the room while she put on a hospital gown. When the nurse came out, she told Sam he could go in. Mary lay on the bed looking smaller than she was.

"I killed him, Sheriff," she whispered as tears rolled down her swollen face. Her right eye was swollen shut, blood oozed from a busted lip, and the left side of her jaw was probably broken.

Sam swore.

"I know, Mary. I need to get some

pictures of you and I'll need to know exactly what happened." Sam took pictures of her and anger flowed through him as he got closer to her and snapped the camera. He pulled a chair up beside the bed and took a seat. "Now tell me what happened, Mary."

"I was in the barn with my pistol because earlier I'd seen a snake and I wanted to be prepared if I saw it again." She shrugged. "Joe came into the barn and told me to fix him something to eat. I was walking out with him when Trick Dillon came by and got on Joe about our cattle being on his property again." Mary gazed at Sam. "I knew what he was doing but you know how Joe is. I couldn't tell him anything. Anyway, Joe would deliberately cut the fence line so the cattle could eat in Trick's pastures." She shook her head. "He cut the fence in several places. Trick came over a few times a week. He'd herd them back to our land and fix the fence, but Joe would just cut it again. Anyway, Trick told him to keep the cattle on our side or he'd call you again. After Trick left, Joe started yelling about everything—the horses, the cattle, Trick, you, and me. He really got mad when I said we should keep our cattle on our side of the fence. He punched me in the eye. I fell down and my gun landed on the ground. I picked it up, aimed it at him, and told him I was tired of him hitting me and I wanted him to leave the ranch. He knew I was scared so he laughed at me. I shot at him, but missed. That's when he kicked the gun from me and started beating on me."

"Son of a bitch," Sam muttered then gave her a nod. "Please go on."

Mary took a deep, shuddering breath. "This time I fought back and bit him on the arm. When he yelled and jumped back, I saw the gun. I crawled to it and turned around. He was coming at me, Sheriff. I aimed the gun at him. I told him to stop and leave me alone. He kept advancing and he told me this time he was going to kill me." She trembled. "I believed him...so I shot him. When he fell to the ground—I'm sorry but I felt good about it. He deserved it. He'd never leave the ranch. It's my ranch so I wasn't going to leave it. My grandmother left it to me years ago. I wasn't going to leave." She repeated. "I'm glad he's dead. I hated him. If you have to arrest me, I'll go peacefully." She stared at him with tears rolling down her face.

Standing, Sam put his hand on her shoulder. "Sounds like self-defense to me, Mary. I'm not charging you with anything. I need to get to the office but if you need me, you call me." He handed her his card.

"Thank you," she whispered and relaxed against the pillow.

Sam patted her shoulder, gave her a smile, and walked out. He was glad the son of a bitch was dead too.

Chapter Ten

When Tessa heard about the shooting at Joe Baker's ranch, she became a total wreck. Jodi told her she'd heard about it when she was at the diner picking up lunch. Connie had a scanner and when the call came across that there had been a shooting out at the Bakers, the entire restaurant went silent. Jodi ran back to the hospital to tell her, only Tessa didn't know who did the shooting or who'd been shot—only that the coroner had been called. She was anxious and so nervous not knowing what was happening that she could hardly breathe. Dear God, she prayed Sam was all right.

"Are you all right?" Jodi asked her.

"I'm scared," Tessa whispered.

"I hope it was Baker who was shot."

"I hate to hear that anyone was shot but I pray it wasn't Sam. Maybe he wasn't even there."

Jodi cleared her throat. "He was. Connie mentioned it right after the call came over the scanner. She said Betty Lou called him while he was there having his lunch."

"Oh, my God. I need to call Betty Lou. She'd know." Tessa reached for the phone and then slammed it down. "I'm too scared."

"Do you want me to call her?" Jodi glanced over her shoulder when she heard the front door open. "I'll be right back." She left to see who had come in.

Tessa put her hands over her face as tears threatened. *Please. Please, don't let it be Sam who was shot.*

"Tessa?"

Placing her hands on the desk, she stared up at him as he stood in the doorway. Jumping up from her chair, she ran around her desk then launched herself at him.

"Sam. I..." She burst into tears.

"What is it?" Sam cupped her face in his hands and stared down at her.

"I heard about the shooting. Jodi was at the diner when it came across the scanner."

"Damn it," he muttered, smoothing back wayward curls from her face that had escaped her ponytail.

"Who was the coroner for?"

"Joe. Mary had finally had enough and shot him."

Tessa wrapped her arms around his waist and pressed her head against his chest. Relief flooded her and she took a deep breath before lifting her head again. "I was so scared." She gasped. "How is she? How's Mary?"

Sam hugged her to him. "I talked to her at the hospital and took pictures. He really beat her this time, looks like he might've even broken her jaw. She said she shot at him twice, missing him the first time. That must have been the one someone called in. The second shot happened just as I was pulling up. She shot him in the chest. She truly believed he was going to kill her this time. Since it was her ranch...been in her family for years...she told him to leave and I guess he told her no, and she no longer had a choice. Terrible thing but frankly, he deserved it."

"I'm glad she's all right. He was a mean bastard."

"Yes, that he was. I have to go write up a report right now but I wanted to ask you if we could have dinner in tonight. I had no idea you knew about the shooting."

"Come to my apartment for dinner, Sam. I'll fix chicken and dumplings." Tessa grinned up at him.

Sam leaned down and kissed her lips. "I love chicken and dumplings. Six-thirty?"

"Yes." She stood on her toes and kissed him. "I'm so glad you're all right."

He grinned against her lips.

"I'll see you later, sweetheart," Sam said on his way out.

Tessa collapsed in her chair and leaned her head back. She had never been so scared in her life. This had been an all-consuming terror, thinking Sam was shot or even worse, dead. She stood and walked out to the lobby. Jodi looked up at her with tears on her cheeks.

"Are you all right, Jodi?"

"I didn't realize how scared I was until I saw Sheriff Garrett walk in here. Joe Baker got what he deserved. I hated him. I don't know anyone in this town who liked him."

"I know. He's gone now and none of us have to worry about him anymore." Tessa sighed. "How many more patients do we have?"

Jodi checked the book. "None. We're done for the day."

"Great. Let's get out of here. I have a dinner to make."

Jodi grinned up at her. "I'd love to get out of here early. I'm going to the movies tonight."

"A date?"

"With the girls." Jodi stood and grabbed her purse. "I'll see you Monday, Doc Mac."

Tessa walked out with her and locked up. She quickly strolled around the building to her car. She needed to head to the grocery store to get what she needed for dinner but she couldn't keep the smile off her face knowing that Sam was all right.

* * * *

When Sam entered the department, Betty Lou came around the counter and hugged him. He kissed the top of her head.

"I was scared to death, Sam. That Joe Baker was a crazy bastard."

Sam burst out laughing. "Watch your mouth, Betty Lou."

She looked up at him and laughed. "Yes, sir." She sobered. "I'm so glad you're all right."

"I'm fine."

"When you called in saying shots fired, I think I lost ten years off my life. Did you tell Tessa about it?"

"She knew. It seems Jodi was in the diner when it came across the scanner."

"Oh, my...I bet she was a wreck."

"She's fine now. I need to write up a report then I'm going to head home. She's going to make me dinner tonight." Sam smiled.

Betty Lou chuckled. "Wonderful. You have a good evening. I'll be leaving in about thirty minutes."

Sam hugged her again then headed

toward his office. He pulled out a report sheet, sat down, and stared at it. Taking a deep breath, he began filling out the form. When he finished, he stood and stretched then left his office.

"I'm leaving Betty Lou. I'll see you Monday."

"All right, Sam. You and Tess have a good weekend." She winked at him.

Shaking his head, he chuckled as he headed out the door then climbed into his SUV patrol cruiser and drove home to take a shower. He couldn't wait to see Tessa again.

At six-thirty, Sam took a deep breath and knocked on Tessa's door. She pulled it open almost immediately and smiled at him.

"Hello, Sheriff," she said as she ran her hand over his black T-shirt. "Why do you have your coat open as cold as it is? Come in."

"I never button my coat." He stepped inside her apartment and took his coat off. Tessa took it from him and hung it on a hall tree beside the door. Sam removed his Stetson and hung it up.

"Come sit down," Tessa said, smiling at him.

Sam wrapped his hand around her wrist. "How about you kiss me first?" He pulled her closer toward him.

Tessa wrapped her arms around his neck. "Anything you say, Sheriff."

"How is that you can make sheriff sound sexy?"

Tessa laughed low in her throat. "Because it's how I want it to sound, I suppose. I love calling you...*sheriff*," she whispered against his lips.

Sam growled. "If I wasn't so hungry, I'd suggest we skip dinner."

"Oh no. I worked my ass off making this dinner."

Sam's hands ran down over her ass and squeezed. "Doesn't feel like it."

Tessa chuckled. "Smartass. Sit down, Sam and I'll get your dinner."

"All right." Sam walked to the sofa and took a seat. He stretched his legs out in front of him. Tessa carried in two plates of steaming chicken and dumplings. She set them on the coffee table and handed Sam a fork.

"I hope you like it. I haven't made it in forever."

Sam took a bite, raised his eyebrows, and chewed. "Fantastic, sweetheart. You can cook for me any time." He smiled and winked at her making her grin proudly.

* * * *

Tessa couldn't keep her eyes off him.

She was still reeling from earlier when he'd been at the Baker ranch. *Dear God!* If he would have been shot or even worse, killed, she wasn't sure she'd survive it. The thought of losing him scared her so much.

Well, you're going to lose him as soon as he finds out your secret! She mentally groaned. *I know. I'll tell him. When? Soon. It has to be soon.*

Sam raised his head to look at her and smiled. She gave him a smile. *No doubt about it, he's going to hate you.*

The evening passed by quickly and later, as they sat on the sofa together watching a movie, Tessa noticed Sam was asleep. Her gaze ran over his face taking in how his thick eyelashes cast little shadows on his cheeks. She'd kill for lashes like those. Sighing, she knew absolutely that she was in way too deep. This was why she never wanted to get involved with him. She knew she'd fall in love with him but then when he discovered the truth about her, he was going to hate her. A tear slid down her cheek as she pushed his hair back from his forehead and his eyes fluttered open.

"I'm sorry. I didn't mean to wake you," she whispered wiping the tear away.

"I didn't mean to fall asleep. This election has been keeping me up nights. I'm more tired than I realized. I'm sorry, Tessa."

"It's okay, Sam. Let's just go to bed." Tessa stood and put her hand out toward him. He took it and stood. She led him to the bedroom where he sat on the edge of the bed and pulled his T-shirt off over his head. Tessa mentally groaned. She loved his hard body.

"I'm going to take a nice long bath, Sam. You just go to sleep."

"Tessa, I'm sorry..."

"Don't be, Sam. We have all weekend. Get some sleep." She smiled as she watched him get in the bed and pull the quilt up to his waist then she entered the bathroom to soak in the tub. As she leaned her head back, tears rolled down her cheeks. She was going to lose him and she was the only one to blame.

* * * *

Sam rolled over, wrapped his arm around Tessa's waist, and pulled her back against him. She moaned in her sleep and his dick woke right up. He nuzzled her hair with his nose and inhaled its sweet vanilla scent.

"I'm trying to sleep here, Sheriff," she murmured in a sleepy voice.

"And I'm trying to wake you up, sweetheart." He chuckled.

Tessa laughed and rolled toward him. "Well, you've succeeded...so now what?"

Sam leaned forward and pressed his lips to hers. When she opened to him, he slid his tongue into her mouth. She moaned and wrapped her arms around his neck as he deepened the kiss. Trailing one hand down over his chest, she smiled when he hissed in a breath as she wrapped her fingers around his hard cock. His fingers encircled her wrist.

"It'll be over before it begins if you keep that up."

"Isn't that what I'm supposed to do? Keep it up?"

"When the hell did you become so evil?"

Tessa laughed. "Since the sexy sheriff of Clifton kissed me."

"Really? I don't think so."

"Okay. Since I first saw the sexy sheriff. How's that?"

Sam grinned against her lips. "That'll work." He rolled on top of her. "God, I need you, Tessa."

"I need you too, Sam."

Sam moved his hand between them and touched her very core. His finger rubbed against her clitoris making her moan. He continued to stroke her until she threw her head back on the pillow and groaned out his name. Leaning over, he reached for his jeans, and retrieved a condom from his wallet.

After sheathing himself, he slowly inched into her.

Sam stared down into her face, leaned in, and gently kissed her. "Damn, you feel so good," he whispered.

"So do you," she said against his lips.

"Do you have any idea how good it feels to be inside you?"

"Sam," she groaned, closing her eyes as he nibbled at her throat.

"There's no one sexier than you, Tessa. No one."

"Sam..."

"You're repeating yourself."

Tessa's laugh rushed out in a breath. "You're so bad."

Sam pressed his lips to hers as he began moving in and out of her with long, slow strokes. Moving to his knees, he placed his elbows on each side of her head. When she hooked her ankles around the back of his thighs, he had to clench his jaw not to thrust hard into her. Instead, he rolled to his back, and pulled her on top of him.

"Ride me, Tessa," Sam said with an eager grin.

Tessa sat up and smiled down at him then slowly moved her hips up and down over him while she ran her hands over his chest.

"You're driving me crazy, Tessa."

Tessa laughed deep in her throat, and gave him an innocent expression. "Me?"

"Christ, you're evil," Sam groaned.

"You told me to ride you, Sheriff. It's what I'm doing."

Sam sat up, wrapped his arms around her, and then flipped her to her back making her cry out in surprise.

"I can't take it anymore. Tessa...baby, I need to do this fast and hard," he growled next to her ear.

"Yes, Sam. Please..." She gasped when he picked up the pace.

It wasn't too much longer before he felt her inner muscles clenching around his cock, and then he pressed his lips to hers hearing her groan out his name as she came. Sam thrust harder and a deep groan tore from his throat as he came hard, his life feeling as if it couldn't get any better. As he came down, he leaned his forehead against hers while trying to catch his breath.

"Are you all right? I didn't hurt you, did I?"

"No, Sam. That was so good." Tessa kissed his chin.

Rolling to his back, he pulled her against him. She rested her head on his chest and draped her arm across his waist. A few minutes went by with just the sound of them trying to catch their breaths filling the room. Sam rolled toward her and she rolled to face him. She smiled at him and his heart skipped a beat. Sam ran his hand over her hair and he pulled strands of her soft hair over her breasts.

"Your hair is so beautiful. I prefer seeing it loose instead of up in a ponytail now that I know what it looks like down." He grinned. "Either spread over my pillow or flowing down your back as you ride me."

"Sam..." Tessa's breath rushed out.

He leaned forward and kissed her, his lips pressing against hers before deepening the kiss, and moving his tongue into her mouth. Groaning low in his throat, Sam moved over her, resting between her thighs again and lifted his mouth from hers, and gazing into her eyes. "You are so beautiful."

Tessa cupped his lightly whiskered cheeks in her hands. "So are you."

Sam drew back with a chuckle. "No—"

Tessa kissed his mouth then laughed. "Yes."

"I'm not going to argue with you."

"Good, because you'd lose."

"Don't bet on it." Sam kissed her quickly. "How about a shower?"

Tessa burst out laughing. "You just want

to take a shower to change the subject."

To prove he was serious about the shower, he climbed from the bed, grabbed her, and sent her into peals of laughter when he picked her up and tossed her over his shoulder before heading to the bathroom.

* * * *

Election Day brought in severe weather. Sam sat in his office and stared out at the snow coming down. The wind was howling and blowing snow sideways. The snow was so heavy he couldn't see the Glaciers. Would today mark the beginning of his last day as Sheriff of Clifton? He hoped not but if it were, he'd deal with it. He loved Tessa and nothing else really mattered.

Sam smiled as he gazed in the direction of the animal hospital. He knew she was over there working and he loved thinking of her caring for the animals. That was something they shared—a love for animals. He loved her for that among so many other reasons. He sighed thinking how he still hadn't told her he was in love with her yet. Once this election was over, he would. Right now, his anxiety over it weighed on him too much.

"Sam?"

He turned to see Betty Lou standing in the doorway. "Yes?"

"You're ahead in the polls," she said

grinning at him with pride.

Sam let out a breath he hadn't realized he'd been holding. "Are you sure?"

Betty Lou put her hands on her hips and glared at him. "Of course, I'm sure, Sam. I just heard it on the radio."

Sam ran his hand over his mouth to hide a grin. "Thanks for letting me know, but it's early yet."

Betty Lou huffed. "I told you. You're going to win."

"What are you...psychic?"

"Don't take that tone with me, Sam Garrett." Indignant, she spun on her heel, and walked away.

"Psycho maybe," Sam muttered.

"I heard that, Sam Garrett."

Sam chuckled. "Of course you did, Betty Lou." He laughed when he heard her laughter. He grabbed his hat. "I'm going to check the roads. I'll be back in a while."

"All right. Be careful. I'll call you if I need you," Betty Lou hollered.

Sam put his hat and coat on, and headed out the back door. *Son of a bitch!* The wind was crazy and now the snow had ice mixed with it. The ice slapped him in the face making it feel as if shards of glass were hitting him. Sam quickly climbed into his SUV, drove slowly out of the parking lot, and headed out of town. The snow was covering the roads quickly and ice was pinging off the hood and roof. Damn. It was going to get a lot worse before it got better.

Coming up behind a pickup truck crawling along the road, Sam stayed back in case the truck stopped quickly. He sure didn't need to run into the back of anyone. When he saw someone toss a green garbage bag out the passenger side window, he frowned. Didn't the fool realize there was a sheriff behind him? Obviously not, since he was littering.

Sam glanced over to the side of the road where the bag lay and he had a strange urge to stop. Quickly memorizing the license plate on the truck, he then pulled off the road. After writing the number down, he pushed his door open and stepped out of the vehicle. He had to be insane to get out in this weather to check what was in all likelihood, just garbage. Holding his hat on his head, he made his way to it. Sam dropped to his knees, tore the bag open, and swore when he saw a tiny kitten inside the bag. Picking up the poor little thing, he put it inside his coat, got back into his SUV, and drove back to town. Pulling up by the front door of the animal hospital, he strode in stopping at the desk.

"Hi, Sheriff." Jodi smiled up at him.

"Hi, Jodi. I need to see Tessa," Sam told her pulling the furry little creature out of the protection of his coat.

"I think she's with a patient." Jodi gasped. "What do you have there?"

"A kitten someone tossed out of a truck. Get her for me, please Jodi."

Jodi nodded and ran from the lobby. A few minutes later, Tessa came running out. "Sam? Jodi said you have a kitten that was tossed from a truck."

Cradling the mewling kitten, he showed it to her. "I'm going after the asshole who tossed the kitten out. Here, you take him and make sure he's okay." Sam handed her the kitten.

"Her."

Sam frowned. "What?"

"She's a calico and a very high percentage of calicos are female. She can't be more than four weeks old. Go get him. I'll take care of her."

"I was behind him, but I guess with the snow blowing the way it was he didn't see me or he didn't care."

Tessa stood on her toes and kissed him. "Be careful out there...please." She turned from him then turned back. "By the way, you're ahead in the election."

She smiled at him and then walked away.

When Sam walked out of Tessa's hospital, he had to hold his hand over his hat since the wind was so strong and he really didn't feel like chasing after it if it blew off his head. The wind nearly ripped the door of his vehicle from his hand when he opened it. Old man winter was showing his ugly side early this year.

Sam climbed inside, shutting out the weather, and talked into his two-way radio.

"I need you to run a tag," he told Betty Lou, and then read it off to her. A moment later, she gave him the information he needed. "Thank you. I'll be back in a while."

Armed with an address for the man who tossed the kitten out, Sam swore aloud as he drove out of town. Some people didn't have any brains was his thought as he drove onto the property of Henry Clark. Sam pulled up close to the front porch, climbed out of his SUV and walked across the porch to knock on the door. A little girl about six years old opened the door and stared up at him. He squatted down and smiled.

"Hi there, is your daddy here?" She nodded and ran away from the door. Sam peered into the house. "Hello? Sheriff's department."

"Hello, can I help you?" a woman asked stepping into view from a room in the back of the house.

Sam removed his hat. "Yes, ma'am. Is Henry Clark here?"

The woman's eyes widened. "Is he in some sort of trouble?"

"I'm Sheriff Garrett. I'd like to speak to him, please."

She nodded. "Henry! There's someone here to see you. Come on in, Sheriff."

Sam nodded and stepped into the foyer, closing the door behind him. "Thank you. I appreciate that."

A large man entered from the direction of the living room and frowned at Sam when he saw his badge pinned to his coat.

"I'm Henry Clark. What can I do for you? Sheriff Garrett, right?"

"Yes, sir." Sam glanced at the woman and little girl. "Could we speak privately?"

"Come on, Tabitha. Let's go into the kitchen so Daddy and the sheriff can talk," the woman said taking the little girl's hand and leading her away.

"Mr. Clark, I was behind you earlier on Moonshine Road. About an hour ago," Sam stated tipping his hat back on his head.

Henry Clark frowned at him. "I wasn't on Moonshine Road then, Sheriff. I haven't been out of the house since early this morning."

Sam scowled. "Who else could have been driving your truck?"

"My son Owen was out today." Henry sighed. "What did he do now?"

"I saw him throw a garbage bag out—"

"Hold on. Let me get him." Henry yelled for his son and a few minutes later, a tall, lanky teenager descended the stairs. He came to a stop when he saw Sam. Henry narrowed his eyes at his son. "The sheriff here says he saw you toss a garbage bag out the truck window today on Moonshine Road."

Sam stared at the boy and saw the fear in his eyes. "You want to tell me why you tossed that bag out, son?"

Owen shrugged coming to stand at the base of the steps. "I didn't throw a bag out."

"I was behind you. I saw you toss the bag out the passenger side window."

"There were only a few things in it." Owen shrugged again.

Sam stepped closer toward him. "There was a kitten in the bag," he said through clenched teeth feeling the muscle in his cheek twitch. Sam knew he needed to rein in his temper. "I can arrest you for animal cruelty."

Owen's eyes widened so much that Sam was surprised they didn't pop out of his head. "I didn't know about the kitten. Warren asked me to throw the bag out when we were together today."

"You didn't question your friend as to why or what was in the bag?"

"No, man. I've done it for him before. I'd just stop by the garbage bin and dump his trash but it was cold out, I didn't want to stop and get out. I just thought it had some trash in it," Owen muttered.

"Well, there was more than trash in it. You didn't notice the bag moving or hear the kitten?" Sam was sure he was being lied to but unfortunately, couldn't prove it.

"I had the radio up and was concentrating on the road because it's so bad out."

"I'm not sure I believe you but I need to know Warren's last name, and I'm also fining you for littering."

"Come on, man—"

"Don't call me *man*. I'm the Sheriff of this county. I'll be right back. I need to get my citation book. The fine for littering in Montana is two hundred dollars." Sam walked out the door and grinned with satisfaction when he heard Henry yelling at his son.

Sam retrieved the book and entered the house again. He wrote the ticket and tore it off, handing it to the teen. "If you go to court, you may just get community service or a reduced fine—if it's your first offense."

"You will go to court, and you'll be working off payment of the fine. I'm sorry, Sheriff Garrett." Henry stuck his hand out.

"Now, what is Warren's last name and where does he live?" Sam said as he shook Henry's hand.

Owen sighed. "Warren Wright. If you turn left out of here, his driveway is three up on the right."

Sam touched the brim of his hat. "Thank you. You both have a good day." He started out the door when Henry spoke.

"I voted for you, Sheriff Garrett. Good luck in the election."

Sam smiled. "Thank you, I appreciate your vote."

Hurrying back to his vehicle, he had a feeling young Owen feared his dad's punishment far more than any handed down by a judge. After stopping to speak with Warren Wright, Sam drove back to town. The kid had been terrified when Sam wrote him a ticket for five hundred dollars for cruelty to animals. Sam told him the same thing he'd told Owen Clark about going to court. Warren's mother was so angry with him, she cried. The only thing Warren wouldn't say was where he got the kitten to begin with. He'd told Sam it was in the bag when he found it but Sam didn't believe that for a minute. Since he couldn't prove any different, he let it drop.

Arriving back in town, he went by the animal hospital before returning to the department. Upon entering the lobby, Jodi glanced up and smiled at him when she saw him.

"I'll get Doc Mac for you, Sheriff," she told him picking up the phone.

Sam took a seat in the waiting area. There was no one else around. He stood when Tessa entered the room and smiled at him.

"What did you find out about who threw Honeybee out?"

"Honeybee?"

Tessa shrugged. "That's what I named the kitten."

Sam frowned. "Some kid threw her out. I couldn't get it out of him where he got her, but he had his friend take the garbage bag. Thing is, his friend didn't know there was a kitten in the bag when he threw it out of the truck, or so he says. Both will have to pay some hefty fines, and most likely appear before a judge."

"Good. Thank you, Sam." Tessa smiled up at him.

Sam leaned down and kissed her. "Can we get together tonight?"

"Why don't you come by after you finish work? We're going to close early. No one else is coming in. Most of the appointments have canceled due to the weather."

"All right but I don't know what time I'll get out of the office though. I'll come by as soon as I can." He kissed her again.

"Can you stay with me tonight?" Tessa whispered.

Sam shook his head. "I have to get home for Bo, but you can stay with me. We can wait for the election returns together." Tessa nibbled on her bottom lip and Sam groaned. "It's okay if you don't want to chance driving out there tonight, I understand," Sam said.

"I can follow you after we have dinner. Will that be all right?"

"Of course."

"I'll see you later then, Sam." She kissed his chin.

Sam leaned down and kissed her. "I'll see you later, sweetheart."

Tessa grinned up at him. "Yes, you will."

Sam smiled and left the hospital then

drove back to the office, entering through the back door. "I'm back, Betty Lou," he called out shaking off the snow before entering his office.

When she didn't answer, he strolled to the lobby and found her chair empty. Sam frowned as he glanced around. He was about to call her cell phone when she came rushing through the front door with the wind howling on her heels.

"What in the hell are you doing out in this?"

"I had to go vote! I'm not an invalid, Sam. Bobbi Jo picked me up out front and just dropped me off."

"Jesus H. Christ, Betty Lou. You could have left me a note," Sam muttered.

"Don't you—"

"Do not say it, Betty Lou. You could have voted on the way home. The polls don't close until late tonight."

Betty Lou marched up to him. "If you had talked to me like this before, I would have voted for Rick!"

"Well, maybe you can work for him then," Sam yelled back, not really knowing why he was feeling so upset, she was a grown woman.

Betty Lou gasped. "Why are you being like this?"

"Because I thought something might have happened to you," Sam shouted.

Her eyes widened as she stared up at him, and then a big grin split her face. "I love you too, Sam Garrett."

Sam reached her in two steps and hugged her. "Don't ever do that again, okay?"

He kissed the top of her head and then strode back to his office. He really did love that woman.

Chapter Eleven

Several days later, Sam sat in his office staring out at the snow swirling around. He'd won the election so life moved along as usual once more. Watching the snow, he thought about Thanksgiving being only two weeks away. The holidays were coming and he looked forward to spending them with Tessa.

The temperatures were supposed to dip into the single digits tonight and he hated the thought of the accidents that would possibly happen because foolish people get out on the road thinking they can handle icy conditions. Sighing, he picked up his pen and continued to fill out reports. He glanced up when Betty Lou stepped into his office wearing a worried expression.

"Something wrong?" Sam asked.

"Rick's here to see you," Betty Lou whispered.

Sam dropped his pen on the desk, leaned back, and frowned. "Did he say why?"

Betty Lou shook her head. "Do you want me to send him back?"

Sam blew out a breath and nodded. Rick

had lost the election to him, and they hadn't spoken since Rick called to congratulate him. Although Sam had threatened to fire him if Sam won, Rick quit before Sam could do it. Sam wasn't sure he actually would have fired Rick but he didn't get the chance to make that decision. Rick was a damn good deputy and now, because of the man's stubbornness, the department was shorthanded due to his leaving. Sam stood when Rick entered the room.

"Have a seat, Rick." He jerked his chin at the chair.

Rick seemed nervous for some reason but he nodded, and took a seat. He glanced around the office and took a deep breath. "Sam, I..." He cleared his throat. "I need a job."

"Do you seriously think I would've fired you, Rick?" Sam raised his hand when Rick started to speak. "I know what I said, but you were one of my best deputies. I admit that I was angry that you would run against me. It makes me question your loyalty, and then you upped and quit..." Sam took a deep breath. "How do I know in another four years you won't try it again?"

Rick shook his head. "I've learned my lesson. This town loves you, Sam. There's no one who could run against you and win."

Sam sat back in his chair and stared at Rick until he shifted in his seat. "I'll tell you right now if I do decide to hire you back, and you run against me again, and I win—I will fire you."

"I understand, Sam, but you don't have to worry. I won't run again—not against you anyway."

"I'll get back to you in a few days," Sam told him and stood. When Rick stuck his hand out, Sam hesitated but then took his hand, and shook it.

* * * *

Tessa walked out of the operating room and almost ran into Jodi. "Whoa, Jodi. What's your hurry?"

"I was looking for you. A dog's just been brought in—hit by a car."

Tessa ran behind Jodi to the waiting room where she came to a stop when she saw a man standing over, what looked to be a Siberian Husky, lying on the floor. He glanced up at Tessa and shook his head.

"He came out of nowhere."

"It's all right. So I gather the dog isn't yours?"

"No ma'am. I was driving on Copper Ridge and as I said, he was just there. I couldn't stop in time."

Tessa nodded and squatted down beside

the dog and put her stethoscope to his chest and listened. "I can hear a heartbeat, that's good." She ran her hands over the dog. "I don't feel any broken bones but I'll need to x-ray him, uh...her." Tessa smiled up at the man.

"I have to get to work. What happens now?"

Tessa felt through the dog's thick fur. "She has a collar. It says her name is Whiskey." Tessa shook her head. Where did people come up with the names for their pets?

The man nodded. "All right. Thanks." He turned to leave.

"Wait," Tessa said and he turned back toward her. "I need to get some information from you. My receptionist will get it from you."

"I just gave you all the information you need. I hit her by accident on Copper Ridge. Look, I really have to get to work. I'm already late because of this dog."

Tessa stood slowly. "Because of this dog? This dog was probably scared to death and trying to find her way home when you came along and hit her. Just how fast were you going? Copper Ridge is a dangerous road and frankly, you should have seen her and been able to stop soon enough if you'd been going slower. It's icy out there today."

The man shuffled his feet. "I wasn't speeding. She ran out in front of me."

"Uh-huh. Well, I happen to know the sheriff pretty well, so would you rather talk to him or my receptionist?"

The man huffed and followed Jodi to the desk. Tessa blew out a breath. What a crock. She couldn't call Sam to report a man most likely going too fast and hitting a dog, but the man didn't know that. Tessa walked to the desk and called her two vet techs so they could take Whiskey to the x-ray room. While she waited for them to come get Whiskey, she called the phone number on the collar only to hear it was no longer a valid number. As she hung the phone up, one of her patient's owner entered and smiled at her.

"Hi, Doc Mac," Shirley Hampton said in greeting.

"Hi, Shirley, I suppose you're here to pick up Piglet?"

"I am." Shirley glanced to the dog lying on the floor of the waiting area and frowned. "Is that Whiskey?"

"You know Whiskey? Who's her owner?" Tessa was relieved someone knew to whom Whiskey belonged.

"Ann Yates, but she moved to Idaho

about three weeks ago. She hit hard times and moved back to her mother's place."

Tessa could feel anger washing over her. "Do you know if she left the dog with someone?"

"I seriously doubt it. I talked to her right before she left and she said she was going to have to turn Whiskey in to the local shelter since she couldn't afford to keep her and her mother wouldn't let her have her there."

"Well, obviously Whiskey wasn't turned in at the shelter. I thought she felt a little thin." Tessa watched as her two techs picked the dog up, laid her on a stretcher, and then wheeled her toward the x-ray room. "Thank you, Shirley. I'll have one of the boys get Piglet for you. I need to help Whiskey."

She practically ran down the hall and when she entered the x-ray room, Tessa asked one of the techs to get Piglet, the cat.

* * * *

That evening, Sam and Tessa lay in her bed. She had her head on his shoulder and he had his arms wrapped around her tight.

"So, Rick wants his job back?" Tessa asked Sam.

"Yes. I suppose I'll let him have it. He is a good deputy but I'm talking with the other men about it first since he left them high and dry."

"Sam, you threatened to fire him," Tessa teased with a chuckle.

"Yeah, I know I was pissed. What can I say? Tell me about your day."

Tessa told him about Whiskey and no one owning her. "She's a beautiful Husky. She has blue eyes like you."

"I'm sure someone will take her."

"Thing is I only have three days to find her a home before I have to take her to the shelter."

"Why?"

"I don't have the room, Sam. There are times we're completely full and even when we're not, I have to keep space open just in case."

"I understand. I hope you don't have to do that though. She doesn't have much of a chance at the shelter. Bo was about to be euthanized when I adopted him. They just don't have the room there."

"I know. I wish I had room for her, but I don't." Tessa sneaked a glance up at Sam and traced a finger along his jaw. "You do though, Sam."

"I already have a dog, Tessa."

"You have so much land and Bo would love her."

"No," Sam said adamantly.

"But Sam—"

"Tessa, I can't take another dog."

Tessa sighed. "All right. I'll figure something out."

Sam pulled her closer and kissed her forehead. Tessa chewed on her bottom lip thinking about Whiskey needing a home and she was going to do all she could to find her one.

"Do you have plans for Thanksgiving?" Sam asked her.

"No. Do you?"

"Katie and Riley invited me to their place. Our parents went on a cruise together. What about your parents?"

Tessa hesitated before answering him. "Uh...my parents go skiing."

"Do you want to go to Katie's with me?"

"Do you think they'd mind?"

"No...not at all."

"I'd love to then."

He rolled so that he was facing her. She smiled at him.

"I want you, Tessa," he said, dipping his head and putting his lips to hers.

"Sam..." she moaned.

"I know when you want me, Tessa," Sam whispered. "I can see it in your eyes. I can feel it in your touch." His hand moved over her chest and down her stomach to between her legs. "I can feel it here, when you're wet for me." His lips pressed against hers and he moved his mouth over hers, parting her lips with his tongue. It dipped inside her mouth. "I love how you taste. Here." He kissed her. "And here." His finger rubbed against her clitoris. When she leaned into him, he reached for a condom.

Tessa groaned low in her throat. "Sam..." His name rushed from her in a breath as he settled between her thighs.

"I can never get enough of you," he whispered against her lips. She took the condom from him and rolled it slowly down over him making him growl. "I think you enjoy doing that way too much."

Tessa chuckled. "I really do." Then she gasped when he slid inside her inch by inch.

"I can't tell you how much I want you every day, Tessa. I think about you constantly. Not a day goes by that my cock doesn't go rock hard when I think of you."

"Sam..."

"I want you any way I can have you—against the wall, on the floor, on the stairs, in the bed...on you, under you, or...behind you. But in all the ways and times I want you, all you'd ever have to say is no, and I'd stop. I'll never hurt you, Tessa. I'd never do anything to make you doubt that."

"I don't doubt it at all, Sam. I know

you'd never hurt me," Tessa whispered in a jagged voice.

"I would hope so, Tessa," Sam said as he pulled out of her and then slammed back into her making her gasp. Her legs wrapped around him as he rode her hard and fast. Both of them groaning as their orgasms hit them.

How was she ever going to tell him the truth? He wanted her to trust him and he trusted her, but she didn't deserve it. He'd never hurt her, but she was going to hurt him. Deeply. If only things were different. If only she could find the right way to tell him the truth.

* * * *

Thanksgiving Day arrived, and the weather was clear and bright. When Sam arrived to pick up Tessa, she told him she needed to stop in at her office to check on something. Sam followed her down the hallway toward her office. When she glanced over her shoulder and smiled, he felt his dick twitch. The tight black skirt she was wearing hugged her ass and the sexy red stilettos had him adjusting his cock as he entered the office behind her. *Damn her.*

"Have a seat, Sam. I'll only be a minute," she said as she set her purse on the desk then put her reading glasses on.

Sam blew out a breath and took a seat in one of the wingback chairs in front of the desk. He watched her walk around her desk and sit down. She shuffled papers around to find the folder she wanted and then proceeded to make notes on a sheet of paper she'd removed. He couldn't take his eyes off her. She was exquisite, even wearing her glasses. The red blouse was unbuttoned just enough to where he was able to see the tops of her breasts. *Shit!* His dick hardened. When he raised his eyes to her face, he found her looking at him. A small smile lifted her lips.

"You're evil as fuck and slowly killing me...and you know it, Tessa," Sam muttered. Her husky laugh had him wanting to jump the desk, lay her across it, and have his way with her. She stood and walked around the desk and sat on the edge of it across from him. He swallowed hard.

"I don't want to kill you, Sam. That would be such a waste," she said in a low voice.

He couldn't take his eyes off those long legs. When she raised one and placed a red stiletto clad foot on the arm of his chair, he about came right there. He could see under her skirt to the small strip of lace barely covering her. His eyes met hers. Tessa leaned toward him and ran her hand over his shoulder and he almost died when she raised the other leg and placed her foot on the other side of him. His dick wanted to explode. Those red stilettos were killing him. Without taking his eyes from hers, he wrapped his hands around each ankle and grinned when he felt her shiver. He slowly moved his hands up her calves, to behind her knees, and up her thighs then he stood and moved between her legs. Leaning toward her, he placed his lips on her neck. When his fingers ran along the elastic in her panties, she moaned.

"Are these new, Tessa?" he asked as his finger pulled on the elastic.

"No," she said breathlessly.

"Good," he whispered right before he ripped them from her, making her gasp. He grasped her legs behind the knees pulling her closer to him, and moved his finger to her wet slit. "You're wet. Do you want me?"

"Sam..."

"Tell me, Tessa."

"Yes," she hissed. "I want you. I want you so much." A sudden frown darkened her expression and her hand reached down and removed his from her.

He frowned at her but then she gave him a small smile as she moved her finger to where his had been. Sam groaned. He wanted to be inside her so much, he was sure he was going to die if he wasn't soon. When she raised her finger to his lips, he took it into his mouth and sucked her essence from her finger.

"Sam, kiss me," she whispered and for some reason, Sam thought he heard a profound sadness there so he decided it was up to him to make it go away.

Moving his lips across her cheek, he took her lips in a deep kiss then moved his tongue into her mouth and tangled it with hers. Her moans set him on fire.

* * * *

Tessa was never going to survive Sam Garrett. The man was too sexy. No man had ever pleased her so much or made her want to surrender to him. She was completely and totally in love with Sam and she had no right to be. As much as she would love to make love to him right now, right here in her office, she felt it was wrong. She was about to spend Thanksgiving Day with his family and didn't deserve that.

She smiled against his lips—his sexy, hot, delicious lips. "You are an amazing man, Sam."

"You're driving me wild with that skirt and those heels."

"My fuck-me shoes?"

Sam chuckled. "If that's what they scream, then wear them more often."

"I will if you like but right now might not be the time to enjoy them," she said, hating herself when she saw him frown in disappointment.

"You're right. We need to get going to Katie's for dinner."

"I'll need to go up to my apartment and get panties on since you ripped mine off."

"Or you could just go without." Sam grinned.

"Not happening, Sam."

Tessa put her hand out to him. When he took it, she started for the door but he pulled her back to him and pressed his lips against hers. She wrapped her arms around his neck as he deepened the kiss. Would she ever get enough of this man? Mentally sighing, she knew she'd have to. No matter how much it would hurt her, she would eventually have to stop seeing him.

Just as they arrived at Riley and Katie's it started to snow. Sam helped her down from the truck and held her hand as they walked up the steps. She suddenly questioned her choice of heels but when she saw Sam's gaze sweep over her, she knew they were the best decision of the day. The door opened and

Riley stood in the doorway.

"Good to see you, Tess," he said as he hugged her.

"You too, Riley."

They stepped inside and Katie hugged her brother and then Tessa.

"I'm so glad you could join us, Tess."

"Thank you for allowing me, Katie. Where's Sadie?"

"Taking a nap but she'll be up soon and she'll be thrilled to see her Unc Sam."

An hour later, they were sitting together at the table, talking about Riley and Sam's friendship when Sam suddenly glared at Riley.

"I was always telling the guys to stay away from my sister. But this one...he didn't listen."

"I rarely talked to her when we were younger." Riley laughed reaching out and squeezing Katie's hand.

"Why was that? Katie is beautiful," Tessa asked with curiosity.

"I was so gangly when I was younger. I never got asked to the prom because I was taller than the boys in my class," Katie mumbled.

Riley leaned over and kissed her cheek. "Aww, darlin', if you hadn't had that frizzy hair, I would have asked you. You were always beautiful."

"No, you wouldn't have, Riley," Sam growled. "It was bad enough when you were seeing her behind my back."

Riley laughed. "Yeah, my chin still hurts."

Katie gasped. "You hit Riley?" She glared at her brother across the table.

"Only once. He deserved it. He hurt you, made you cry. Or don't you remember?" Sam shrugged.

"I made up for it. I married her." Riley laid his arm across the back of his wife's chair and kissed her cheek.

"Dada," Sadie screamed.

Riley stood, took Sadie from her highchair, and held her. He kissed her cheek too. "I love you too, squirt," he said, making Sadie giggle.

After dinner, everyone retired to the living room, to relax and let full bellies settle. When things grew quiet, Sam stood.

"I need some fresh air to wake me up." He looked at Tessa. "Join me?"

Tessa smiled. "I'd love to, that delicious turkey is about to put us all to sleep. I'll be right back, Katie, and will help you clean up," she said as Sam helped her into her coat.

"Don't worry about it. Riley will help me."

"Yep," Riley said while stifling a yawn.

Once outside, Sam took her hand in his and they carefully walked down the steps coated with a thin layer of snow. Tessa stared up at the moon in the now clear sky.

"It is so beautiful here."

"Yes. Even though this was a bad place for Riley when he was a kid, he built a beautiful home here."

"Katie told me about his childhood. I'm glad he found out Roscoe wasn't his real father. But to think of that man beating him when he was younger is just heartbreaking."

"He'd stay with us more than he stayed at home. He hated Roscoe, but he loves Jordon now. They have a good relationship."

"I'm so glad." Tessa wrapped her arms around his waist. "I love Clifton. I'd be truly sad if I ever had to leave it now." She loved the town almost as much as she loved him but knew it would be hard to stay here if he hated her.

"Well, you've no reason to leave. You've got a good business, friends, and me, right? So that means you'll be sticking around."

Tessa stared up at him. "Oh, I will if the sexy sheriff says so."

Groaning, Sam shook his head. "Don't call me that."

Tessa burst out laughing. "Sexy sheriff?

It's what all the women around here call you."

"I sure as hell hope not," Sam muttered.

"I am not kidding, Sam. It's what they all call you, and I totally agree."

Sam shook his head and led her back up the steps. They entered the house and stayed a while longer visiting with his family before going home. If she couldn't be with her own family during the holidays, it was wonderful to be with Sam's instead. After returning home, the turkey finally caught up with them, and they fell asleep holding each other.

Chapter Twelve

Sam parked his vehicle in the back lot of the animal hospital then ran up the stairs to Tessa's apartment, and knocked on her door. It'd been four days since he'd last seen her and he missed her terribly. He heard her unlocking the door and then it opened wide enough for him to enter. Without a word or even a kiss, he strode past her and stopped in the middle of the room. The door closed behind him and he spun around to look at her. Whatever he'd been planning to say stuck in his throat when he saw her standing there, leaning back against the door, staring at him. He watched as her gaze ran down his body and he knew she saw his hard cock straining against the fly of his jeans.

"Sam?" she said softly.

Swallowing hard, he ran his eyes over her from the top of her mussed hair, down over her white T-shirt, her long legs and back up lingering on the juncture of her thighs. Slowly, his gaze moved up and he could see her nipples harden under her shirt. His eyes met hers as he moved slowly toward her.

"Nothing on under that shirt?" he asked with raised eyebrows.

"Nope." Her eyes never left his. He nodded. "Why—?"

Her question ended in a gasp when he lifted her to place her back against the door and held her there with his big body as he moved a finger between her slit and moved it up and down along her slit, making her wet and causing her to moan. Unzipping his jeans, and after quickly rolling on a condom he then inched into her.

"I've missed you so much," he said against her lips before taking them in a deep kiss and slowly sliding his tongue into her mouth. Her arms wrapped around his neck as her legs enfolded his waist. Sam knew he should slow down but he needed this...needed *her* too much to stop. Pounding into her, he could feel her clench around him as she tore her mouth from his and cried out his name. He growled low in his throat as his orgasm ripped through him, feeling as if he was shattering into a million pieces. As they both gasped for breath, Sam leaned his forehead against hers and smiled.

"Hi," he said breathlessly.

Tessa smiled at him. "Hi, yourself. Maybe we should stay apart more often."

Sam helped her stand, zipped up his

jeans, and then headed to her bathroom to dispose of the condom. Walking back into the room, he halted in front of her.

"I can't take being away from you that long again." He kissed her fast and hard. "These have been the worst four days of my life. I'd reach for you at night, only to find your side of the bed empty." He pressed his lips to hers then moved them across her cheek to her ear and down her neck. She smelled wonderful. "I don't want to be away from you that long *ever* again." Lifting his head, he stared into her eyes. "You've wiggled deep into my heart, darlin'."

Tessa inhaled, her eyes fluttered shut for a moment, and then she gazed up at him while leaning into him. "I have to...it was terrible being apart so long. It seemed like we were both so busy," she said then smiled at him. "Let's take a shower, Sheriff."

Sam groaned. "I wish I could but I can't, sweetheart. I have to get back to the office. Later, though." He kissed her quickly and left the apartment, hurrying down the stairs then climbing into his vehicle and driving to the office.

When he entered the front doors, he saw Betty Lou scowling at him.

"What's up?" Sam asked, hoping it wasn't something serious. He was in too good a mood to have it ruined.

"Rick is in your office. Didn't you tell him you'd think about giving him his job back?" she whispered leaning forward on her elbows.

Sam smiled. "Yes, and I told him to come in so don't get your panties in a wad."

Betty Lou burst out laughing. "My panties haven't been in a wad in a very long time."

Sam winced. "Too much information, Betty Lou...way too much," he said with a chuckle then proceeded on to his office. When he entered, Rick stood.

"Have a seat, Rick," Sam told him as he hung up his coat and dropped his hat on his desk.

"Thanks, Sam." Rick sat back down in the chair located in front of the desk.

"I talked with the men and they're willing to let you slide this time. We're shorthanded and they'd all like to get back to regular hours so I'll let you come back, Rick but I hope it's understood that if you want more responsibility, more duties...I'll be more than happy to give them to you. You don't have to be sheriff to be weighed down with work. Any insubordination and you're gone."

Rick blew out a breath and stood then

stuck his hand out toward Sam. "Understood, Sam and I appreciate it. I really need the job."

Sam shook his hand. "Be here tomorrow morning for your shift."

"I get the day shift back?" Rick asked, reacting surprised.

"Mark and Paul love nightshift so yes, I'll need you on days with Brody. Maybe then I can actually get some work done in here."

Rick grinned. "Thank you, Sam. You won't regret it."

"You're a damn good deputy, Rick. I hated losing you. But as I said, I won't be so nice the next time."

"There won't be a next time. I'll see you tomorrow, Sam." Rick strode from the office.

Sam smiled as he watched him go but he wasn't worried so much about getting an attitude from Rick as much as from Betty Lou. Because the odds were she wouldn't let him live it down that Sam had given Rick another chance.

* * * *

Tessa carried the little calico kitten she'd named Honeybee upstairs to her apartment. She hadn't been able to part with the little kitten so she decided to keep her. After entering the apartment, she showed

Honeybee where the litter box was, and then fed her. The little kitten was eight weeks old now and had grown quite a bit turning into a sweet little ball of energy. Tessa took a seat on the sofa and Honeybee quickly climbed up to settle into her lap. Tessa stroked her soft fur of orange, black, brown, and white. The kitten had just closed her eyes to sleep when someone knocked on the door.

Carefully getting to her feet, she slid Honeybee onto the sofa, and then peered through the peephole. Grinning, she opened it letting Sam in. He gave her a quick kiss and proceeded to enter but stopped in his tracks when he saw Honeybee stretching out on the sofa.

"You have a cat," he muttered as his face twisted in distaste.

Tessa laughed. "You might not be a cat person but I fell in love with her. She was so pitiful and sweet. I had to bring her home. I still haven't found a home for Whiskey though."

"Do you still have her at the hospital?"

"Yes, but she's going to the shelter tomorrow. I've kept her a lot longer than I should have. I just can't find anyone to take her."

Sam sighed, pulled her close, and stared down at her. "I'll take her," he grumbled.

"You will?"

He ran his hand around the back of his neck and shrugged. "I have no idea why but yes, I'll take her."

Tessa squealed and threw her arms around his neck, kissing and hugging him. "You'll love her and so will Bo."

"The things you manage to talk me into." Sam pressed his lips to hers.

Tessa moaned against his mouth. "How long can you stay, Sheriff?"

"Not long enough. I have to get back to the office. I hired Rick back."

"I knew you would. You're a nice man, Sam Garrett."

"*Sheriff* Sam Garrett." He grinned. "I'll see you later. Do me a favor and don't go out unless you absolutely have to, and call me if you don't want to go out alone. The weather is horrible and I'd rather you're not out on the roads."

"Yes, sir," she whispered against his lips.

Sam smiled at her. "One more day and we'll have the weekend."

"Speaking of which...how would you like to go to Kalispell for the weekend?"

"Kalispell?" Sam furrowed his brow as if to show he didn't understand why Kalispell, and Tessa couldn't wait to explain about the cabin.

"My Aunt Lil, well, she's actually my godmother, owns a cabin there and she's invited me to visit. We could leave after work tomorrow and come back Sunday night."

"Your aunt wouldn't mind if you bring me?"

"No. I already asked her about you." Tessa kissed his jaw.

"That does sound good," Sam said against her lips. "Let's do it."

Tessa hugged him. "I'll let her know. You'll love her and the judge."

"The judge?"

"Her husband. That's what we all call him. He was a very well-known judge in Pennsylvania. They've been married forever. Her family is rich from oil in Texas. I love her and the judge."

"Sounds good, angel, we'll leave tomorrow right after work. I'll let the office know."

"Great! I'll call Doc Carter. If there's a problem and he can't cover for me, we can go some other time. We can even take Bo and Whiskey. Aunt Lil loves animals. She owns an animal sanctuary in Texas."

Sam kissed her. "All right. I'll see you later. Please call me if you have to go out."

After Sam left, Tessa locked the door, and leaned back against it. She was in way too deep with Sam and she'd been thinking about going to Kalispell for a while. Getting him away where they were less likely to be interrupted, she thought it would be easier to tell him the truth but now she wasn't sure she had the courage. Maybe being with Lil and the judge, they would help her sort this all out. Their relationship had come to the point where she knew she'd have to tell him the truth, and she hoped beyond hope that she wouldn't lose him forever.

You are not only lying to him but to yourself. You need to stop this, Tessa!

"I can't." She sobbed. "I love him so much."

* * * *

Sam trotted down the steps from Tessa's apartment and mentally shook his head. He couldn't believe he'd just agreed to take in another dog. He needed another dog like he needed a hole in his head but the look on her face when he said he'd take the dog was worth it. He'd do anything he could to see her smile at him.

Back at the office, he was happy to see he only had one more hour before he could head home. He'd pick up the dog tomorrow since today had been a long day. Everyone except Betty Lou was gone but he had some paperwork to finish. He called Brody and told him about the weekend so they could coordinate things. Having Rick back on the job was going to help a lot. At nights, the local 9-1-1 office took any calls while Mark and Paul were usually out on patrol. Sam only heard from them if it were a really bad situation. He knew he could depend on his deputies.

Finished for the day, he stopped by Betty Lou's desk.

"Betty Lou? I'll be out of town for the weekend. Brody knows and he'll let the other men know but please, I don't want any calls."

"Where are you going?"

"Kalispell."

"What's in Kalispell?"

Sam grinned. "Tessa."

Betty Lou laughed. "You're going away together for the weekend?"

"Yes, ma'am."

Betty Lou stood, walked around the counter, and hugged him. He wrapped his arms around her as she gazed up at him.

"That's wonderful, Sam."

He kissed the top of her head. "I think so."

"You have a good time and don't worry about anything here."

"I promise not to let Clifton enter my head. You go now and go home but be careful. Have a great weekend."

"Sam, I'm so happy for you and Tess. She's a wonderful woman. The whole town is happy for you both. It's about time you had a good woman in your life."

"Yeah, you've been on me long enough about it." Sam laughed.

"I know I aggravate you, Sam, but it's only because I love you."

"Betty Lou, if we didn't argue like we do, I don't know what I'd do. You know I love you. You're my favorite godmother."

She hugged him tighter. "I'm your only godmother. Personally, I love aggravating you."

"I know you do," Sam said and chuckled. "Now, go home. I'll see you Monday."

"I can have tomorrow off?"

"Yes. Go. Before I change my mind." Sam laughed when she scurried around the counter, grabbed her purse, kissed him on the cheek, and practically ran out the door.

Finished up for the day, he headed to the diner to get something to eat before heading home. He entered the diner and everyone called out to him as usual, making him grin. He took a seat on a stool at the counter and ordered a coffee and burger to go. Sam glanced around and saw the stranger seated at a back booth again. This time there was a second man with him. Wondering who he was and whether he had family here, Sam was never happy to see strangers in his town unless it was during the summer and the Clifton Bed and Breakfast was open. As long as neither caused any trouble, he had no reason to deny them visiting the town. Mentally shrugging his shoulders, he turned back to the counter when Connie said his name.

"Do you think Betty Lou is ready for her birthday party?" Connie asked him as she set his coffee down in front of him.

"I'm sure. It's all she's been talking about lately. She said it's not every day she turns seventy. I swear the woman is going to outlive me."

Connie laughed. "I can't wait for this party. I love Betty Lou and Bobbi Jo. What characters they are."

"I know. I've known them both forever. Betty Lou is actually my godmother but at times, she's worse than my own mother at butting into my business." Sam laughed.

"She loves you, Sam, and you know you love her too."

"I do. When my mom suggested I hire her, I thought she was crazy but Betty Lou's been a rock in the department."

"I'm sure it will be a wild party."

"And packed. She's invited everyone."

Connie handed Sam his burger in a Styrofoam to-go box. He stood, paid for his meal, and after giving everyone a wave, started for the door but turned back to look at the two strangers. The men were eating their meals and talking but neither glanced his way. Sam had an uneasy feeling about them but until they did something wrong, Sam wouldn't bother with them.

* * * *

The next afternoon, Tessa walked out to the lobby stopping at the desk. "Are we done for the day?"

Jodi smiled up at her. "Yes. I'm so glad too. It's been a long week. Are you seeing Sheriff Garrett this weekend?"

Indeed Tessa was. He'd been in earlier today to pick up Whiskey and she was pleased that he and the dog seemed to hit it off immediately. She looked forward to seeing them again soon and heading up to the cabin.

"I am. We're going away for the weekend so Doctor Carter will be on call. You can go ahead now and leave, Jodi. I'll lock up. You have a good weekend."

"Great. I'm going out on a date tonight." Jodi laughed pulling her coat on and heading out the door.

"Good for you. Have fun." Tessa locked the door behind her and started walking back toward her office. She frowned when someone knocked on the door. Spinning around to see Jodi standing there waving her hand frantically, she opened the door to let her back inside.

"Is there something wrong, Jodi?"

Jodi smiled at her. "I was in such a hurry when I left that I think I left my cell phone in my desk."

Tessa smiled and Jodi hurried past her and headed straight for her desk. Jodi grinned as she held the phone up having found it. Tessa laughed at her. The girl wouldn't survive without her cell phone. Tessa was sure it was a permanent fixture to her hand.

"Thanks, Doc Mac. I'll see you Monday. Have a nice weekend with Sheriff Garrett." Jodi waved as she left.

Tessa smiled, happiness spreading through her, with just a hint of worry but with her aunt Lil and the judge as support, she hoped it would all go well. She knew she was going to have a great weekend since she was spending it with Sam. Tessa reached out to lock the door again, and froze. Her heart clutched in her chest, her breath caught in her throat, and she felt the blood drain from her face as she looked at the one person she feared most in life. Ryan Kirkland. Her husband.

Chapter Thirteen

"Aren't you going to say hello, Tess?" Ryan Kirkland said as he stepped inside the hospital closing and locking the door behind him.

Tessa trembled as she stepped back and quickly moved behind the counter.

"Wha-what are you doing here?" She cursed herself for the tremor in her voice and wished she had her cell.

Ryan chuckled as he stared at her. "What you mean is...how did I find you?"

Tessa didn't say anything. Her eyes glanced from him to the door and back again. He continued to stare at her.

"It took me over two fucking years to find you," he hissed, his anger showing, making her tremble with fear.

Terror engulfed Tessa, her worst nightmare had come true, and he stood in front of her. Mentally shaking her head, she couldn't let him see her fear because it gave him control. She straightened up, squared her shoulders, and glared at him.

"Get out of my hospital." Her jaw

clenched as she ordered him and wishing they weren't alone. *Never let him see your fear* was her mantra. It had taken her too long to realize she shouldn't show fear since he thrived on it.

Ryan burst out laughing. "Finally growing some balls, huh?" He walked forward and leaned across the counter. "Too little, too late, babe...I spent every waking minute looking for you. I've had men searching every corner of this country. One of them has been here since July, but it took time to discover if it was you or not. The name change was a clever idea but you can't hide those looks. I would've come sooner but *business* kept me tied up and I couldn't leave. But I'm here now, and you and I are going to take up where—"

"No," Tessa shouted. "I want you to leave or I'll call the sheriff."

"Is that the same sheriff you've been fucking? Does he know about me?"

"Get out, Ryan. Now!"

"Let me tell you something, Tess. No one walks away from me and you should know that. My guy has told me all about you and him. I've seen the pictures, and I know you've been screwing the sheriff. At first, I thought he was just a deputy until I saw him in the diner. You always went for the top shelf, didn't you, Tess. No deputy would do for you. You had to have the sheriff. I'll ask you again, does he know about me?"

Tessa picked up the phone. "I'm calling the sheriff," she repeated, her hand shaking as she pressed the numbers on the pad.

Ryan stared at her and then gave a terse nod. "Fine, but this is not over. You and I will talk, and I have a feeling you haven't been truthful with him." He spun on his heel and walked out the front door leaving it standing open.

Tessa dropped the phone back into its cradle and collapsed into the chair behind the counter. Her heart was pounding in her head so loud she barely heard anything else. How had he found her? She thought she'd covered her tracks. She placed her hands over her face.

Dear God! What was she going to do? Knowing it was the only thing that she could do now, she had to tell Sam the truth, and he was going to hate her for it. A tear slid down her cheek. If only she'd been honest from the start. She loved him so much and by lying to him all this time, he would feel betrayed. Not that she could blame him. She was a fool. Tears flowed freely as she cried as if her heart were breaking. In all likelihood, it was.

* * * *

Sam heard the front door open and since he was the only one available, he stepped out of his office into the hall where he could see directly to the lobby. There he saw one of the strangers he'd seen in the diner, standing in the lobby.

"May I help you?" Sam asked leaning against the doorway leading to the hall, but he kept one hand on his holstered weapon. Something about the man rubbed him the wrong way and he wanted to be prepared.

"I want you to stay away from my wife," the man said through clenched teeth.

"Your wife?" Sam straightened. His gut never led him wrong.

"Tess is my wife."

Feeling as if he'd been slammed in the chest, Sam tried his best to stay calm and hoped the man was talking about someone else named Tess. "Tess?"

"You know who I'm talking about...Tessa Kirkland...right, you know her as Tessa McGuire," the man said stepping closer. "Whatever name she's going by, she's my wife."

"I don't believe you," Sam said, even as his gut clenched and he feared it was the truth.

"Ask her. We'd been married for two years when she disappeared. We...we had an argument and she just took off. It took me a long time to find her but now that I have, she'll be coming home to Pennsylvania with me."

Sam didn't move. "If she left you then, what makes you think she'd return with you now?" His head was beginning to throb and he actually felt sick to his stomach.

"She will, I'll persuade her. She belongs with me."

"You can't make her go if she doesn't want to. I'll see to that." Sam knew he'd do his job if Tessa didn't want to leave with this man, if he was truly her husband. That he would have to hear from her lips. He hated the thought that she'd been lying to him all these months.

"I'm not afraid of you."

"You should be," Sam said with deadly calm.

"Is that a threat, Sheriff?"

Sam pushed away from the wall and stepped forward. "You're God damn right it is. Now, get out of here."

"Tess belongs to me. Her running off doesn't change that. I *will* take her home with me. She belongs with me, and not in this shit hole town."

"You need to grow some balls, realize she doesn't want to be with you, and just let her go."

"Why? So you can have her? Over my dead body."

Sam sneered. "Deal."

"You have no idea who you're fucking with—other than my wife."

"Why would you want her if she's fucking around on you?"

"Because she belongs to me," the man shouted in anger and frustration.

"She's not a possession." The muscle in Sam's cheek twitched as he tried to hold on to his anger.

"The hell she isn't. She is my possession, she's my fucking wife, and she'll leave here with me."

"Not if I have anything to say about it."

"You won't have any say in it at all. You ask Tess about me. Ryan Kirkland." He stared at Sam. "A real shame if something should happen to you, Sheriff."

Sam clenched his fists. "Are you threatening an officer of the law?"

Kirkland smirked. "Oh, no. That's not a threat at all, Sheriff." He turned and walked out letting the door swing shut behind him.

Sam put his hands on his hips, hung his head, and took deep breaths then he raised his head, drew a fist back and punched a hole in the wall. Shaking his hand to ease the pain, he entered his office where he jerked his coat from the hall tree, nearly making it fall. He grabbed his hat and slapped it on his head as he stormed out the back door, slamming it behind him. Once outside, he sucked the cold air into his lungs and climbed into his vehicle. Wrapping his hands around the steering wheel, he swore as he started the vehicle, threw it into gear, and drove to Tessa's. Sam was angry, confused, and hurt. If what this man said was true, she'd lied to him—every day—straight to his face. He wanted answers.

Did you lie to me, Tessa?

He swore as he drove around to the back of the hospital and slammed on the brakes, making the vehicle slide sideways. Shutting off the engine, he sat there staring out the windshield seeing nothing. He clenched his jaw as he thought about walking up those stairs and confronting her. Taking a deep breath, in all fairness, he had to give her the benefit of the doubt. This guy...this Ryan Kirkland...might be a fruitcake who was yanking his chain. He'd give her a chance to explain or deny.

Taking another deep breath, he exhaled, threw the door open, and stepped out of the vehicle. He stared up the metal stairs toward her door then started to climb them.

Stopping in front of her door, he hesitated then pounded on it. The door opened and she stood there smiling at him. He pushed down the anger and the hurt. He loved her and didn't want any of this to be true. He moved past her into the room.

"Sam?"

"I had a visitor at the station," Sam said without turning around.

"Who?" Her voice wavered and his heart sank when he heard the anxiety in her voice.

Sam spun around to face her. "Ryan Kirkland, your husband."

Tessa gasped, her hands flying to her face. "Sam, please, you have to let me explain."

"Explain what, exactly? Explain that you're married. Are you married?" When she didn't answer him, he shouted. "Are you?"

"Yes, but..."

"You lied to me. You lied every day—straight to my face. All this time, all you've done is lie."

"From the beginning, I told you I didn't want to get involved with you, Sam. I had my reasons." A tear rolled down her cheek but he didn't care.

"Then you should have told me."

"I didn't know how."

"How hard was it to say you were married? You should have told me the first time I kissed you. Hell, any fucking time before or after would have done. I don't fool around with married women." He laughed without humor. "Apparently I do. *Fuck!*"

He strode away to the door.

"Please...listen to me, Sam. Please," she begged. "I'm terrified. I don't know what to do."

Sam hesitated because of her plea. He didn't want to hear any more of her lies, and although he kept his hand on the doorknob, he couldn't bring himself to open it.

"I'm sorry, Sam. I couldn't take the chance of filing for divorce and letting him find me...and kill me."

"Kill you? That sounds a little over dramatic."

"No. You don't know him, Sam. He's ruthless. He has associations with the mob."

"Yet, you married him." He refused to turn around and look at her.

"I didn't know that when I married him. He's the CEO for Santros." Sam had heard of Santros, it was a large beverage distributor. "I figured that's where all his money came from, not dealing in murder and money laundering. It's why I know he'd kill me if he found me. No one leaves Ryan Kirkland unless he wants them to."

"I can't believe you didn't tell me this." Sam hung his head.

"Aren't you listening to me? As far as I am concerned I haven't been married for years, Sam."

"Bullshit," he roared as he turned to face her. "Just because you're not with him doesn't mean you aren't married. You have a legal piece of paper stating the opposite. *Son of a bitch*," he muttered as he shook his head and turned away from her. He couldn't bear to look at her because he hurt so much he couldn't bear it.

"That piece of paper doesn't mean anything to me," she said, her voice trembling.

Sam turned and glared at her. "Well, it does to me. If only you'd told me, maybe..."

"Sam—"

Sam threw his hand up. "No. I don't want to hear any more of this." He took a shuddering breath. "I can't fucking believe this. If you cared at all you wouldn't have lied to me, Tessa."

"I do care. I couldn't tell you. I didn't know how, I was afraid to tell you."

Sam watched another tear roll down her cheek. "All you had to do was tell me.

Where did you think this was going, Tessa?"
He waved his hand between them.

"This is why I didn't want to get involved, Sam. I thought we'd just—"

"Just what? Fuck?" Sam clenched his jaw so hard he was surprised his teeth didn't shatter. "We both knew after the first time we had sex, it was different...at least, I thought it was. Holy hell, Tessa...I'm in love with you," he shouted.

"Sam, I love—"

"Do not say it," he snarled.

"Sam, please. He found me and I'm scared."

"Get a restraining order."

"A piece of paper isn't going to stop him," Tessa shouted.

"It sure as hell didn't stop you either, did it?"

"Please listen to me. Please. I should have listened to my parents. They didn't like him—not at all. Daddy hated him on sight. Mom told me he was bad news." She shrugged. "I thought I was in love. Since my dad refused to give me away to Ryan, we got married at the courthouse. Not the dream wedding I'd always wanted, but it was all I could do. I hated hurting my parents, but they forgave me when I crawled home to them."

"Crawled?" Sam asked then could have kicked himself because he didn't want to care anymore.

"A month after we were married, I found out he had a mistress but he refused to leave her. I didn't understand it. I thought he loved me."

Sam hissed in a breath because it reminded him of Katie's first husband. "He just wanted to own you—control you."

Tessa nodded. "Yes, that's what Mom said too. I told him I was leaving him and he said he'd never let me go. He always worked long hours so I knew I had a chance to get out while he was gone...or at least, I thought I did. He came home just as I was about to walk out the door and he...he beat me and told me I would always belong to him and that if I tried to leave him again, he'd kill me. He told me there was no sense in reporting him for domestic violence because the police were his friends, and they'd take his side. I believed him, but it didn't stop me, Sam. I played it cool for a while with him. I acted as if I was fine with everything. I hated letting him touch me.

It was Aunt Lil, who saved me. She's so rich it's actually rather mind-boggling. The cabin, the one she owns in Kalispell where we were going to visit her, is where I hid for almost six months, she had me flown there. She has a private jet so no one knew. I told Ryan I was going to have lunch with Mom one day and since he thought everything was fine, he was all right with it. I knew he'd have me followed because I was anytime I left the house. My aunt Lil and Mom had come up with this elaborate scheme. I hid in the trunk of Aunt Lil's car, which she'd parked in the garage. When she left my mom's house, I knew the man following me would think she was alone since he could only see Aunt Lil when she drove past him. She drove me straight to the airport and gave me money to buy clothes because I had left everything behind. She actually gave me one of her credit cards to use. I only sent text messages to my parents and her, on a burner phone.

I stayed in Kalispell until Aunt Lil got things set up for me. She paid for everything. I don't know what I would've done without her. I had my last name changed to my great-grandmother's maiden name. Aunt Lil helped me with that too, and she said he'd never know about it. She has the money to do anything she wants and being married to the judge helped. He was the one who did the name change, off the books I guess you could say. I wanted to work and I saw the ad for the hospital for sale here in Clifton. Doc

Carter suggested I come here and work with him before I made a decision to buy it. One more thing Aunt Lil helped me with that she refuses to let me pay her back. Doc Carter said since it was a small town I might not like it. Honestly, I didn't at first but then I made friends, and it's grown on me. I love it here now. It's my home. Sam, I've been looking over my shoulder for two years hoping he'd never find me here..."

He glanced at her when her voice faded off. Tears streamed down her cheeks and she stared at the floor, wringing her hands.

"I knew not to get involved with you. I told you I thought you'd be easy to fall for, and I did. I know you hate me right now, but I wouldn't change one minute of the time I've had with you. I love you, Sam. Do you know why I love you? I love you because of the way you look at me—like I'm the most important thing in the world to you."

Sam couldn't look at her again because he knew if he did, he'd take her in his arms. His heart ached so hard he thought he was going to die. She'd betrayed his trust, his love. He needed to go.

"Say something, Sam," she whispered on a quiet sob.

"You want me to say something? All right, I will. All of this has been a fucking lie.

You said you didn't want to get involved yet you let me get involved. You say you love me, how can you when you couldn't trust me enough to tell me the truth? Okay, it's true that if you'd told me you were married, I might not have pursued you but then again, had I known the circumstances, maybe I could have helped you. But no, you used me, betrayed me, led me to believe that you cared and that you were free to be with me. You knew how I'd feel about you not being free to be with me one hundred percent, and then you lied to me about it." Tessa started to say something but he held up his hand, stopping her. "Lying by omission is lying all the same. All you had to do was say two simple words— I'm married. Maybe I would have walked away, maybe not but now we'll never know. Instead, you took my heart and crushed it." She had indeed crushed his heart and he needed to distance himself, and fast. "I'm done with this, Tessa. I'm done with you."

Sam opened the door then glanced back over his shoulder. "Goodbye."

He pulled the door closed and after taking a deep breath, walked down the stairs and away from the woman who he knew would always hold his heart, but not his trust.

Chapter Fourteen

Tessa ran to the door and pulled it open. She watched him walk down the steps and called out his name. He hesitated but then continued down the steps and climbed into his SUV. Without even glancing in her direction, he drove off. Tears tore at her throat as she stepped back inside, closed the door, and leaned against it before sliding to the floor where she released gut wrenching sobs.

Sam was right. She should have told him right away. He might have walked away leaving her to never know what a truly amazing man he was and how it was possible to love someone as much as she loved him but then again, he might have stayed. He might have helped her solve her problem but she screwed it all up, and now her life would never be the same. Without Sam in it, it was no life at all.

Monday morning brought snow and gloomy skies, which didn't help the sense of doom weighing heavily on her shoulders. Her weekend had consisted of not much sleep, lots of tears, and begging the universe to bring Sam back. Tessa's heart was broken and Ryan knew where she was. Life couldn't get any worse but still she tried to smile as she entered the hospital.

"So how was your weekend?" Jodi's expression fell when Tessa's turned to a frown with tears threatening. "Oh, not good, huh? Sorry. You have a guest in your office," Jodi told her pointing in that direction with a pencil over her shoulder.

Tessa came to a halt, feeling the hairs on her neck rise and her gut twist. "Who?"

Jodi shrugged. "I don't know who he is. He said he was a friend of yours."

Tessa glanced back to her office, and then back to Jodi. "Call the sheriff's department and tell them I need someone here right now."

"Did I do something wrong?" Jodi asked in alarm while grabbing for the phone.

Tessa tried to smile. "No, Jodi. I don't know what I'd do without you. Just make the call."

Glancing toward her office again, Tessa knew, without a doubt, it was Ryan waiting for her. Taking a deep breath, she nodded at Jodi hearing her talking to Betty Lou and headed back to her office. When she opened the door and stepped inside, she found Ryan sitting in one of the chairs in front of her desk. He glanced over his shoulder at her, and when Tessa left the door open, he smirked.

"What are you doing here?" Tessa glared at him staying in the doorway.

He glanced around the office. "We have things to settle."

"Get out." She clenched her jaw. "I had Jodi call the sheriff's department and someone will be here soon."

"Do you think I fucking care who you called? I'm not afraid of them. You and I have unfinished business."

"You and I have been finished for a long time."

"I own you, Tess, and I intend to take you back home with me." Ryan stared at her.

Tessa shook with anger. She was about to respond when she heard someone's boot heels clacking down the hall then Sam was standing beside her glaring at Ryan.

"Is there a problem here, Doctor McGuire?" Sam asked her, his tone purely professional but she saw the muscle tick in his jaw.

Pain ripped through her heart at Sam using her name as if they were only acquaintances.

"Yes, *he's* here without my permission."

"I didn't think stopping in to say hello to my wife was something I needed permission to do." Ryan smirked.

"Wrong. If Doctor McGuire doesn't want you here, I'll have to ask you to leave," Sam said moving to clear the doorway and making Tessa move aside in the hallway. She realized he was putting himself between her and Ryan. He knew how to do his job.

Ryan stood and moved through the door into the hall. He looked at Tessa over Sam's shoulder. "You and I will finish this later," he said narrowing his eyes before turning to leave the hospital.

"Thank you for coming over, Sam," Tessa said wanting to throw her arms around his neck and feel his strong arms comforting her.

Sam stared at her for a few seconds, and then nodded. "It's my job. I'll have one of the guys walk you home later. Don't leave here until I send someone over." He put two fingers to his hat brim, turned, and walked away, nodding to Jodi on the way out through the front doors.

Tessa entered her office, collapsed in her chair, rested her forehead on her folded arms, and sobbed. He didn't even want to walk her home later. He was sending one of his deputies over to do that and he'd only come here because it was his job, not for her—never again for her.

* * * *

Sam sat in his office and grumbled under his breath how he'd liked to kill Kirkland with his bare hands. Damn it. The thoughts running through his head were that he shouldn't care one way or the other, but he did. He loved her so much but her lies, her betrayal was too much, and it was tearing him apart. He'd never fooled around with a married woman before because he believed them off limits. He'd always steered clear and looked for that wedding band. A wedding band was a sign of commitment, an important commitment deserving respect.

Fuck! How in the hell was he going to get past loving her? Granted, her husband was a dick, but she should have been upfront with him from the beginning. *Then you never would have had her.*

Sam shook his head. He couldn't tell himself that. She'd lied and now the son of a bitch was here. It was true that she seemed honestly frightened but he'd sent Rick over to walk her home and to inform her that someone would also walk her to work in the mornings. He would do whatever he needed to do to protect her because he certainly didn't trust Kirkland but he also loved her. If anything happened to her, he'd never survive the guilt. He knew the type Kirkland was since he'd dealt with them enough when he'd been a Marshal. The man was scum and he was just the type to do what Tessa had told him he would do.

"Sam?"

"What is it, Betty Lou?"

"What's going on?"

Sam glanced up at her. "Nothing."

"I know when you're lying, Sam Garrett."

"Betty Lou, let it go. Please."

"Did something happen between you and Tess?"

Sam swore under his breath. "I said let it go," he gritted out between clenched teeth.

"I don't like seeing you hurting, Sam."

"I'll be fine."

"You're not fine..."

Standing slowly, he glared at her. "I will be. Just leave it alone."

"Sam—"

"Holy hell, Betty Lou...it's over, okay. She lied to me. Tessa's married," Sam shouted then took a deep breath in an attempt to calm his angry mood.

"Married?"

Sam sat back down and ran his hands down his face. "Yes, married. She's been on the run from him for a long time, changed her name, and moved here to hide from him. She claims she couldn't divorce him because she feared he'd find her. Well, he found her anyway. He's here—in Clifton."

"Will he hurt her?" Betty Lou's voice trembled, and Sam knew she was thinking of how Joe Baker treated Mary.

"Not if I can help it. I've got the men watching her, and I'm hoping for her sake that he'll eventually give up and leave."

"What if he doesn't?"

"Then I'll deal with him."

Sam picked his pen up and got back to the paperwork in front of him. He knew Betty Lou had left the office and he was sure it would be all over town soon enough about Tessa being married. What possessed him to tell Betty Lou? He had no clue but his anger simply got the better of him. The woman didn't know when to quit. He knew the minute the words came out of his mouth, he'd made a mistake then again, maybe he wanted Tessa to hurt like he was hurting. *Shit!*

On his way home that afternoon, he refused to look toward the hospital. It was best if he just stayed away from her. His deputies could watch over her until Kirkland left town. Driving out of town, Sam put his sunglasses on and pulled the visor down as he drove in the direction of the setting sun. How in the hell had he gotten himself into this situation? If only she'd been truthful from the start. If only she had just told him she was married, he would have backed off. Sam tightened his jaw as he thought about how she'd lied. Would he have backed off? He had to wonder—had she told him the truth and explained the situation, would he have still gotten involved with her? He'd never been the kind of man to go after another man's woman since he'd never want it to happen to him.

Now, he was in love with a married woman and it pissed him off more than he could imagine. Sure, he'd wanted her from the time he'd first set eyes on her, but he'd have gotten over it if she'd just been honest up front, he would have just walked away and found someone else.

Bullshit! She's the woman you're meant to love for the rest of your life.

"It doesn't matter anymore," he murmured to himself. "Forget about her."

Yeah, right.

As he drove around the curve on Copper Ridge, he saw a car sitting on the side of the road and swore as he recognized Ryan Kirkland leaning against the vehicle. Sam pulled off the road in front of him. Only after inhaling a deep calming breath, he exhaled and stepped out of his vehicle. He placed his hat on his head and strode toward Kirkland. Stopping by the back of his vehicle, Sam folded his arms across his chest, and leaned against his SUV.

"This isn't by coincidence. What do you want, Kirkland?"

"Simple, Sheriff. I want my wife."

"You don't seem to understand that she doesn't want to leave with you."

"Do you think that matters to me? Tess belongs to me. Always has. Always will. I think if you tell her you don't want her anymore, she'll go back with me."

Sam blew out a laugh. "Well, there you go thinking. I'm not seeing her anymore and she still won't leave. What does that say about you?"

Kirkland shrugged. "Maybe she thinks she has a chance with you again. I don't know and I don't fucking care. She is my wife and she will leave with me," he shouted.

"Wow. Temper, temper. It doesn't take much to set you off, does it? You know, I hate a man who thinks he owns a woman, or one who beats her. Why do you suppose men do that? Are they just pussies and know they can't beat up a man, so they beat a woman?" Sam knew he was making Kirkland angry when he saw the muscle twitch in his cheek and his hands clench into fists.

"Don't push me, Garrett."

"That's Sheriff Garrett to you, and I'll push you all I want. This is *my* town and I want you out of it."

"I'll gladly get out of here once Tess is ready to go—"

"So you can beat her again? Because I have a gut feeling that *if* she does leave with you that's exactly what will happen. Do you beat your mistress too?" Sam pushed his coat back to show his weapon and placed his hand on it. "My sister's first husband had a mistress. The son of a bitch died on this very road—kind of funny how you decided to stop me here." He straightened up. "I want you out of Clifton."

"I haven't done anything wrong, Sheriff. I have a lot of money, you know."

"So? Is that supposed to impress me?"

"Just saying. I'm sure a small town sheriff doesn't make a lot of money."

Sam smirked. "I make enough."

"You could make more."

"Are you attempting to bribe me? Because if you are, I'll haul your ass in so fast your head will spin."

"Not at all. It was just a statement."

"Was there a reason you wanted me to stop? I don't particularly want to waste any more of my time talking to someone like you—a thug and a man who beats up women. You know—scum."

Kirkland narrowed his eyes at him. "You only have Tess's word on that."

"And I'd believe her any day over a man like you. Thing is, you aren't a man. You're a damn pussy. How about we just go at it and see just how tough you are?"

"You have, at least, fifty pounds on me. How would that be fair?"

Sam stepped forward. "How many did you have on Tessa?" Kirkland backed up, making Sam sneer. "Get in your car and drive off before I haul you in just for the hell of it."

He watched as Kirkland climbed into his car, started the engine, and tore out on the road. Sam took a deep breath and blew it out, forming it into a puff of air. He hadn't even realized how cold it was since he'd been so angry talking with that prick. Walking back to his SUV, he watched the disappearing taillights of Kirkland's car moving further down the road then climbed in behind the wheel, and drove home.

Later that evening, Sam sat in his living room watching TV, when he saw headlight beams flash across his ceiling. *Who the hell?* Pushing himself up from the recliner, he picked up his weapon then walked to the kitchen, opened the back door and swore when he saw Riley getting out of his truck then walk up the porch steps.

"What are you doing here, Riley?"

"I was in the neighborhood," Riley said as he entered the kitchen then took off his coat and hat.

"Bullshit. There's no reason for you to be in my neighborhood. We live in opposite directions of town." Sam walked to the refrigerator, yanked the door open, and grabbed a beer. He didn't even ask Riley if he wanted one. After twisting the cap off, he took a long pull.

"No, thanks...I didn't want a beer," Riley said with a sneer.

"You're leaving, and you know how I feel about drinking and driving. The roads are bad enough without you on them after drinking."

"How many have you had, Sam?"

"What the hell is this, Riley? I'm in my own damn house and not going anywhere."

"Not only are you my friend, you're also my brother in-law, so I can tell you that we're worried about you."

"I'm fine. Go home."

"You're not fine, Sam. You're hurting. You love her. Why don't you go get her back?"

Sam slammed the beer bottle down so hard, beer sloshed out of the top. "Go the fuck home. I'm fine."

Riley sighed then put his coat and hat back on. "Your sister is worried about you so I promised I'd stop by."

"Tell Katie I'm all right or I will be eventually—whatever you want. I'll get past this. Seriously, Riley, go home to your wife and daughter."

"I'm worried about you too," Riley said.

Sam huffed, pulled a chair out from the table, and took a seat. "If I hadn't just won the election, I swear I'd quit."

"You love the job, Sam."

"It doesn't mean much to me anymore but I won't let the people of Clifton down."

"I can't begin to know why she lied—"

"No, you sure as hell can't but the point is she did lie." Sam shook his head. "Now go home. I'll get past this."

"Not for a long time."

"You're right about that but I will, eventually."

"Are you drunk?"

Sam smirked. "Not yet, but I'm working on it. Go home. Please."

Riley nodded and slapped him on the back then left. Sam just wanted everyone to leave him alone. He'd get through this on his own. Somehow.

* * * *

Tessa stood and stretched as her stomach growled. "Jodi, I'm going to the diner for lunch. Do you want anything?" she asked as she entered the lobby.

Jodi smiled and told Tessa what she wanted, but then her smile slipped. "Are you all right?"

"I just haven't been sleeping much lately." Tessa said. It wasn't a lie. She hadn't slept at all since Sam had left and that was almost a week ago. She absently rubbed the spot over her heart. Would the pain ever go away? Ryan was still in town but he couldn't get to her with the deputies around her all the time. Rick was in the waiting room keeping an eye out.

Jodi nodded. "Breakups are a bitch."

"Excuse me?" Tessa said with astonished surprise.

Jodi waved her hand. "Everyone knows you and Sheriff Garrett broke up. We were all hoping for a wedding, but since you're already married..." Jodi shrugged and glanced away.

"I guess news travels fast in a small town,"

Tessa muttered.

Jodi nodded. "Everyone probably knew the minute it happened."

"I'm sure you're right. Jodi, I'm sorry I didn't tell you the truth..."

Oh hey, Doc Mac, don't worry about it. I'm sure you had your reasons. I just hate it that you and Sheriff Garrett are over. Anyone could see how much he loved you."

Tessa felt sick. Jodi, in all likelihood, was telling the truth. The people of Clifton knew everyone's business. It wasn't so much of a rumor mill as it was the actual events. It was never malicious, it just *was.* Tessa nodded to Jodi and left the hospital with Rick in tow to get lunch.

She kept her eyes straight ahead so she wouldn't glance toward the Sheriff's department. The thought of Sam sitting in there was killing her. As they walked down the street, Tessa glanced around and almost stumbled when she saw Ryan up ahead, leaning against a building, smoking a cigarette. He straightened up when he saw her. A smirk lifted his lips making her wonder how she could ever have found him attractive. He was nothing compared to Sam. She placed her hand on Rick's arm to stop him. He glanced at her and then to where she was staring. He placed his hand over his weapon and stepped in front of her.

"Don't move, Doc."

"Is there something wrong, Deputy?" Ryan asked him as he kept his eyes on her.

"Move along, Kirkland," Rick growled.

"Surely, it's not against the law to stand here."

"I'll arrest you just for the hell of it."

Ryan laughed. "You sound just like your boss. That's some watchdog you have there, Tess."

"Ryan, leave me alone," Tessa said, her voice trembling.

"I'm not doing anything...yet." Ryan tossed his cigarette down and ground it under the heel of his shoe then he picked it up and tossed it into the trashcan. "See, you can't even arrest me for littering, Deputy." He chuckled as he strode away.

The air whooshed out of her and Rick touched her arm. "Are you all right, Doc?"

"Yes," she lied. She knew Ryan would do whatever he could to get to her and he was letting her know that no one was going to stop him. He wasn't going to go about it in a flamboyant style. He'd sneak in when no one was looking—like a snake. They continued on to the diner.

Rick opened the diner door, and waited for Tessa to step inside before following her.

The place went quiet as everyone stared at her. She felt self-conscious as she glanced around then she saw him. Sam was sitting in a back booth with Brody.

Tessa quickly took a seat at the counter and placed her orders with Connie. She was doing everything in her power not to glance his way. Rick sat down on the stool next to her. A few minutes later, Tessa was paying for her orders when she felt him beside her. She didn't have to turn to see him. She knew he was there because the aroma of his aftershave had encircled her and made her heart ache. He reached past her to pay Connie for his lunch then she heard Rick telling him about their encounter with Kirkland. She heard Sam mutter something but she couldn't make it out.

"Hey, Doc Mac," Brody said to her with a smile when she glanced over to him.

Tessa tried to smile but it was too hard. "Brody."

Her eyes strayed to Sam. He gave a terse nod and walked out the door.

Brody tightened his lips. "Sorry, Doc," he said before following his boss out the door.

Tessa's eyes followed Sam across the street. She flinched when Connie touched her arm. Tessa looked to her expectantly.

"Your change, Tess." Connie held out

her hand and gave her a sympathetic look.

Tessa nodded and took the change then picked up the bag, left the diner, and strolled down the street to her hospital with Rick quietly walking just behind her. A winter storm was moving in. Tessa glanced toward the Glaciers and saw the snow coming over them. The cold air had a snap to it with a promise of dropping temperatures. It was mid-December and it could bring a lot of snow. The winter usually brought the blues for some. Tessa snorted. She definitely had those and with the holidays nearly upon them, it was worse. With Sam so angry with her, she'd never hurt more. The thought of going on without him in her life was heartbreaking. They'd loved each other but it all fell apart because she'd lied. She knew it was inevitable that eventually she'd have to tell him. There was no other way they could have a future together. Not that she ever actually saw a real future with Sam, not as long as Ryan was still searching for her.

You should have stayed away. Now you both have broken hearts and it's your fault!

Jodi sat behind the counter talking on the phone. After leaving Rick with his lunch, Tessa handed Jodi her bag with a burger in it, and then headed for her office. Closing the door behind her, she let the tears fall. She seriously hoped that once the New Year arrived, it would heal her broken heart.

A few minutes later, a shadow passed over her desk and she glanced up to see Katie Madison standing in the doorway.

"Hi, Katie," she greeted her with as much of a smile as she could muster. She genuinely liked Katie.

Katie entered the room then stood in front of Tessa's desk and narrowed her eyes at her.

"I can't tell you how upset I am about all of this," Katie said placing her hands on her hips.

"I am too—"

"Don't give me that, Doctor. McGuire. I thought you were my friend. I thought you loved my brother—"

"I do, Katie," Tessa said as she stood becoming annoyed that everyone seemed to be sticking their noses where they don't belong.

"No, you don't because if you truly loved him, you wouldn't have hurt him. I do love my brother, and it kills me to see him this way and all because of you. He may not look like he's hurting but I know him, and he is. How could you do this?"

Tessa watched as Katie's hands clenched into fists. She raised her eyes to look at her.

"You have to believe me, Katie...I didn't plan any of this. I knew I shouldn't have gotten involved with him."

"But yet you did," Katie said, her tone carrying more than a hint of anger.

"Actually, it's really none of your business, Katie."

Katie reared back as if struck. "*None of my business?* Sam is my brother, and I thought you were my friend. It seems you fooled a lot of us, Doctor McGuire."

"We are friends, Katie."

"Wrong. We *were* friends. You don't deserve someone as special as Sam. He's too good for you." She spun on her heel and strode from the room.

Tessa slumped back down into her chair and stared at the doorway. How many more friends would she lose over hurting Sam? A lot was her bet. This town loved Sam, just as much as she did.

Chapter Fifteen

Sam was working at his desk in his office when the phone rang. He answered since he could see that Betty Lou was on another line.

"Sheriff Garrett."

"This is not over between us, Sheriff. Tess is *my* wife and she will be leaving with me," Kirkland's voice said in his ear.

Sam gripped the phone. "If she doesn't want to leave and you take her, it will be against her will. Kidnapping is a federal offense, and I'd take great pleasure in arresting your ass."

"You'd never find me, Garrett. You seriously need to find someone else's wife to fuck, because mine will be leaving this podunk town." Kirkland hung up.

"*Son of a bitch!*" Sam roared. He knew the bastard was goading him as if he wanted Sam to come after him. He wasn't going to give him the satisfaction. This was one of the many reasons, he never got involved with married women—until Tessa.

Betty Lou appeared in the doorway. "Are you okay? What happened?"

"Nothing, Betty Lou. Don't worry about it." Sam tried to smile but he couldn't.

She stared at him until she finally sighed and walked away. Sam shook his head. This shit needed to end and end soon. He stood and pulled his coat on then placed his hat on his head. He walked to the back door.

"I'll be back in a little while, Betty Lou," he called out.

"All right, Sam."

When he opened the back door, snow flurries hit him in the face and the cold air seeped into his lungs. He climbed into his SUV and drove to Tessa's apartment. Once there, he stepped from the vehicle and walked to where Rick was sitting in his cruiser.

"Hey, Sam...everything okay?" Rick asked Sam after he let the window down.

"I'm going up to talk to Tessa. Go get some food. I'm sure you're hungry."

"How long will you be here? I'd love to go home and have dinner with my family."

"Go ahead. I'll stay with her until Paul comes on duty."

Rick saluted and smiled then closed the window and minutes later, drove off toward home. Sam climbed the steps and knocked on the door. It opened almost immediately. Without a word, he strode in past her stopping in the middle of the living room and turning.

"Did you even look to see who was at the door?"

"Yes. I'm not stupid, Sam."

Sam nodded as he glanced around the apartment. He'd always loved being here with her but now as he took in her standing there looking beautiful and sexy, his heart ached knowing he couldn't touch her.

"Kirkland called me at the office. I also had a run-in with him a few days ago on Copper Ridge. He says you're going home with him and it didn't matter what I said. He's determined to take you back."

"I won't go. I hate him. I decided a long time ago that I didn't want to be married to him anymore. He doesn't love me. He just hates to lose."

"I can understand that. He's a real prick." Sam glanced away from her. "Could I get some coffee?"

"Where's Rick?" Tessa asked him as she moved to make him coffee.

"I sent him away so I'll stay until Paul gets here." He removed his hat and coat then draped them over the back of a chair.

Tessa stared at him. "Don't do me any favors, Sam Garrett."

"That's Sheriff Garrett, and it sure as

hell isn't a favor. I'm doing my job."

He watched as she nodded and wiped a tear away as she moved around the small kitchen. Damn it. What the hell was he thinking by telling Rick to go and he'd stay? He knew Paul was due to be on watch in two hours. Sam could make it two hours. Couldn't he? The thought of being here was slowly killing him. The smells were so familiar to him. Inhaling deeply, he took a seat on the sofa. Honeybee jumped up beside him, staring up at him so Sam stared back.

"I think she knows you're the one who rescued her," Tessa said from beside him as she handed him his coffee.

Sam took the cup from her, making sure not to touch her. "Thanks." He looked back at the cat. "She's grown a lot."

Tessa sat in the chair across from him. "Yes. She's a good kitten. It kills me when people do things like what happened to her. How is Whiskey doing?"

"Great. Bo loves her. They run together all the time." Sam hated trying to make small talk.

"I'm glad. I knew they'd get along."

Sam nodded but didn't say anything more. He took a sip of coffee and kept his eyes off her. Sipping the coffee reminded him of the first time he'd been here. The first time he'd kissed her. *The night she should have told me, she was a married woman.*

He couldn't look at her. She was so beautiful and he loved her more than life but she'd cut his heart out with a lie.

"Sam? I'm sorry I didn't tell you about Ryan. It was wrong of me not to trust you with it and when I finally did, I didn't know how. I just wanted to forget him—"

"Forget him? He's your husband, Tessa. You don't just *forget* about a husband," Sam growled, and then clenched his jaw so hard, he could feel the muscle twitching in his cheek.

"I know I hurt you. Things between us happened so fast. Yes, I should have told you from the beginning but...I didn't know how, and after...well, I wanted to be with you so much." She stood and moved closer to the sofa.

Sam quickly stood and set the cup down. "Don't," he said staring down at her but unable to move further away.

Tessa stepped closer to him and placed her hands on his chest. "I miss you so much, Sam." She stood on her toes and kissed his jawline.

Sam closed his eyes, trying to block out the touch of her lips on his jaw because it was killing him. He clenched his hands into fists to keep from reaching for her. When she bit the lobe of his ear, he grabbed her arms and pushed her away.

"I said, don't." He moved away from her and stared at her. "I hate what you did to me. It's all about trust, Tessa. How am I ever to trust you after this," Sam said, his heart aching when he saw the tears glistening in her eyes.

"Sam..." She whispered his name while her eyes and body pleaded with him.

"Tessa, you lied to me. Maybe you were scared but you should've known you could trust me. I've never lied to you and I've told you I never would. I'm a strong man, Tessa, but not when it comes to you. I'm too weak because I love you, and I'm just going to have to work past that. The entire time we were together, you lied to me and you don't seem to understand how it's torn me apart."

When she made a move toward him, he held his hand up, stopping her. He watched her take a deep breath while her eyes pleaded with him to forgive her. He wished he could but...

"I am so sorry. I'll file for divorce, Sam. He knows where I am anyway so it doesn't matter now. I don't know if he'll cause more trouble, but I'll try. I'll file as soon as possible," she told him, taking another step forward.

Sam shook his head and stepped away from her. "It's not that easy, Tessa. Like I said, it's about trust. You didn't trust me with your secret and now I don't know if I can trust you with my heart."

"I know I've lied. I led you to believe my name was something other than my own even though legally, it is mine now and I lied by omission by not telling you that I was married." Tessa took a deep breath and he noticed she was shaking. "Everything else about me is true. The greatest truth being that I love you more than I've ever loved anyone. And I do trust you...I trust you with my life. I wish you could trust me again. I'm sorry, Sam. I know I keep saying it, but I am. It's killing me that you don't want to be with me anymore. I love you." Tessa turned her back to him and he saw her shoulders shake. She was crying and his body wanted to go to her, wrap his arms around her, and comfort her but his brain and his heart told him not to.

"You had so many opportunities to tell me the truth. I know we never talked about the future but eventually, I would have and maybe then, you would have told me but you knew that any woman that I wanted forever had to be mine—one hundred per cent. You're not even mine a small percentage because you're legally bound to another man. Maybe if you would have explained it to me in the beginning, I could have helped you...*something*." Sam thrust his fingers through his hair. "But you didn't." He swallowed hard. "I waited a long time for you to come into my life but it was all for nothing."

He wished he knew for sure he could get over her but with her still here in town, it was going to be hard, and if he was truthful to himself, if she divorced tomorrow, he might want to try again. However, he wasn't going to give her the satisfaction of knowing that.

A knock on the door startled them both. Sam quietly walked to the door and peered through the peephole. He blew out a breath when he saw Paul, and Sam silently thanked him for being early.

"I'll be right out, Paul," Sam called out through the closed door.

"Okay, I'll be in the cruiser, Sam." Paul's voice came through the door, and then Sam heard him walk down the stairs. He picked up his hat and coat.

"Paul will watch over you tonight," Sam said as he opened the door. As he shrugged his coat on, he looked back at her and it took every ounce of his willpower not to go to her. Slapping his hat onto his head, his heart broke just a little bit more when he saw tears streaming down her face.

"Goodbye, Tessa." He walked out, closing the door behind him.

* * * *

Tessa slumped to the floor in the middle of her living room, and wept. The one man she loved and wanted in her life, didn't want her—not anymore. He couldn't forgive her for lying to him. *You're so stupid, Tessa! You had the man you wanted to spend your life with and you screwed it up by lying to him.*

If only she'd just stayed away from him but no, she couldn't resist him. Fate had a warped sense of humor in that when she'd finally escaped a man who treated her like a possession and never like a woman, she encounters a man who makes her feel special. Was that what she first sensed about Sam and why she put up such an unfriendly barrier between them from the start? He was the man she was meant to be with and if it took her the rest of her life to make it up to him, she would. One thing was for certain, she was not leaving Clifton.

However, she was terrified of what Ryan was planning and she knew he was planning something. He'd hunted her down and was certainly just not going to walk away. He never let go of anything or anyone unless he wanted to or tired of it. It was never anyone else's decision. It was his and his only. If he didn't want her anymore, he'd make sure no one else would have her either. Ryan would make sure she disappeared. He was the type of man who tossed away things or people, like most people threw out the trash. If he didn't want it, he made sure no one else had a chance to have it.

When she'd first discovered he had a mistress, she also found out just how possessive he was. He'd told her he'd never give her or his mistress up and if she ever thought of divorcing him, he'd make sure she'd regret it. Thinking she'd simply divorce him and disappear, she'd actually gone to see an attorney but once the man found out who her husband was, he refused to take the case. He warned her that no other attorney in Pennsylvania would take the case either. No one went against Ryan Kirkland—no one. Tessa knew then she had no choice but to run.

She'd left everything behind. She hadn't seen her parents in over two years because they couldn't take the chance that Ryan would have them followed, and find her.

Tessa still didn't know how he'd found her, and she didn't really care anymore. All she cared about now was ridding him from her life. She'd get a divorce, stay in Clifton and run her hospital, and maybe—just maybe—win back Sam Garrett.

Pushing up from the floor, she walked to her bedroom and stood in the dark feeling exhausted but knowing she wouldn't sleep. Her apartment still smelled of Sam's aftershave.

Dear God! How can I go on without him? This is all my own fault. More tears fell as she curled up on the bed and sobbed.

Later, she went to stand in front of her window and gazed down at the street. Paul was in his cruiser keeping a watch over her. Tessa gasped when she saw Ryan standing against the lamppost across the street. The same lamppost she'd thought she'd seen someone standing against in the rain back in July. Now she knew it hadn't been just her imagination that she'd felt someone watching her at the festival or standing there that night. It most likely had been one of Ryan's many minions.

Her thoughts drifted back to that evening last summer. Sam had been worried about her, worried enough, and caring enough, to check on her when she'd gone home early because she'd told him she was sick. *Another lie!* Well, she had felt somewhat ill, upset, nervous, scared, or whatever that night so it wasn't an actual lie, but it hadn't been the truth either. That had been the occasion of their first kiss and if she were able to go back in time...she'd still let him kiss her. Sam was such a wonderful man and sometimes, she even wondered if she'd fallen in love with him that first time he came to the hospital to welcome her to town. Maybe that was why she'd been so unfriendly.

As she peered out at Ryan, the snow came down heavily but he didn't seem to mind it as he stood there staring up at her window. She wondered if she should alert Paul to his being there but before she could decide, she watched as he glanced away then back to her. Suddenly, he gave her a salute then he disappeared around the corner. A sheriff's cruiser driving by told her why Ryan had walked off.

Dear God! Please make him go away and leave me alone. Please.

Taking a deep breath, she moved away from the window and took a seat on the sofa. She hoped no emergency calls came in, because although Paul would follow her, she feared Ryan would try something. The safest place she could be for now was right where she was—holed up in her apartment.

* * * *

Later that night, Sam lay awake in his bed on his back with his hands clasped behind his head. He stared up at the ceiling fan whirling above him but he didn't see it because his thoughts were with Tessa. He could have had her this afternoon. All he'd had to do was wrap his arms around her and they would have made love. The sex had always been good between them. The pull to her was strong, and knowing he'd never experience the same level of lovemaking with any other woman didn't help. It was best if he just stayed away from her and ignored her any time he saw her.

"Yeah, right."

Sam shook his head, like that was going to be easy. He couldn't stop thinking about her when she wasn't here, how was he going to see her nearly every day and ignore her— resist her. It was wrong. He'd never been the kind of man to fool around with another man's woman and to think how she'd compromised him with a lie cut him to the quick. Clenching his jaw, he swore.

Sitting up, he swung his legs over the bed, ran his hands down his face, then stood, and walked to the kitchen. The light from the microwave clock was the only light to see by and when he entered the kitchen, Bo and Whiskey whimpered at him. He opened the door to the fridge, reaching in for a bottle of water. Glancing at both dogs, he closed the door and leaned back against the counter. After twisting the cap off, he took a long swig. Both dogs moved to sit in front of him and looked up at him with questioning eyes.

"I'm fine," he said to them. They continued to stare up at him. He pointed at Whiskey with the water bottle. "*You* shouldn't even be here but *she* wanted me to take you in, so I did and now you're just a reminder of her."

Whiskey lay down on the floor, put her head on her paws, and stared up at him with sad eyes as if she understood his pain. Bo lay down beside her and did the same thing.

"You two are no help at all. If I can't pour my heart out to you two, who can I? Damn it. I'm so in love with her that I can hardly think straight, but what am I supposed to do. I can't allow her back into my life. I can't." He shook his head. "I just can't. How can I ever trust her to be honest with me after this? She lied to me and I despise liars. But, I don't despise her...no, I'll love her as long as I live. She's the one and no other will come close, even if I tried to find someone else."

The dogs looked up at him. Blowing out a breath, Sam stared down at them. "Like I said, you're no help at all. I can't sleep. I can't eat. I miss her..." His voice caught in his throat.

"Shit," he muttered. "I may as well just stay up now. I know it's damn cold out, but I'm going for a horseback ride. You two behave." The dogs whined but didn't get up.

Sam strode with determination back to his bedroom, dressed, and returned to the kitchen to pull his coat, hat, and gloves on. Stepping onto the porch, he shivered at the cold. Taking in a deep breath, the cold air poured into his lungs then he blew it out, and watched it form into a puff of air.

You have to be crazy to be out in this.

"I am, but I need to get her out of my head. What better way than a ride in freezing weather with the cold air whipping through my head?" Sam murmured as he walked down the steps and headed for the barn. After saddling his horse, he gave his horse free rein, raced out of the barn, and headed for the north pasture. He was going to get her out of his head—somehow, even if it destroyed him first.

* * * *

That Friday night found Sam sitting in Dewey's Bar, nursing a beer he'd ordered an hour earlier. When someone tapped him on his shoulder, he was ready to tell whomever it was to fuck off, but he was surprised to see Sandy standing beside him.

"Hi, Sandy," he said looking back to his now flat beer.

"Do you mind if I sit with you?" she asked, smiling.

Sam shrugged. "Suit yourself but I'm not very good company right now."

Sandy slid onto the stool next to him and signaled for the bartender to bring her a beer. He set it in front of her, along with a glass, and walked off.

"What happened, Sam?"

"Nothing," he mumbled but looked at her when she laughed.

"I know you better than that. You wouldn't be here sulking if it was nothing."

"I am not sulking," Sam growled.

"I just thought you'd want to talk. I heard about you and Doc McGuire. I'm sorry things didn't work out."

"If you knew already then why did you ask?"

"Because I'm here if you want to talk. I'd like to think we're still friends, Sam, and I think I know you fairly well. We were together six months after all." She shrugged.

"She lied to me about being married.

What else is there to say?"

Sandy sat beside him and didn't say anything more. Sam sat at the bar wishing he could go home but all he'd do there was sit and think. He huffed. Much like he was doing here. Twirling the bottle around on the bar, he paid no attention to anything or anyone around him.

Why couldn't she have just told me the truth? Trusted me. Damn it! He was sure he'd never hurt this bad ever before in his life. Glancing to Sandy, he wondered if he'd hurt her this badly?

"Did I hurt you, Sandy?"

She seemed startled by the question. "Truth?" He nodded. "Yes, you did."

Sam winced. "I'm sorry. Maybe this is payback for hurting you and Lydia."

"Oh, Sam...it doesn't work that way. At least, I don't think it does. We know we didn't belong together. You just figured it out sooner than I did, but it did hurt me all the same because I was hoping we had something. Apparently, we didn't or we'd still be together." She placed her hand over his. "You will always have a place in my heart because you are one of the best men I've ever met. You hate hurting people and you love this town. Clifton is your town and people know you care about them. When we first started dating, it amazed me how people would just stop you on the street and tell you how much they appreciated you. I'm sure the town is hurting because you're in pain. I really hate seeing you like this, Sam. I wish I knew what to do to take your pain away."

Sam stared at his beer bottle. "I wish you did too."

"You love her very much," Sandy said in a quiet voice that told him she knew the answer but didn't really want to hear it. He really had hurt her.

"Yeah, I do, Sandy and I wish to hell I didn't. I just can't get past the fact she didn't trust me enough to tell me about her past. Now her...*husband* is here and threatening to take her back to Pennsylvania with him whether she wants to go or not. He's a real prick and he's going to push and push until it comes to a head."

"You'll protect her though. I know you will."

"Shit. I am already. I have my deputies staying with her until he leaves or..." Sam shrugged as he looked at Sandy. "I'm sorry for hurting you. It was never my intention."

"Maybe it wasn't hers either."

Sam blew out a laugh. "Might not have been but she succeeded. All she had to do was tell me the truth in the beginning."

"Then you never would have had her in your life. To her way of thinking, she'd left her husband years ago and didn't think of herself as married anymore...and you, Sam Garrett, are a very hard man to resist. I know she should have been up front with you, but think back to when you first started to pursue her. Was she all for it or did she seem hesitant? If she was all for it, then yes, she hurt you deliberately...but if she was hesitant, she was probably trying to convince herself not to get involved with you. I think you two are meant to be together and that's why she eventually gave in, and started seeing you. Take it from a woman who knows. You're easy to fall for, Sam." She leaned over and kissed his cheek. "Think about it. Everyone deserves a second chance, don't you think?"

Sam watched her walk away and swore. As much as he wanted her to be right, she was wrong. Tessa had lied to him. As he sat there, however, he thought back to her telling him it wasn't a good idea to get involved with him, and that she hadn't been looking for a relationship.

You'd be far too easy to fall for, Sam. Her words echoed in his mind and made him wonder.

To hell with it, he was going home and heading to bed. This night couldn't end soon enough.

"Sam?"

Sam swore. "What the hell are you doing here, Riley?"

"I was driving by and saw your SUV. You're not drunk, are you?"

"You sure as hell seem awfully interested in my drinking lately," Sam growled as he glared at his brother in-law.

"Kaitlyn and I are worried about you. You know she loves her big brother, though I can't figure out why."

Sam tightened his lips as he looked at Riley. "Yeah, well I don't get what the hell she sees in you either." Sam chuckled when Riley grinned.

"Seriously, how many have you had? Do I need to drive you home?"

Sam held up the bottle. "This is the only one I've had and as you can see, it's almost full. Now, go home to your wife and daughter."

"Did you know that Kaitlyn stopped in to see Tess?" Riley said giving him a smirk that told him that he'd been itching to tell him.

"What for?"

"To give her hell, for hurting her big brother."

Sam laughed. "We Garretts are a loyal

bunch."

"No shit. Come on, Sam. I'll walk out with you. You need to go home. One day, this will all blow over and things will be right as rain again."

"You think so? Because I sure as hell don't," Sam muttered as he stood and pulled his coat on then his hat. He walked out with Riley following him.

Chapter Sixteen

Saturday night in Clifton brought everyone to the town hall for Betty Lou's birthday party. Sam stood against the back wall with his friends—Jake, Gabe, Wyatt, Ryder, Riley, Brody, and Trick. They all looked as if they were holding the wall up since they all leaned against it with their arms folded across their chests scanning the crowd.

"How the hell did so many people fit in here?" Trick muttered.

"You know damn well, if there's a party of any kind, the people of Clifton find a way," Ryder said with a chuckle.

"What I want to know is why is there a band, when there's no real room to dance?" These words came from Gabe.

Jake laughed. "Close dancing for sure. Though, I wouldn't mind that with Red." Sam watched as Jake's eyes scanned the crowd until he found his wife, Becca.

"What do you suppose they're up to?" Wyatt asked them as they all watched their wives talking and laughing.

"No fucking good, that's for sure,"

Brody muttered as he pushed himself away from the wall and walked off toward his wife.

Sam wanted to be anywhere but here. He was keeping an eye on Tessa and it was killing him as he watched her smile at people and dance with her friends.

"Are you doing all right, Sam?" Riley asked him, leaning closer.

"I'm fine. We've been over this, Riley."

Riley snorted. "You're not fine. You love that woman."

"Doesn't matter...now back the hell off," Sam muttered and straightened up when he saw Tessa walking toward him.

* * * *

"I need to walk over to the hospital and check on the cat I operated on this afternoon," Tessa said when she reached Sam.

Sam stared at her. "You know you can't go anywhere alone right now."

"I know," Tessa gazed up at him, hoping against hope that he'd go with her.

"I'll get Brody. Stay here."

Tessa sighed as she watched him move through the crowd. He'd made it clear that he wanted nothing to do with her. He wouldn't even volunteer to walk her over to the hospital. She wished she hadn't come to the party. She wanted to be anywhere but

here only Sam had insisted. She and Sam
had even argued about her being here which
was actually kind of encouraging that he'd put
that much emotion and energy into a
conversation with her. Most talking events
between them lately were just a few words
here or there.

"You damn well will go," he'd shouted
when she said she wasn't going.

"Everyone in this town hates me. Why
should I go?"

"Because my deputies are going to be
there and taking turns patrolling. This is a big
deal for Betty Lou, and they all love her and
want to be there for her. Besides, I seriously
doubt that the town hates you."

"You do, Sam," she'd said staring up
into that gorgeous face, and eyes which took
that moment to look at the floor. Then he
said something that gave her heart a little bit
of hope.

"I wish to hell I did," he'd said before
slamming out of her apartment.

"Are you doing all right, Tess?" Trick
asked her, bringing her back to the present.

"Yes." She nodded, even though it was
yet another lie.

"I don't think so," Trick said as he put
his arm around her shoulders.

"Oh, Trick. It's just that I lied to Sam

and he can't forgive that."

"Give him time..."

Tessa shook her head. "It doesn't matter how much time I give him, I know he'll never forgive me or give me a second chance."

"I don't believe that for a minute," Trick said giving her a squeeze.

She was about to respond when she saw Sam strolling toward her with Brody following behind him.

"Brody will go with you. If you both aren't back in fifteen minutes, I'll be coming after you." He looked at Brody. "Got it?"

"Yes sir. We'll be back in fifteen," Brody said to him then indicated to Tessa to accompany him to the door.

Tessa nodded. She walked to the door with him where she put her coat on then together, the two of them ventured outside, and strolled up the street to the animal hospital. Snow flurries swirled around them and the temperature was close to freezing. Glancing over her shoulder, she saw Brody scanning the street, which made her nervous so she hurried her steps. He kept up with her and finally, they reached the hospital.

"I'll just be a minute, Brody. Come in from the cold." She unlocked the doors to enter the hospital then flipped on the bright overhead lights.

Brody nodded at her as they entered, and he secured the doors behind them. "No problem, Doc Mac. I'll be right here," he said, leaning against the counter to wait.

Tessa entered the room the cat was in and slowly walked toward the cage. Kneeling down, she smiled when the cat meowed at her.

"Hi, sweet girl, how are you feeling?"

"You always did love animals more than people, Tess."

Tessa let out a small squeal as she stood and spun around to find Ryan standing behind her grinning with a gun in his hand. She glanced at the door and he shook his head.

"Don't even think about it. I know you're not alone and it's a real bitch that I have to kill him."

"No," she hissed. "What do you want?"

"Oh, Tess, you know I want you. You're going to leave with me and be my wife again."

"Doc Mac?" Brody yelled from the lobby.

"Tell him you're fine," Ryan said in a lowered voice and moving closer so the gun was that much nearer.

Tessa cleared her throat looking at the gun too close to her midsection now. "I'm fine, Brody. I'll be right there."

"Very good." Ryan smiled at her.

"How did you get in here?"

"I've always been good at picking locks but that one on your apartment upstairs is a bitch, so I picked the one on the back door here instead. I knew you'd come in sooner, or later. I'm just glad you came in on a day off. I'd hate to have to kill everyone who worked here just to get to you. Now, I only have to kill that man out front."

"Please don't. I'll go with you, no problem," Tessa pleaded.

"I don't have a choice, Tess. He'll figure it out soon enough even if we slip out the back. Who is he anyway? I was really hoping you'd show up with the sheriff. I'd love to take him out."

Tessa shivered at the thought of anyone being hurt, but Sam most of all. "The man out front is the sheriff's deputy. You'll get in a lot of trouble killing him." God, she hated the thought of anything happening to Brody. His wife, Madilyn, would be devastated.

"It would be the same no matter who I had to take out. Don't try that bullshit on me. I'm smarter than that. Let's go. We're going to walk out front so I can take care of him, and then we're leaving out the back." He waved the gun at her. "Come on, go. Now!"

"Please, Ryan. We can slip out the back

door and be gone before he realizes it. I'll just tell him the cat needs her bandages changed and that it will take a while."

"No. I don't like loose ends and he is one. Once he figures out we're gone, he'll be looking for us and as much as I hate to admit it that damn sheriff of yours is one smart son of a bitch. I really wish he'd been the one with you. I'd love to put a fucking bullet in his head."

Tessa trembled and tried to think. She had to stall. If she and Brody weren't back in the fifteen minutes Sam allotted, he'd come after them, but then Ryan would surely kill him too. *Shit!*

"We could be long gone, Ryan, if we just leave by the back door now. I'll go back to Pennsylvania with you and be...be your wife again." Good Lord, she wanted to throw up at just the thought of doing that.

"You really deserve to be punished for leaving me, Tess. Janet always does what I ask. You, on the other hand, argue constantly and resist me. I don't like that in a woman. Your place is to do your husband's bidding."

"I will if we go back. Please. I'll be a good wife. Let's just go," she begged, knowing no matter what she said, he was going to make her pay for leaving him.

"I'm done with this conversation. We're

going out there so I can take care of this
deputy and once you and I are home, I'll
figure out what to do with you—decide your
punishment."

"If we go out into the lobby, someone
will see in from outside."

"Everyone's at that damn party, Tess.
Let's go," he ordered her, shoving the gun
against her ribs and grabbing her arm.

Taking a deep breath, she tried to pull
away from him but he pushed her through
the door and made her walk in front of him,
the cold metal of the gun muzzle pressed
against her back just about kidney height.
One shot could kill her. When they got to
the lobby, Brody was still leaning against the
counter. When he saw Ryan behind her, he
straightened up and his hand went for his
weapon, drawing it from his holster. As if
everything were happening in slow motion,
she rapidly blinked tears away and mouthed
'I'm sorry' to him. Brody halted his
movements when he realized Ryan had a gun
pointed at her. He gave a brief nod of his
head as he shifted his eyes to Ryan who
brought the muzzle up to alongside her head.

"You're not getting out of here with her,"
Brody said in a menacing voice pointing his
gun at them.

"Don't bet on it, Deputy." Ryan stood

just behind her, gun to her head and in control—for now. "You won't take the chance shooting me with Tess right here so close to me." Suddenly, he pointed his gun at Brody. "I hate like hell killing you, but I don't have a choice in the matter since I know you'll try to stop me."

"You're damn right about that," Brody's stance widened as he stared at Ryan. Tessa was shaking.

"Drop the gun, Deputy or I'll kill her and you."

"Please, Brody, just let us go," she pleaded, as tears trickled down her cheeks.

"You know I can't do that, Doc Mac. Sam wouldn't like it," Brody said without taking his eyes off Ryan.

"Sam doesn't care about me—not anymore, but he cares what happens to you," Tessa said trying to convince him.

"The man apparently has morals, if he quit fucking you when he found out you were married," Ryan said sarcastically.

"Doesn't matter, Doc. Kirkland's not leaving here with you," Brody muttered and Tessa saw a muscle tick in the man's jaw. Brody was as forthright as Sam was, and would die trying to stop Ryan.

"Drop the fucking gun," Ryan shouted grabbing Tessa by her ponytail and yanking her head back on her neck making her cry out.

Tessa could see the defiance in Brody's eyes but he let out a breath, and slowly lowered the gun to the floor.

"Christ, you do have balls, Deputy. I really hate like hell to do this," Ryan said then he fired his gun. Tessa screamed and watched in horror as Brody fell to the floor. Ryan grabbed her ponytail tighter, and pulled her over toward where Brody lay bleeding on the floor.

"Damn it. You're quick I'll give you that, Deputy, but now I just have to shoot you again." Tessa watched Brody as he struggled to brace himself even as he bled from a gunshot wound to his arm. Ryan stood over him aiming the gun down toward Brody's head.

"Please, Ryan, don't. He's hurt enough. He has a wife and son. Please. Let's just go. The sheriff is going to know it's you anyway. You don't have to kill Deputy Morgan."

"Oh, but I do. I told you, I don't like leaving loose ends. You know—"

The sound of a gunshot went off at the same instant the glass in the front door shattered. Blood spattered on her face then Ryan released her hair and fell backward onto the floor. She turned to look down at him. A bullet to the forehead had ended his life.

* * * *

When the fifteen minutes had passed, Sam got worried that Brody and Tessa hadn't returned so he slipped out of the town hall and walked to the hospital. The streetlights lit the way for him and he could see light spilling out onto the sidewalk from the hospital's lobby windows. Something told him to use the opposite side of the street so he could see inside without being easily detected. He walked beside the cars parked along the sidewalk.

When he reached the location directly across from the hospital, he swore aloud when he looked in to see Kirkland yanking on Tessa's hair, and pointing a gun at her head while yelling at Brody who stood with his weapon pointed at Kirkland. Sam withdrew his weapon and moved to the center of the street. He knew with the bright lights inside, no one would see him outside in the street, and with two streetlights out, he was virtually invisible. Suddenly, everything inside seemed to speed up, and then Sam watched in horror as Brody laid his gun on the floor and Kirkland shot him causing him to fall to the floor.

"Son of a bitch," Sam muttered as he

raised his weapon, moved closer to the doors, rolled his shoulders, and took aim at Kirkland. He watched the bastard drag Tessa by her ponytail over to where Brody was struggling to get up. Tessa was saying something but Kirkland took aim at his deputy. Kirkland planned to kill Brody. Sam widened his stance, took a deep breath, and slowly blew it out, knowing he couldn't wait any longer. He fired and saw Kirkland's head snap back just after the bullet shattered the glass doors striking him right between the eyes. As Sam ran to the hospital doors, he saw Kirkland fall back onto the floor and heard Tessa scream. Stepping through the broken glass, crunching it beneath his boots, he reached Brody and knelt down beside him.

"Are you all right, Brody?"

"I'll live but I'm bleeding pretty badly."

Sam nodded, and stood then spoke into the two-way radio hooked on his shoulder calling for an ambulance and the coroner. He turned his eyes to Tessa.

"Are you all right?" She nodded but her face was pale and he saw she was trembling. Giving her something to do was the best way to keep her from losing it completely. "Could you get some gauze for Brody's wound and wrap it until the ambulance gets here?"

"Yes...I...yes." She disappeared down the hallway.

"Let me look at it," Sam told Brody as he helped him sit up then assisted him in shrugging out of his jacket. "Shit—not through and through. You'll need surgery to remove the slug, my friend."

"I'll be fine. Just get Maddie for me," Brody's speech was beginning to slur due to shock and blood loss.

"I'll call Rick and have him get her. She can meet you at the hospital." Sam made a quick call to Rick.

"He was hiding in the back, Sam. He probably would have waited as long as it took," Brody murmured.

"You're probably right. Save your strength. The ambulance is on the way."

Sam quickly stood when Madilyn came running through the door and he glared at Rick.

"She refused to go to the hospital. She said she knew he was here." Rick shrugged.

Sam watched as Madilyn sank to her knees beside Brody with tears streaming down her face.

"He'll be fine, Madilyn," Sam said as he squatted down beside them, patting her on the back.

"He'd better be, Sam Garrett," she said

and glared at him. He saw Brody smile.

Sam ran his hand over his mouth. "Yes, ma'am."

Tessa returned to the room with supplies, cleaned up the blood on Brody's arm, and then wrapped the gauze around it. Sam swore when he saw all the blood and he saw Madilyn's face go pale. He put his hand on her shoulder to lend comfort.

"How did he miss you?" Sam asked Brody.

"Well, he obviously didn't, but I dodged when I knew he was going to shoot. I watched his eyes. I was ready for it," Brody told him.

"Good job." Sam watched Tessa wrap tape around the gauze. The next thing Sam knew, there were people trying to crowd into the hospital. He stood and faced them raising his hands to reassure folks.

"Everything is fine. Go back to the town hall. Brody got himself shot, but he'll be fine."

"Is that Kirkland?" Wyatt asked him, jerking his chin at the man on the floor.

Sam glanced over his shoulder to the man lying in a pool of blood. "Yes."

"Good shot, Sam," Wyatt told him and turned to the crowd. "Come on, everyone. This is completely under control—back to the party."

Sam sighed. He knew everyone considered him and Wyatt to be the best sharpshooters around this part of Montana. Wyatt had helped Sam out on more than one occasion and Sam had saved Madilyn when a lunatic had her. Sam didn't like killing anyone but to see Kirkland with his gun pointed at one of his deputies made him see red, and there was also no way he was getting out of here with Tessa. Sam glanced down at her while she worked on Brody.

"I'm so sorry, Brody," she said to him as she finished the bandaging.

"Don't worry about it, Doc Mac. I'll be fine."

Sam watched as Tessa looked to Madilyn. "I'm so sorry, Madilyn. It's my fault."

"No, Tess. Please don't think that. You didn't pull that trigger."

Sam glanced away. Tessa blamed herself for Kirkland shooting Brody. He mentally shook his head as he saw the ambulance pull up. When the EMTs rushed in with a stretcher, they all moved back. They checked Brody over then lifted him onto the stretcher and rolled him out. Madilyn followed and climbed into the back of the ambulance with Brody.

Sam would wait for the coroner. He exhaled long when he realized only he and Tessa remained. Watching her stare down at Kirkland, Sam saw a tear roll down her cheek. Was she upset he was dead? She raised her eyes and looked at him.

"I'm sorry I had to kill him, Tessa. I couldn't take the chance, if I just shot to wound, he might have been able to still kill Brody—or you," Sam told her.

Tessa moved to stand close to him staring up at him. "Don't apologize for killing him. He deserved it. I'm glad he's dead. He was an evil, evil man." She walked around him and started out the door. Her words reminded him so much of Mary Baker's.

"I'll need you to come in and file a report, Tessa."

Hesitating in the doorway, she nodded and then walked out, the glass crunching under her shoes. Sam muttered under his breath then sat behind the counter to wait for the coroner. Tossing his Stetson onto the counter, he leaned back in the chair and propped his feet up on the desk, hoping it wouldn't take them long to get here.

Chapter Seventeen

It was a late Saturday afternoon and Tessa lay on her sofa dozing off when her cell phone rang.

"Doctor McGuire," Tessa answered in a voice barely above a whisper and full of sleep.

"Doc Mac?"

Tessa cleared her throat and blinked herself fully awake. "Yes. I'm sorry, who's this?"

"It's Wyatt. There's something wrong with Bear. Would you mind coming out or do you want me to bring him to you?"

"I'll be right there, Wyatt." Tessa hung up.

She was happy to do anything right now to get her mind off Sam. Anger rushed through her when more tears rolled down her face. It was certain now he wanted nothing more to do with her. Since the shooting last month, she hadn't seen him at all. Rick had taken her statement.

Shaking anger, frustration, and the rest of the sleepiness from her head, she retrieved her medical bag and headed for Wyatt's ranch. When she arrived, Olivia came running out to meet her. It was snowing heavily around them.

"Thanks for coming, Tess. We don't know what's wrong with him. He won't eat and he's just lying on the straw. He doesn't want to get up or anything."

Tessa could hear the panic in her voice. "Let me see him, Liv. I'll do what I can."

She followed Olivia into the barn to where the dog lay. Crouching down alongside the animal, she rubbed Bear's head. "What's going on with you, Bear? Did you eat something you shouldn't have?"

"He hasn't eaten since yesterday," Wyatt told her. He squatted down beside her. "He's only six years old." He glanced at Tessa. "Do what you can, Tess. Please."

An hour later, Bear was up and eating. He'd had a stomach virus of some sort so Tessa had given him some medicine to help. After checking him out again, she stood and told Wyatt and Olivia that he'd be fine but to keep an eye on him and let her know if there was any change.

"How's your beautiful son, Liv?" Tessa had wanted to have children one day and had even imagined doing so with Sam but she'd obviously messed up that chance.

Olivia smiled at her. "He's gorgeous of course. He looks just like his daddy."

"You were lucky that Sam..." She couldn't say anything more. Just saying his name made her heart ache.

Olivia hugged her then pulled back from her raising an eyebrow at her. "Are you all right, Tess?" Olivia whispered close so it was between just them.

Tessa started to nod but then a tear rolled down her face as she shook her head. Olivia wrapped her arms around her as Tessa cried. Tessa heard Olivia telling Wyatt that everything was okay, and that she'd be in soon then handed him the baby monitor.

Tessa pulled back. "I'm sorry, Liv. I'm trying not to fall apart..."

"I was hoping you two could've worked it out by now," Olivia said.

Tessa gazed at her and shook her head. "He's done with me. I lied to him so he doesn't trust me anymore. He'll never forgive me."

"Why the fuck not?" Olivia exclaimed. "You love him. He loves you. End of story."

Tessa laughed without humor. "I've apologized so many times, Liv. He just can't get past my lying to him, especially about being married." She shook her head knowing all was lost.

"That man adores you. I can only imagine how he's feeling knowing you lied to him, but love is about forgiveness. You had your reasons, Tess, and eventually he'll understand that." She put her arm around Tessa's shoulders. "Don't let the love of your life get away. Please don't do that, Tess. Sam's a wonderful man and you're lucky to have found each other. That's a huge feat in today's world."

"He doesn't want me," Tessa whispered.

"I don't believe that. You know I'm your friend, Tess," Olivia said.

"I know, Liv."

"So, I wouldn't say anything to hurt you, but I have to say this—if you let a man like Sam Garrett, get away—you're a damn fool."

"Liv—"

"No. You listen to me. You love each other. The entire town was so happy about you two being together. We've all had our hearts broken at one time or other. It's a part of life. You need to do whatever it takes to get Sam back." Olivia took a deep breath. "Look at Wyatt. He swore he'd never love again, but he loves me and gave love another chance. I read somewhere that one day the right person will come along and make you realize why the others didn't work out. Tess, don't let love with this man slip through your fingers. Sam is an amazing man. You know how I feel about that sexy sheriff. You need to grab onto him and hold on before someone else does. Make him realize you two are meant to be together."

Tessa shook her head. "It's too late now, Liv."

"That is a crock of shit. I don't believe that. It's never too late for real love. Sam's loved you since the first time he saw you—I knew that even if he didn't," she said laughing. "And his love for you isn't going to disappear because you hurt him." Olivia took her hand in hers. "Go after him, Tess. Don't let the love of your life go."

"I've hurt him too badly. He'll never forgive me." Tessa was so certain about that it hurt to say it.

"Of course he will. He loves you. Look, Tess...I almost lost Wyatt, and when I think about what my life would be like without him...well, I just can't imagine it. We were both so very stubborn. I was tired of him not committing and he was too proud to ask me to stay. Don't let Sam walk away. Go after that man. You won't regret it."

"I'll think about it," Tessa whispered even as she wondered if what Olivia was saying was true. Could it be that she needed to just keep at him until he got past his pride?

"You'd better think damn fast because there's not a woman in the entire county who wouldn't jump at the chance to have Sam."

"You don't know how badly he was hurt when he found out," Tessa whispered.

"All of us have worked hard for the love of our lives. Take a look at your friends right here in Clifton. Becca once accused Jake of stealing her horses and ransacking her home. Emma took Sophie and left Gabe because she didn't believe he loved her and only married her because of their daughter. Madilyn wouldn't leave here and go with Brody and she suffered miserably until he finally came back to town. Ryder made Kelsey leave him because he didn't believe they could make it together. Katie wouldn't move to Texas with Riley and almost lost him until he came to his senses. Wyatt treated me like shit but I hung in there until he listened to his heart. We've all had pain in our relationships but we all learned to forgive. Sam *wants* you, he loves you, and like Wyatt, he needs to get past his pride and listen to his heart." Olivia sighed. "I'm trying to make a point here, Tess. Sam is your *one* and you are his. You need each other. It was fate you came to Clifton and met him just as it was for Becca, Kelsey, and me. Don't let him go. If you don't at least try, I promise you that you'll regret it forever."

Tessa stared at Olivia and suddenly, she knew Olivia was right. Sam was the best thing to happen to her and yes, she had hurt him but if he really loved her, he'd forgive her. She had been without him long enough. She had to give saving what they had one more try. Tessa nodded and hugged Olivia.

"Thank you, Liv. I have to go find Sam, I'll beg him if I have to."

Olivia grinned and hugged her back. "You go girl. Invite us to the wedding."

Tessa smiled, and for the first time in what felt like forever, she laughed as she ran to her SUV. As she tore out of the driveway, nervous energy filled her as she drove toward Copper Ridge Road, where she hoped Sam was running radar. If she didn't find him there, she'd go to the station or his home. Sam Garrett needed to know how much she loved him. If he didn't want anything more to do with her after one more attempt to save what they had then at least, she'd know she tried.

* * * *

Lately, the days seemed to run into each other, one after the other. Sitting at his desk on a Saturday, Sam stared at the form in front of him. He couldn't concentrate. Thoughts of Tessa kept filling his head.

Running his hand over his jaw, he tried to remember when he last shaved—the day before yesterday maybe. He really didn't care, sighing as he picked up the form.

Rick had filled it out and all Sam had to do was sign it. *So, do it already.* It was just a formality. A form used for DUI charges. Sam swore and signed the form. That finished up his day and that was why he'd taken so long to sign it. Knowing once he did, he could go home, and sit in that house—alone.

Jesus! You miss her.

Sam shook his head and stood telling his inner voice to shut up and get over her. Getting over her wasn't going to be easy to do since they lived in a two-lane town, and he was doing his absolute best not to run into her as it was. He swore and strode from his office glancing at Betty Lou who stood when she saw him.

"Sam—"

Sam held up his hand. "I don't want to hear it, Betty Lou. I know how much you care about Tessa..." *Christ, it hurt to say her name.* "But it's over and done with."

"I love you, Sam. You're the son I never had. I hate seeing you hurt, and you *are* hurting, Sam. I can see it in your eyes." She moved closer to him. "Those beautiful blue eyes of yours have lost their sparkle." Betty

Lou put her hand on his arm. "Don't end up like me and Bobbie Jo, Sam. We're lonely because we never took a chance on love. Please don't end up like us. You love that girl, so you go get her back. Yes, she lied about her past, and yes, that was something important but she had her reasons, and you know that now. You need to forgive her."

Sam shook his head and smiled sadly. "It's not that simple, Betty Lou. It's about far more than her lying to me. It's about trust. Even if she couldn't tell me in the beginning, then once we were together and building something, she should have been upfront with me. Her not trusting me enough to tell me—that's hard to forget." He hugged her and pressed a kiss to the top of her head. "I'll be fine."

He moved toward the back door. "I think I'm going to set up radar on Copper Ridge for a while before I head home. Call me if you need me." Pulling on his coat and gloves, he put on his hat then headed out the door.

The snow was coming down harder but not doing much more than coating grassy areas, the roads were still all right. Sam climbed into his patrol cruiser. He had to do something to keep his mind off her and going home, sitting alone in that house, wasn't the way to do it. He drove to Copper Ridge, backed his vehicle into a spot off the road, and left the engine running then leaned back in the seat.

It wasn't long before the radar gun went off. Sam sat up and watched as Tessa drove by in her SUV. He grumbled under his breath. Forget it there was no way he was pulling her over. She was probably on an emergency run anyway.

Smiling sadly, he remembered the day he rode with her to Wyatt's to take care of the sick horse. She'd paid absolutely no attention to the posted speed limit. The smile left his face when he remembered that was also, the night they'd almost made love. Sam swore as his cock twitched. Damn, all he had to do was think of her.

He slunk back down in the seat and less than a minute later, Tessa's vehicle flew by again heading in the opposite direction. *What the hell?*

Sam shook his head. Nope, it was none of his business.

Leaning his head back, he pulled his hat down over his eyes. He was tired. Maybe he'd be able to sleep...

The radar gun went off again. Swearing, he lifted his hat and his jaw went slack when he saw Tessa's SUV fly by again—this time fifteen miles per hour over the limit. Swinging his legs up on the seat, he lowered his hat again. He didn't know what she was doing, and didn't care. It wouldn't matter if she were fifty miles per hour over he wasn't going after her.

Maybe she was lost. Why else would she be running up and down the damn road? He sure as hell didn't care. Sitting up, he looked out at the road. Thing was, he did care. He cared a lot but he wasn't going to give in. His lips twisted pushing back what surprised him as a grin when he saw her speed by going in the other direction again. What was she doing? A few minutes went by and she didn't come back.

Sam sighed, assuming she must have figured out where she was going.

Deciding to call it a day, Sam sat up and even though he hated the thought of going home, he couldn't put it off any longer. He was about to drive out onto the road when the radar gun went off again.

Son of a bitch! What now?

Copper Ridge was never this busy. Of course, the only vehicle he'd seen today belonged to Tessa. Sighing, he waited for the vehicle to approach and when Sam glanced at the gun, it read the speed as twenty-five miles over the limit. He was ready to flip the lights on when he saw Tessa's SUV fly by again. Sam hit the steering wheel with the palm of his hand. This time there was no way he could let her get away with it. No matter how much he wanted to let her go, he had to pull her over. She was breaking the law.

Shit! Shit! Shit!

Sam flipped the lights and siren on then tore out behind her. Surprising him, she steered the vehicle off to the side immediately. He pulled in behind her then sat there staring at the back of her SUV. Taking a deep breath, he threw the door open, stepped out, and put his hat on. As he started toward her vehicle, her door flew open and she emerged. Sam bit back a groan. He had missed her so much. Everything seemed to slow down around them as if time itself was slowing. Snow fell heavily around them and the world seemed to disappear.

"You in a hurry today, Doctor McGuire?" Sam halted by the back of her car, leaned against it, and folded his arms across his chest.

"Maybe." She shrugged while chewing on her lower lip.

"Driver's license, registration, and proof of insurance, please," Sam said in a no nonsense voice pulling out his citation pad.

"Are you serious?" Tessa asked turning

to face him.

"Yes, ma'am...clocked you at twenty-five miles over the limit. I can take your license right here, right now, if I want to."

"I was twenty-five miles over the limit because you didn't come after me when I was ten or fifteen over," Tessa said.

Sam stared at her without saying a word. She'd done this on purpose to get his attention. Tessa marched to him and stood right in front of him, looking up at him.

"Take those damn sunglasses off." She poked him in the chest.

Sam stepped back. "Do I need to remind you what happened the last time you assaulted an officer of the law?"

"No, you don't need to remind me. You handcuffed me and took me to the office, but you didn't frisk me, Sheriff. Why was that?"

Sam frowned. What was she up to? "License, registration, and proof of insurance—now."

Tessa growled and stepped closer. "Frisk. Me. Sheriff." She emphasized each word with a poke to his chest.

"I don't need to frisk you for a speeding violation."

Tessa burst out laughing. "How about for assaulting an officer then?"

"I'm going to let that go since you seem

to be having a bad day. You went up and down the road several times. Are you looking for something?"

"Am I—? Oh, Sam, isn't it obvious? I was looking for you." Then she smiled at him. "I wanted you to come after me."

"Why?" He took a step back from her when she stepped closer. She smelled so good.

"Because I love you."

Sam nodded. "So you said, at the same time you were lying to me."

"I will beg you to forgive me if I have to. Love is about forgiving," Tessa whispered.

He didn't move but when she moved closer to him, he took a step back. Suddenly, she placed her hand over her mouth on a sob.

"I really did ruin it all, didn't I? You really don't want me anymore."

Turning away, she rushed away and climbed back into her SUV. Sam followed her, reached across her, and took the keys from the ignition.

"What are you doing?"

"I thought that would be obvious, Doc. I'm arresting you—twenty-five miles over the speed limit, and assaulting an officer. Please step from the vehicle."

"I will not," Tessa shouted.

Sam stepped back holding the door open wide. "Yes, you will. Don't add resisting arrest to it too."

Tessa stepped from the car and stared up at him. "I love you, Sam. Please tell me it's not too late for us."

Sam watched as tears streamed down her face. He spun her around, pressing her to the side of the vehicle so fast he was sure she got dizzy. "I'm taking you in."

"Sam Garrett, you let me go. This is ridiculous."

Sam put his lips close to her ear. "That's *Sheriff* Sam Garrett, and I will never let you go."

Tessa turned her head to gaze at him. "What?"

"I'm never letting you go," he whispered. He couldn't be without her a minute longer. Yes, they would have to work out some issues between them but he realized he was a fool to let her go. She was his *one.*

Tessa squealed and spun around, throwing her arms around his neck and her legs around his waist. She removed his sunglasses, gazed into his eyes, and then rained kisses over his face. Sam grinned, and then lowered his head to kiss her.

"I love you, Tessa. I can't be without you any longer," he whispered against her lips.

"I've been so miserable without you in my life."

"Sam, I love you."

"I believe you do, so what do you say, we start over?"

"Start over?"

"Yeah, start from the beginning. I mean, I suppose we could skip all the usual courtship stuff and get right to the making love part of a relationship but...you know, get to know each other again. Trust each other again."

"That sounds like a great idea. I'm single and not involved with anyone right now. How about you, Sheriff?"

"Well, there is this animal doctor that I think is kind of hot."

Tessa laughed. "I happen to be an animal doctor."

"Really, come to think of it, you look kind of familiar," Sam said leaning back to give her face a good look. "Yeah, you're the one. Weren't very friendly when I first met you but I think I've been in love with you since I first saw you."

"Me too, Sam, me too," Tessa said against his lips.

He took a deep breath. "I want you in my life for as long as I live but I'm serious about us working through our trust issues then maybe in say six months or so—will you marry me, Tessa?"

"Yes. Yes, Sam. I will," Tessa cried then showered his face with kisses. "I trust you completely. I knew that the night of the shooting. I knew you'd come for us. I was terrified that you would, but I knew it. I just hope you can learn to trust me as completely, Sam. I will always trust you with everything, my secrets, my heart, my love..." Suddenly, she punched his bicep. "I thought you were seriously going to arrest me."

"Oh, I am arresting you, angel. It's for a life sentence and even that's not long enough. You're where I belong, Tessa."

"Does this mean you will forgive me for lying to you, Sam?"

Sam swallowed hard but knew he would—that he had.

"I have already. I know you had your reasons. Crazy as they may be, but I realized if you had told me the truth, this never would have happened between us and to use your words, I wouldn't change one minute of the time I've spent with you. Maybe I made it a bit hard for you to tell me the truth too, with all of my talk of honesty and hating deceit but from now on, you can tell me the truth...even if it's not something I want to hear. I will never want any other woman in my life,

Tessa. I love you."

"You are everything to me, Sam." Tessa kissed him and moaned when he deepened the kiss. Someone drove by and blew the horn. Sam and Tessa waved without breaking the kiss. It would soon be all over Clifton that the sheriff had caught his woman.

Epilogue

Tessa stood in Katie and Riley's bedroom staring at her image in the mirror. She was in awe of the reflection staring back at her. Nearly eight months had passed since that day on the road when she'd literally thrown herself down like a gauntlet to win Sam back, but it had been worth it.

"You look so beautiful, Tess," Katie said from beside her.

"I'm so glad you forgave me for hurting Sam, Katie.

"I was hurting too, Tess. Everyone knows I adore my big brother. I'm truly glad you're going to be my sister in-law though."

"I didn't get a wedding like this the first time. My dad hated you know who so much that we got married at the courthouse." Tessa refused to speak his name. She was letting go of that time in her life. "This gown is so beautiful."

"So is the bride wearing it," Olivia said from where she sat on the bed.

"Thank you, Liv." Tessa smiled over her shoulder at her dear friend.

The gown was white with a tight bodice and scooped neck. The sleeves were three quarter length and made up of lace. A long train flowed out behind her. The top of the dress was silk and the full skirt matched the lace on the sleeves. Around her neck, she wore a tear-drop shaped diamond necklace that Sam had given her for a wedding gift. She smiled as she thought back to him giving her the necklace along with one other gift.

"I love the necklace, Sam," she had whispered as she kissed him.

"It's the only teardrop I ever want to see on you again."

"What about tears of joy?"

Sam nodded. "Well, okay but only those and I'm hoping there will be many of those."

"I know there will be. I have the man I love and I'm never letting him go again."

"I have one more thing for you. Come with me." He had held his hand out to her. Narrowing her eyes and wondering what he was up to, she had followed him as he led her to the barn. Stopping by one of the stalls, he had jerked his chin toward it with a smug grin. She stepped up and looked inside. Her eyes went to Sam, wide with delight.

"You bought me a horse?"

"Yes. You said you always wanted one so I bought her from Ryder. She's a three-year-old Paint."

Tessa had laughed as she hugged him. "I love her. Thank you, Sam." She had kissed him filled with joy. "I can't wait to ride her. Sam, you once asked me about my tattoo, well, I want to tell you about it. It represents my freedom from *him*. A butterfly emerges from a chrysalis to begin a new life. It's what I did when I left him—started a new life."

"That new life is with me," Sam had whispered against her lips right before he kissed her.

The door to the bedroom flew open bringing her back to the present, and Becca, Kaylee, Kelsey, Emma, and Madilyn entered. Each of them carried a flute of champagne, and then her mother, Poppy O'Brian, Sam's mother, Genevieve Garrett, and Tessa's aunt Lil followed them in. Poppy handed one of two flutes to Tessa.

"Are you nervous, honey?" Poppy asked her daughter setting her own glass down. Tessa watched her mother attach the beautiful veil she'd chosen over her long hair, which was pulled up in a loose bun with tendrils falling down around her face.

"No. Not at all, Mom," Tessa said sipping her champagne.

"I can't tell you how happy I am that you're marrying my son," Genevieve said smiling at her.

Tessa smiled back. She already loved her future in-laws. "I love him so much, Genevieve. I think that's why I'm not nervous."

"I wasn't nervous on my wedding day either," Olivia said. "I knew I finally had the man I wanted—easy peasy."

All of the women laughed and nodded their heads in agreement. Tessa glanced at all of them. "I'm so happy to have all of you in my wedding." She slipped her arm through Katie's and hugged her. "Thank you for being my matron of honor, Katie. I think I'll love having you as a sister in-law."

"Of course you will. I'm wonderful." Katie laughed. "I was a little worried that Sam might not ask Riley to be his best man...they were always so close growing up...but he did, so I guess they're finally good again. All the guys are close, but Riley and Sam were always the closest."

"Sam loves him like a brother. I'm glad Riley had your family to lean on when he was growing up," Tessa said.

"He's happier now since he has his parents in his life, especially his real dad. Jordon adores Riley."

"Tess? I have something for you and Sam for a wedding gift," her aunt Lil said stepping forward.

"You have done more than enough for me, Aunt Lil. I can never repay you for all you've done."

"And you don't need to. I love you like a daughter. This is for you and Sam together." She handed Tessa an envelope. "Go on...open it."

Everyone stood around her waiting while she tore open the envelope and unfolded the paper. It was a deed. Tessa skimmed over it then raised surprised eyes.

"Are you serious?"

"Of course I am. The judge and I rarely go there. It can be your place to get away together."

"Oh, Aunt Lil," Tessa cried hugging tight the woman who had done so much to give her freedom.

"What is it?" Olivia asked, ever curious.

Tessa looked at her friends and smiled with pure joy. "The deed for the cabin in Kalispell. Sam and I had planned to go there when everything went wrong. It's a perfect place and I can't wait to tell him. Thank you so much, Aunt Lil." She looked at her mom with suspicion. "Did you know?"

"Of course I did." Poppy laughed then hugged her daughter.

"Hello, beautiful ladies," Sean O'Brian

said from the doorway.

Tessa moved forward to greet him. "Daddy, you look so handsome."

Sean kissed her cheek. "I see Lil gave you her present." He winked at Lil over Tessa's shoulder then looked lovingly into his daughter's eyes. "Let's get you married, baby girl. I'm sure Sam is getting anxious."

Waiting for everyone else to file out before them, Tessa placed her arm in his when he extended it to her. She smiled up at him and let him lead her from the room.

* * * *

To say Sam was anxious would be a huge understatement. Running his fingers through his hair and cursing himself for doing it yet again, he paced the floor in the back room of the church. He stopped for a moment when his groomsmen returned to the room after seating everyone.

"Would you relax?" Riley chided him.

Sam started again and stopped, narrowing his eyes at his best man, brother-in-law, and best friend—still. "If we weren't in church, you know what I'd say to you."

Riley laughed. "I'm surprised you don't anyway. Why are you so nervous?"

"What if she doesn't show?"

Riley snorted. "Come on, Sam. You know better than that."

"Do I?"

"She loves you, Sam," Wyatt said taking a seat then hopping back up and smoothing the back of his tux jacket.

"I know, but—"

The men laughed in unison making Sam glare at them, making them laugh even harder. The door opened and Jonathan Garrett stepped into the room. He halted when he saw Sam glaring and his friends laughing. Jonathan sighed and rolled his eyes.

"He's not sprouting that bull...uh...stuff about her not showing up again, is he?"

"He is for sure," Jake said as he leaned against the wall with his arms folded.

"I seriously doubt she's going to change her mind, son. She has all of you in tuxedos and seven attendants. The woman is getting her dream wedding." Jonathan put his hand on Sam's shoulder. "Besides, from the story I heard, she worked too hard to get you to let you slip away now."

"I know. It's just—" His father was right. Tessa had gone above, and beyond to get him to realize they were supposed to be together.

The door opened and the reverend stuck his head in. "Let's get you married, Sam. Your bride is here."

Sam sighed with relief. "Thank God," he

muttered as the men headed toward the door that led to the altar.

Following them out, he took his place and his gaze skimmed over the guests. His mother and Betty Lou were already crying into tissues. He winked at his mom when she looked over to him making her smile as she wiped away tears.

"Why do women cry at weddings?" he whispered, tilting his head toward Riley.

"They cry at the drop of a hat. Who knows?" Riley whispered back and shrugging his broad shoulders.

The music started and Sam watched as each beautiful woman walked down the aisle. When Katie took her place at the altar, Sam saw her blush so he leaned toward Riley.

"Stay away from my sister," he murmured with a grin.

"Not a chance." Riley chuckled and put a hand on Sam's shoulder. Sam glanced at him and nodded. He was glad his best friend was at his side.

When Sam looked to the back of the church as the music changed, he hissed in a breath when he saw Tessa start down the aisle with her father.

"Holy shit," he murmured.

"You're in church, Sam," the reverend reminded him.

"Sorry, Padre." Sam couldn't take his eyes off her as she moved toward him. She smiled up at him when her father brought her to a stop in front of him. Sam stepped forward to take her hand.

"I know you'll be good to my baby girl, Sam. Enjoy Kalispell," Sean O'Brian whispered then he took a seat next to his wife in the front pew.

"Kalispell?" Sam whispered wondering about what his about to be new father-in-law was referring.

"Aunt Lil gave us the deed to the cabin for a wedding gift."

"No shit—"

"Jonathan Sam Garrett," the reverend reprimanded grabbing his attention. The man frowned at him.

Sam winced. "Sorry."

He looked back to Tessa. "She gave it to us?"

"Yes. Maybe we'll make it there this time," Tessa whispered and smiled.

"I know we will. Ready to do this, angel?"

"More than ready, Sheriff. How about you?" Tessa smiled at him.

Sam grinned. "I was born ready."

Tessa squeezed his hand and Sam squeezed back then they repeated their vows to each other.

"I now pronounce you husband and wife. You may now kiss your bride," the reverend told Sam.

"With pleasure," Sam murmured as he lifted her veil, and cupped her face in his hands. He pressed his lips to hers. When Tessa moaned, he deepened the kiss. Her arms wrapped around his neck and continued kissing him until someone cleared their throat. Sam slowly lifted his lips from hers and gazed out toward the guests. "What?"

The guests laughed and started applauding. People outside who couldn't fit inside the church started cheering. Sam and Tessa laughed. It had become a tradition with Jake and Becca's wedding. Whoever couldn't fit in the church stood outside, no matter how hot or cold it was. It was a hot August day, but they didn't care. No one was going to complain because the town's favorite sheriff and veterinarian were just married.

Sam took Tessa's hand and led her down the aisle, stopping in the doorway as more cheers erupted. Sam kissed her hand. Tessa smiled at him and his heart skipped a beat.

"I love you, Tessa."

"I love you, Sam Garrett."

Sam grinned and pulled her to him then put his lips close to hers. "*Sheriff* Sam Garrett."

"Anything you say...Sheriff," Tessa said in a husky tone.

"I'll make a list," Sam whispered as he put his lips to hers. She groaned into his mouth when he deepened the kiss.

Life couldn't be better. Sam finally had the woman he loved and he'd make sure she was happy every single day as long as he had a breath in his body. She'd never go without and he'd make sure he'd never be without her. Gazing into her beautiful dark eyes, he smiled, truly happy. The only thing that could make this better was to have some babies with this beautiful woman who was now his wife. That would come in time, since he wanted her for himself for a while first. He knew most people went through hard times when love was involved but together, they had worked through it. Saving their love had been worth it.

The End

About the Author

Susan was born and raised in Cumberland, MD. She moved to Tennessee in 1996 and now lives in a small town outside of Nashville, along with her husband and their two rescued dogs. Although, writing for years, it was recently she decided to submit to publishers and signed a three-year contract with Secret Cravings Publishing. Since SCP closed their doors in August 2015, Susan decided to self-publish. She is a huge Nashville Predators hockey fan. She also enjoys fishing, taking drives down back roads, visiting Gatlinburg, TN, her family in Pennsylvania, and her hometown. Susan started a new six book series in January 2015, The Bad Boys of Dry River. Although Susan's books are a series, each book can be read as standalone books. Each book will end with a new story beginning in the next one. She would love to hear from her readers and promises to try to respond to all. She would also appreciate reviews if you've read her books.

You can visit her Facebook page and website by the links below:

Facebook: http://bit.ly/2BtlyP7

www.susanfisherdavisauthor.weebly.com

Email: susan@susanfisherdavisauthor.com

Made in the USA
Columbia, SC
15 October 2020

22930471R00202